J.G. Ballard was born in 1930 in Shanghai, China, of English parents, and he lived there until he was fifteen. After the attack on Pearl Harbor he was interned by the Japanese in a civilian prison camp. He moved to England in 1946, and after leaving school he read medicine at King's College, Cambridge. Thereafter he worked as a copywriter, a porter in Covent Garden and, after a spell in Canada with the RAF, as an editor of technical and scientific journals. His first short story appeared in 1956, and in 1962 he published *The Drowned World*, a brilliant novel that won him instant critical acclaim. His semi-autobiographical novel, *Empire of the Sun*, won the 1984 *Guardian* Fiction Prize and James Tait Black Award, and was filmed by Steven Spielberg. His controversial 1973 novel *Crash* was also made into a film, directed by David Cronenberg. *Cocaine Nights*, a *Sunday Times* bestseller in both hardback and paperback, was shortlisted for the 1996 Whitbread Novel Award.

The Terminal Beach

J.G. BALLARD

PHŒNIX

A PHOENIX PAPERBACK

First published in Great Britain in 1964
by Victor Gollancz Ltd
This paperback edition first published in 1984
by J. M. Dent & Sons Ltd
Reissued 1992

Reissued by Indigo in 1997
an imprint of Orion Books Ltd,
Orion House, 5 Upper St Martin's Lane,
London WC2H 9EA

Reissued 2001 by Phoenix,
an imprint of Orion Books Ltd

A CIP catalogue record for this book
is available from the British Library.

ISBN 0 57540 131 1

Printed and bound in Great Britain by
The Guernsey Press Co. Ltd, Guernsey, C.I.

CONTENTS

A QUESTION OF RE-ENTRY

ALL day they had moved steadily upstream, occasionally pausing to raise the propeller and cut away the knots of weed, and by 3 o'clock had covered some seventy-five miles. Fifty yards away, on either side of the patrol launch, the high walls of the jungle river rose over the water, the unbroken massif of the mato grosso which swept across the Amazonas from Campos Buros to the delta of the Orinoco. Despite their progress—they had set off from the telegraph station at Tres Buritis at 7 o'clock that morning—the river showed no inclination to narrow or alter its volume. Sombre and unchanging, the forest followed its course, the aerial canopy shutting off the sunlight and cloaking the water along the banks with a black velvet sheen. Now and then the channel would widen into a flat expanse of what appeared to be stationary water, the slow oily swells which disturbed its surface transforming it into a sluggish mirror of the distant, enigmatic sky, the islands of rotten balsa logs refracted by the layers of haze like the drifting archipelagoes of a dream. Then the channel would narrow again and the cooling jungle darkness enveloped the launch.

Although for the first few hours Connolly had joined Captain Pereira at the rail, he had become bored with the endless green banks of the forest sliding past them, and since noon had remained in the cabin, pretending to study the trajectory maps. The time might pass more slowly there, but at least it was cooler and less depressing. The fan hummed and pivoted, and the clicking of the cutwater and the whispering plaint of the current past the gliding hull soothed the slight headache induced by the tepid beer he and Pereira had shared after lunch.

This first encounter with the jungle had disappointed Connolly.

His previous experience had been confined to the Dredging Project at Lake Maracaibo, where the only forests consisted of the abandoned oil rigs built out into the water. Their rusting hulks, and the huge draglines and pontoons of the dredging teams, were fauna of a man-made species. In the Amazonian jungle he had expected to see the full variety of nature in its richest and most colourful outpouring, but instead it was nothing more than a moribund tree-level swamp, unweeded and overgrown, if anything more dead than alive, an example of bad husbandry on a continental scale. The margins of the river were rarely well-defined; except where enough rotting trunks had gathered to form a firm parapet, there were no formal banks, and the shallows ran off among the undergrowth for a hundred yards, irrigating huge areas of vegetation that were already drowning in moisture.

Connolly had tried to convey his disenchantment to Pereira, who now sat under the awning on the deck, placidly smoking a cheroot, partly to repay the Captain for his polite contempt for Connolly and everything his mission implied. Like all the officers of the Native Protection Missions whom Connolly had met, first in Venezuela and now in Brazil, Pereira maintained a proprietary outlook towards the jungle and its mystique, which would not be breached by any number of fresh-faced investigators in their crisp drill uniforms. Captain Pereira had not been impressed by the UN flashes on Connolly's shoulders with their orbital monogram, nor by the high-level request for assistance cabled to the Mission three weeks earlier from Brasilia. To Pereira, obviously, the office suites in the white towers at the capital were as far away as New York, London or Babylon.

Superficially, the Captain had been helpful enough, supervising the crew as they stowed Connolly's monitoring equipment aboard, checking his Smith & Wesson and exchanging a pair of defective mosquito boots. As long as Connolly had wanted to, he had conversed away amiably, pointing out this and that feature of the landscape, identifying an unusual bird or lizard on an overhead bough.

But his indifference to the real object of the mission—he had given a barely perceptible nod when Connolly described it—soon became obvious. It was this neutrality which irked Connolly, implying that Pereira spent all his time ferrying UN investigators up and down the rivers after their confounded lost space capsule like so many tourists in search of some non-existent El Dorado. Above all there was the suggestion that Connolly and the hundreds of other investigators deployed around the continent were being too persistent. When all was said and done, Pereira implied, five years had elapsed since the returning lunar spacecraft, the *Goliath* 7, had plummeted into the South American land mass, and to prolong the search indefinitely was simply bad form, even, perhaps, necrophilic. There was not the faintest chance of the pilot still being alive, so he should be decently forgotten, given a statue outside a railway station or airport car park and left to the pigeons.

Connolly would have been glad to explain the reasons for the indefinite duration of the search, the overwhelming moral reasons, apart from the political and technical ones. He would have liked to point out that the lost astronaut, Colonel Francis Spender, by accepting the immense risks of the flight to and from the Moon, was owed the absolute discharge of any assistance that could be given him. He would have liked to remind Pereira that the successful landing on the Moon, after some half-dozen fatal attempts—at least three of the luckless pilots were still orbiting the Moon in their dead ships—was the culmination of an age-old ambition with profound psychological implications for mankind, and that the failure to find the astronaut after his return might induce unassuageable feelings of guilt and inadequacy. (If the sea was a symbol of the unconscious, was space perhaps an image of unfettered time, and the inability to penetrate it a tragic exile to one of the limbos of eternity, a symbolic death in life?)

But Captain Pereira was not interested. Calmly inhaling the scented aroma of his cheroot, he sat imperturbably at the rail, surveying the fetid swamps that moved past them.

Shortly before noon, when they had covered some 40 miles, Connolly pointed to the remains of a bamboo landing stage elevated on high poles above the bank. A threadbare rope bridge trailed off among the mangroves, and through an embrasure in the forest they could see a small clearing where a clutter of abandoned adobe huts dissolved like refuse heaps in the sunlight.

9

" Is this one of their camps? "

Pereira shook his head. " The Espirro tribe, closely related to the Nambikwaras. Three years ago one of them carried influenza back from the telegraph station, an epidemic broke out, turned into a form of pulmonary edema, within forty-eight hours three hundred Indians had died. The whole group disintegrated, only about fifteen of the men and their families are still alive. A great tragedy."

They moved forward to the bridge and stood beside the tall Negro helmsman as the two other members of the crew began to shackle sections of fine wire mesh into a cage over the deck. Pereira raised his binoculars and scanned the river ahead.

" Since the Espirros vacated the area the Nambas have begun to forage down this far. We won't see any of them, but it's as well to be on the safe side."

" Do you mean they're hostile? " Connolly asked.

" Not in a conscious sense. But the various groups which comprise the Nambikwaras are permanently feuding with each other, and this far from the settlement we might easily be involved in an opportunist attack. Once we get to the settlement we'll be all right —there's a sort of precarious equilibrium there. But even so, have your wits about you. As you'll see, they're as nervous as birds."

" How does Ryker manage to keep out of their way? Hasn't he been here for years? "

" About twelve." Pereira sat down on the gunwale and eased his peaked cap off his forehead. " Ryker is something of a special case. Temperamentally he's rather explosive—I meant to warn you to handle him carefully, he might easily whip up an incident —but he seems to have manoeuvred himself into a position of authority with the tribe. In some ways he's become an umpire, arbitrating in their various feuds. How he does it I haven't discovered yet; it's quite uncharacteristic of the Indians to regard a white man in that way. However, he's useful to us, we might eventually set up a mission here. Though that's next to impossible —we tried it once and the Indians just moved 500 miles away."

Connolly looked back at the derelict landing stage as it disappeared around a bend, barely distinguishable from the jungle, which was as dilapidated as this sole mournful artifact.

"What on earth made Ryker come out here?" He had heard something in Brasilia of this strange figure, sometime journalist and man of action, the self-proclaimed world citizen who at the age of forty-two, after a life spent venting his spleen on civilization and its gimcrack gods, had suddenly disappeared into the Amazonas and taken up residence with one of the aboriginal tribes. Most latter-day Gauguins were absconding confidence men or neurotics, but Ryker seemed to be a genuine character in his own right, the last of a race of true individualists retreating before the barbed-wire fences and regimentation of 20th century life. But his chosen paradise seemed pretty scruffy and degenerate, Connolly reflected, when one saw it at close quarters. However, as long as the man could organize the Indians into a few search parties he would serve his purpose. "I can't understand why Ryker should pick the Amazon basin. The South Pacific yes, but from all I've heard—and you've confirmed just now—the Indians appear to be a pretty diseased and miserable lot, hardly the noble savage."

Captain Pereira shrugged, looking away across the oily water, his plump sallow face mottled by the lace-like shadow of the wire netting. He belched discreetly to himself, and then adjusted his holster belt. "I don't know the South Pacific, but I should guess it's also been oversentimentalized. Ryker didn't come here for a scenic tour. I suppose the Indians are diseased and, yes, reasonably miserable. Within fifty years they'll probably have died out. But for the time being they do represent a certain form of untamed, natural existence, which after all made us what we are. The hazards facing them are immense, and they survive." He gave Connolly a sly smile. "But you must argue it out with Ryker."

They lapsed into silence and sat by the rail, watching the river unfurl itself. Exhausted and collapsing, the great trees crowded the banks, the dying expiring among the living, jostling each other aside as if for a last despairing assault on the patrol boat and its passengers. For the next half an hour, until they opened their lunch packs, Connolly searched the tree-tops for the giant bifurcated parachute which should have carried the capsule to earth. Virtually impermeable to the atmosphere, it would still be

11

visible, spreadeagled like an enormous bird over the canopy of leaves. Then, after drinking a can of Pereira's beer, he excused himself and went down to the cabin.

The two steel cases containing the monitoring equipment had been stowed under the chart table, and he pulled them out and checked that the moisture-proof seals were still intact. The chances of making visual contact with the capsule were infinitesimal, but as long as it was intact it would continue to transmit both a sonar and radio beacon, admittedly over little more than twenty miles, but sufficient to identify its whereabouts to anyone in the immediate neighbourhood. However, the entire northern half of the South Americas had been covered by successive aerial sweeps, and it seemed unlikely that the beacons were still operating. The disappearance of the capsule argued that it had sustained at least minor damage, and by now the batteries would have been corroded by the humid air.

Recently certain of the UN Space Department agencies had begun to circulate the unofficial view that Colonel Spender had failed to select the correct attitude for re-entry and that the capsule had been vapourized on its final descent, but Connolly guessed that this was merely an attempt to pacify world opinion and prepare the way for the resumption of the space programme. Not only the Lake Maracaibo Dredging Project, but his own presence on the patrol boat, indicated that the Department still believed Colonel Spender to be alive, or at least to have survived the landing. His final re-entry orbit should have brought him down into the landing zone 500 miles to the east of Trinidad, but the last radio contact before the ionization layers around the capsule severed transmission indicated that he had under-shot his trajectory and come down somewhere on the South American land-mass along a line linking Lake Maracaibo with Brasilia.

Footsteps sounded down the companionway, and Captain Pereira lowered himself into the cabin. He tossed his hat onto the chart table and sat with his back to the fan, letting the air blow across his fading hair, carrying across to Connolly a sweet unsavoury odour of garlic and cheap pomade.

"You're a sensible man, Lieutenant. Anyone who stays up on deck is crazy. However,"—he indicated Connolly's pallid face and' hands, a memento of a long winter in New York—" in a way it's a pity you couldn't have put in some sunbathing. That metropolitan pallor will be quite a curiosity to the Indians." He smiled agreeably, showing the yellowing teeth which made his olive complexion even darker. " You may well be the first white man in the literal sense that the Indians have seen."

" What about Ryker? Isn't he white? "

" Black as a berry now. Almost indistinguishable from the Indians, apart from being 7 feet tall." He pulled over a collection of cardboard boxes at the far end of the seat and began to rummage through them. Inside was a collection of miscellaneous oddments—balls of thread and raw cotton, lumps of wax and resin, urucu paste, tobacco and seed-beads. " These ought to assure them of your good intentions."

Connolly watched as he fastened the boxes together. " How many search parties will they buy? Are you sure you brought enough? I have a fifty-dollar allocation for gifts."

" Good," Pereira said matter-of-factly. " We'll get some more beer. Don't worry, you can't buy these people, Lieutenant. You have to rely on their good-will; this rubbish will put them in the right frame of mind to talk."

Connolly smiled dourly. " I'm more keen on getting them off their hunkers and out into the bush. How are you going to organize the search parties? "

" They've already taken place."

" What? " Connolly sat forward. " How did that happen? But they should have waited "—he glanced at the heavy monitoring equipment—" they can't have known what—— "

Pereira silenced him with a raised hand. " My dear Lieutenant. Relax, I was speaking figuratively. Can't you understand, these people are nomadic, they spend all their lives continually on the move. They must have covered every square foot of this forest a hundred times in the past five years. There's no need to send them out again. Your only hope is that they may have seen something and then persuade them to talk."

Connolly considered this, as Pereira unwrapped another parcel. " All right, but I may want to do a few patrols. I can't just sit around for three days."

"Naturally. Don't worry, Lieutenant. If your astronaut came down anywhere within 500 miles of here they'll know about it." He unwrapped the parcel and removed a small teak cabinet. The front panel was slotted, and lifted to reveal the face of a large ormolu table clock, its Gothic hands and numerals below a gilded belldome. Captain Pereira compared its time with his wrist-watch. "Good. Running perfectly, it hasn't lost a second in forty-eight hours. This should put us in Ryker's good books."

Connolly shook his head. "Why on earth does he want a clock? I thought the man had turned his back on such things."

Pereira packed the tooled metal face away. "Ah, well, whenever we escape from anything we always carry a memento of it with us. Ryker collects clocks; this is the third I've bought for him. God knows what he does with them."

The launch had changed course, and was moving in a wide circle across the river, the current whispering in a tender rippling murmur across the hull. They made their way up onto the deck, where the helmsman was unshackling several sections of the wire mesh in order to give himself an uninterrupted view of the bows. The two sailors climbed through the aperture and took up their positions fore and aft, boat-hooks at the ready.

They had entered a large bow-shaped extension of the river, where the current had overflowed the bank and produced a series of low-lying mud flats. Some two or three hundred yards wide, the water seemed to be almost motionless, seeping away through the trees which defined its margins so that the exit and inlet of the river were barely perceptible. At the inner bend of the bow, on the only firm ground, a small cantonment of huts had been built on a series of wooden palisades jutting out over the water. A narrow promontory of forest reached to either side of the cantonment, but a small area behind it had been cleared to form an open campong. On its far side were a number of wattle storage huts, a few dilapidated shacks and hovels of dried palm.

The entire area seemed deserted, but as they approached, the cutwater throwing a fine plume of white spray across the glassy swells, a few Indians appeared in the shadows below the creepers trailing over the jetty, watching them stonily. Connolly had expected to see a group of tall broad-shouldered warriors with white markings notched across their arms and cheeks, but these Indians were puny and degenerate, their pinched faces lowered beneath their squat bony skulls. They seemed undernourished and depressed, eyeing the visitors with a sort of sullen watchfulness, like pariah dogs from a gutter.

Pereira was shielding his eyes from the sun, across whose inclining path they were now moving, searching the ramshackle bungalow built of woven rattan at the far end of the jetty.

"No signs of Ryker yet. He's probably asleep or drunk." He noticed Connolly's distasteful frown. "Not much of a place, I'm afraid."

As they moved towards the jetty, the wash from the launch slapping at the greasy bamboo poles and throwing a gust of foul air into their faces, Connolly looked back across the open disc of water, into which the curving wake of the launch was dissolving in a final summary of their long voyage up-river to the derelict settlement, fading into the slack brown water like a last tenuous thread linking him with the order and sanity of civilization. A strange atmosphere of emptiness hung over this inland lagoon, a flat pall of dead air that in a curious way was as menacing as any overt signs of hostility, as if the crudity and violence of all the Amazonian jungles met here in a momentary balance which some untoward movement of his own might upset, unleashing appalling forces. Away in the distance, down-shore, the great trees leaned like corpses into the glazed air, and the haze over the water embalmed the jungle and the late afternoon in an uneasy stillness.

They bumped against the jetty, rocking lightly into the palisade of poles and dislodging a couple of water-logged outriggers lashed together. The helmsman reversed the engine, waiting for the sailors to secure the lines. None of the Indians had come forward to assist them. Connolly caught a glimpse of one old simian face regarding him with a rheumy eye, riddled teeth nervously worrying a pouch-like lower lip.

He turned to Pereira, glad that the Captain would be interceding between himself and the Indians. "Captain, I should have asked before, but—are these Indians cannibalistic?"

Pereira shook his head, steadying himself against a stanchion. "Not at all. Don't worry about that, they'd have been extinct years ago if they were."

"Not even—white men?" For some reason Connolly found himself placing a peculiarly indelicate emphasis upon the word 'white'.

Pereira laughed, straightening his uniform jacket. "For God's sake, Lieutenant, no. Are you worrying that your astronaut might have been eaten by them?"

"I suppose it's a possibility."

"I assure you, there have been no recorded cases. As a matter of interest, it's a rare practice on this continent. Much more typical of Africa—and Europe," he added with sly humour. Pausing to smile at Connolly, he said quietly. "Don't despise the Indians, Lieutenant. However diseased and dirty they may be, at least they are in equilibrium with their environment. And with themselves. You'll find no Christopher Columbuses or Colonel Spenders here, but no Belsens either. Perhaps one is as much a symptom of unease as the other?"

They had begun to drift down the jetty, over-running one of the outriggers, whose bow creaked and disappeared under the stern of the launch, and Pereira shouted at the helmsman: "Ahead, Sancho! More ahead! Damn Ryker, where is the man?"

Churning out a niagara of boiling brown water, the launch moved forward, driving its shoulder into the bamboo supports, and the entire jetty sprung lightly under the impact. As the motor was cut and the lines finally secured, Connolly looked up at the jetty above his head.

Scowling down at him, an expression of bilious irritability on his heavy-jawed face, was a tall bare-chested man wearing a pair of frayed cotton shorts and a sleeve-less waistcoat of pleated raffia, his dark eyes almost hidden by a wide-brimmed straw hat. The heavy muscles of his exposed chest and arms were the colour of tropical teak, and the white scars on his lips and the fading traces of the heat ulcers which studded his shin bones provided the only lighter colouring. Standing there, arms akimbo with a sort of jaunty arrogance, he seemed to represent to Connolly that quality of untamed energy which he had so far found so conspicuously missing from the forest.

Completing his scrutiny of Connolly, the big man bellowed: "Pereira, for God's sake, what do you think you're doing? That's my bloody outrigger you've just run down! Tell that steersman of your's to get the cataracts out of his eyes or I'll put a bullet through his backside!"

Grinning good humouredly, Pereira pulled himself up on to the jetty. "My dear Ryker, contain yourself. Remember your blood-pressure." He peered down at the water-logged hulk of the derelict canoe which was now ejecting itself slowly from the river. "Anyway, what good is a canoe to you, you're not going anywhere."

Grudgingly, Ryker shook Pereira's hand. "That's what you like to think, Captain. You and your confounded Mission, you want me to do all the work. Next time you may find I've gone a thousand miles up-river. And taken the Nambas with me."

"What an epic prospect, Ryker. You'll need a Homer to celebrate it." Pereira turned and gestured Connolly on to the jetty. The Indians were still hanging about listlessly, like guilty intruders.

Ryker eyed Connolly's uniform suspiciously. "Who's this? Another so-called anthropologist, sniffing about for smut? I warned you last time, I will not have any more of those."

"No, Ryker. Can't you recognize the uniform? Let me introduce Lieutenant Connolly, of that brotherhood of latter-day saints, by whose courtesy and generosity we live in peace together —the United Nations."

"What? Don't tell me they've got a mandate here now? God above, I suppose he'll bore my head off about cereal/protein ratios!" His ironic groan revealed a concealed reserve of acid humour.

"Relax. The Lieutenant is very charming and polite. He works for the Space Department, Reclamation Division. You know, searching for lost aircraft and the like. There's a chance you may be able to help him." Pereira winked at Connolly and steered him forward. "Lieutenant, the Rajah Ryker."

"I doubt it," Ryker said dourly. They shook hands, the corded muscles of Ryker's fingers like a trap. Despite his thick-necked stoop, Ryker was a good six to ten inches taller then Connolly. For a moment he held on to Connolly's hand, a slight trace of wariness revealed below his mask of bad temper. " When did this plane come down? " he asked. Connolly guessed that he was already thinking of a profitable salvage operation.

" Some time ago," Pereira said mildly. He picked up the parcel containing the cabinet clock and began to stroll after Ryker towards the bungalow at the end of the jetty. A low-eaved dwelling of woven rattan, its single room was surrounded on all sides by a veranda, the overhanging roof shading it from the sunlight. Creepers trailed across from the surrounding foliage, involving it in the background of palms and fronds, so that the house seemed a momentary formalization of the jungle.

" But the Indians might have heard something about it," Pereira went on. " Five years ago, as a matter of fact."

Ryker snorted. " My God, you've got a hope." They went up the steps on to the veranda, where a slim-shouldered Indian youth, his eyes like moist marbles, was watching from the shadows. With a snap of irritation, Ryker cupped his hand around the youth's pate and propelled him with a backward swing down the steps. Sprawling on his knees, the youth picked himself up, eyes still fixed on Connolly, then emitted what sounded like a high-pitched nasal hoot, compounded partly of fear and partly of excitement. Connolly looked back from the doorway, and noticed that several other Indians had stepped onto the pier and were watching him with the same expression of rapt curiosity.

Pereira patted Connolly's shoulder. " I told you they'd be impressed. Did you see that, Ryker? "

Ryker nodded curtly, as they entered his living-room pulled off his straw hat and tossed it on to a couch under the window. The room was dingy and cheerless. Crude bamboo shelves were strung around the walls, ornamented with a few primitive carvings of ivory and bamboo. A couple of rocking chairs and a card-table were in the centre of the room, dwarfed by an immense victorian mahogany dresser standing against the rear wall. With its càstellated mirrors and ornamental pediments it looked like an altarpiece stolen from a cathedral. At first glance it appeared to be leaning to one side, but then Connolly saw that its rear legs had been carefully raised from the tilting floor with a number of small wedges. In the centre of the dresser, its multiple reflections receding to infinity in a pair of small wing mirrors, was a cheap three-dollar alarm clock, ticking away loudly. An over-and-under Winchester shotgun leaned against the wall beside it.

Gesturing Pereira and Connolly into the chairs, Ryker raised the blind over the rear window. Outside was the compound, the circle of huts around its perimeter. A few Indians squatted in the shadows, spears upright between their knees.

Connolly watched Ryker moving about in front of him, aware that the man's earlier impatience had given away to a faint but noticeable edginess. Ryker glanced irritably through the window, apparently annoyed to see the gradual gathering of the Indians before their huts.

There was a sweetly unsavoury smell in the room, and over his shoulder Connolly saw that the card-table was loaded with a large bale of miniature animal skins, those of a vole or some other forest rodent. A half-hearted attempt had been made to trim the skins, and tags of clotted blood clung to their margins.

Ryker jerked the table with his foot. "Well, here you are," he said to Pereira. "Twelve dozen. They took a hell of a lot of getting, I can tell you. You've brought the clock?"

Pereira nodded, still holding the parcel in his lap. He gazed distastefully at the dank scruffy skins. "Have you got some rats in there, Ryker? These don't look much good. Perhaps we should check through them outside...."

"Dammit, Pereira, don't be a fool!" Ryker snapped. "They're as good as you'll get. I had to trim half the skins myself. Let's have a look at the clock."

"Wait a minute." The Captain's jovial, easy-going manner had stiffened. Making the most of his temporary advantage, he reached out and touched one of the skins gingerly, shaking his head. "Pugh....Do you know how much I paid for this clock, Ryker? Seventy-five dollars. That's your credit for three years. I'm not so sure. And you're not very helpful, you know. Now about this aircraft that may have come down——"

Ryker snapped his fingers. "Forget it. Nothing did. The Nam-

19

bas tell me everything." He turned to Connolly. "You can take it from me there's no trace of an aircraft around here. Any rescue mission would be wasting their time."

Pereira watched Ryker critically. "As a matter of fact it wasn't an aircraft." He tapped Connolly's shoulder flash. "It was a rocket capsule—with a man on board. A very important and valuable man. None other than the Moon pilot, Colonel Francis Spender."

"Well...." Eyebrows raised in mock surprise, Ryker ambled to the window, stared out at a group of Indians who had advanced half-way across the compound. "My God, what next! The Moon pilot. Do they really think he's around here? But what a place to roost." He leaned out of the window and bellowed at the Indians, who retreated a few paces and then held their ground. "Damn fools," he muttered, "this isn't a zoo."

Pereira handed him the parcel, watching the Indians. There were more than fifty around the compound now, squatting in their doorways, a few of the younger men honing their spears. "They are remarkably curious," he said to Ryker, who had taken the parcel over to the dresser and was unwrapping it carefully. "Surely they've seen a pale-skinned man before?"

"They've nothing better to do." Ryker lifted the clock out of the cabinet with his big hands, with great care placed it beside the alarm clock, the almost inaudible motion of its pendulum lost in the metallic chatter of the latter's escapement. For a moment he gazed at the ornamental hands and numerals. Then he picked up the alarm clock and with an almost valedictory pat, like an officer dismissing a faithful if stupid minion, locked it away in the cupboard below. His former buoyancy returning, he gave Pereira a playful slap on the shoulder. "Captain, if you want any more rat-skins just give me a shout!"

Backing away, Pereira's heel touched one of Connolly's feet, distracting Connolly from a problem he had been puzzling over since their entry into the hut. Like a concealed clue in a detective story, he was sure that he had noticed something of signficance, but was unable to identify it.

"We won't worry about the skins," Pereira said. "What we'll do with your assistance, Ryker, is to hold a little parley with the chiefs, see whether they remember anything of this capsule."

Ryker stared out at the Indians now standing directly below the veranda. Irritably he slammed down the blind. "For God's sake, Pereira, they don't. Tell the Lieutenant he isn't interviewing people on Park Avenue or Piccadilly. If the Indians had seen anything I'd know."

"Perhaps." Pereira shrugged. "Still, I'm under instructions to assist Lieutenant Connolly and it won't do any harm to ask."

Connolly sat up. "Having come this far, Captain, I feel I should do two or three forays into the bush." To Ryker he explained: "They've recalculated the flight path of the final trajectory, there's a chance he may have come down further along the landing zone. Here, very possibly."

Shaking his head, Ryker slumped down on to the couch, and drove one fist angrily into the other. "I suppose this means they'll be landing here at any time with thousands of bulldozers and flame-throwers. Dammit, Lieutenant, if you have to send a man to the Moon, why don't you do it in your own back yard?"

Pereira stood up. "We'll be gone in a couple of days, Ryker." He nodded judiciously at Connolly and moved towards the door.

As Connolly climbed to his feet Ryker called out suddenly: "Lieutenant. You can tell me something I've wondered." There was an unpleasant downward curve to his mouth, and his tone was belligerent and provocative. "Why did they really send a man to the Moon?"

Connolly paused. He had remained silent during the conversation, not wanting to antagonize Ryker. The rudeness and complete self-immersion were pathetic rather than annoying. "Do you mean the military and political reasons?"

"No, I don't." Ryker stood up, arms akimbo again, measuring Connolly. "I mean the *real* reasons, Lieutenant."

Connolly gestured vaguely. For some reason formulating a satisfactory answer seemed more difficult than he had expected. "Well, I suppose you could say it was the natural spirit of exploration."

Ryker snorted derisively. "Do you seriously believe that, Lieutenant? 'The spirit of exploration!' My God! What a fantastic idea. Pereira doesn't believe that, do you, Captain?"

Before Connolly could reply Pereira took his arm. "Come on,

Lieutenant. This is no time for a metaphysical discussion." To Ryker he added: "It doesn't much matter what you and I believe, Ryker. A man went to the Moon and came back. He needs our help."

Ryker frowned ruefully. "Poor chap. He must be feeling pretty unhappy by now. Though anyone who gets as far as the Moon and is fool enough to come back deserves what he gets."

There was a scuffle of feet on the veranda, and as they stepped out into the sunlight a couple of Indians darted away along the jetty, watching Connolly with undiminished interest.

Ryker remained in the doorway, staring listlessly at the clock, but as they were about to climb into the launch he came after them. Now and then glancing over his shoulder at the encroaching semi-circle of Indians, he gazed down at Connolly with sardonic contempt. "Lieutenant," he called out before they went below. "Has it occurred to you that if he had landed, Spender might have wanted to stay on here?"

"I doubt it, Ryker," Connolly said calmly. "Anyway, there's little chance that Colonel Spender is still alive. What we're interested in finding is the capsule."

Ryker was about to reply when a faint metallic buzz sounded from the direction of his hut. He looked around sharply, waiting for it to end, and for a moment the whole tableau, composed of the men on the launch, the gaunt outcast on the edge of the jetty and the Indians behind him, was frozen in an absurdly motionless posture. The mechanism of the old alarm clock had obviously been fully wound, and the buzz sounded for thirty seconds, finally ending with a high-pitched ping.

Pereira grinned. He glanced at his watch. "It keeps good time, Ryker." But Ryker had stalked off back to the hut, scattering the Indians before him.

Connolly watched the group dissolve, then suddenly snapped his fingers. "You're right, Captain. It certainly does keep good time," he repeated as they entered the cabin.

Evidently tired by the encounter with Ryker, Pereira slumped down among Connolly's equipment and unbuttoned his tunic. "Sorry about Ryker, but I warned you. Frankly, Lieutenant, we might as well leave now. There's nothing here. Ryker knows that.

22

However, he's no fool, and he's quite capable of faking all sorts of evidence just to get a retainer out of you. He wouldn't mind if the bulldozers came."

"I'm not so sure." Connolly glanced briefly through the port-hole. "Captain, has Ryker got a radio? "

"Of course not. Why? "

"Are you certain? "

"Absolutely. It's the last thing the man would have. Anyway, there's no electrical supply here, and he has no batteries." He noticed Connolly's intent expression. "What's on your mind, Lieutenant? "

"You're his only contact? There are no other traders in the area? "

"None. The Indians are too dangerous, and there's nothing to trade. Why do you think Ryker has a radio? "

"He must have. Or something very similar. Captain, just now you remarked on the fact that his old alarm clock kept good time. Does it occur to you to ask *how*? "

Pereira sat up slowly. "Lieutenant, you have a valid point."

"Exactly. I knew there was something odd about those two clocks when they were standing side by side. That type of alarm clock is the cheapest obtainable, notoriously inaccurate. Often they lose two or three minutes in 24 hours. But that clock was telling the right time to within ten seconds. No optical instrument would give him that degree of accuracy."

Pereira shrugged sceptically. "But I haven't been here for over four months. And even then he didn't check the time with me."

"Of course not. He didn't need to. The only possible explana-tion for such a degree of accuracy is that he's getting a daily time fix, either on a radio or some long-range beacon."

"Wait a moment, Lieutenant." Pereira watched the dusk light fall across the jungle. "It's a remarkable coincidence, but there must be an innocent explanation. Don't jump straight to the con-clusion that Ryker has some instrument taken from the missing Moon capsule. Other aircraft have crashed in the forest. And what would be the point? He's not running an airline or railway system. Why should he need to know the time, the *exact* time, to within ten seconds? "

23

Connolly tapped the lid of his monitoring case, controlling his growing exasperation at Pereira's reluctance to treat the matter seriously, at his whole permissive attitude of lazy tolerance towards Ryker, the Indians and the forest. Obviously he unconsciously resented Connolly's sharp-eyed penetration of this private world.

"Clocks have become his idée fixe," Pereira continued. "Perhaps he's developed an amazing sensitivity to its mechanism. Knowing exactly the right time could be a substitute for the civilization on which he turned his back." Thoughtfully, Pereira moistened the end of his cheroot. "But I agree that it's strange. Perhaps a little investigation would be worthwhile after all."

After a cool jungle night in the air-conditioned cabin, the next day Connolly began discreetly to reconnoitre the area. Pereira took ashore two bottles of whiskey and a soda syphon, and was able to keep Ryker distracted while Connolly roved about the campong with his monitoring equipment. Once or twice he heard Ryker bellow jocularly at him from his window as he lolled back over the whiskey. At intervals, as Ryker slept, Pereira would come out into the sun, sweating like a drowsy pig in his stained uniform, and try to drive back the Indians.

"As long as you stay within earshot of Ryker you're safe," he told Connolly. Chopped-out pathways criss-crossed the bush at all angles, a new one added whenever one of the bands returned to the campong, irrespective of those already established. This maze extended for miles around them. "If you get lost, don't panic but stay where you are. Sooner or later we'll come out and find you."

Eventually giving up his attempt to monitor any of the signal beacons built into the lost capsule—both the sonar and radio meters remained at zero—Connolly tried to communicate with the Indians by sign language, but with the exception of one, the youth with the moist limpid eyes who had been hanging about on Ryker's veranda, they merely stared at him stonily. This youth Pereira identified as the son of the former witch-doctor ("Ryker's more or less usurped his role, for some reason the old boy lost the confidence of the tribe"). While the other Indians gazed at Connolly as if seeing some invisible numinous shadow, some extra-corporeal nimbus which pervaded his body, the youth was obviously aware that Connolly possessed some special talent, perhaps not dissimilar from that which his father had once practised. However, Connolly's attempts to talk to the youth were handicapped by the fact that he was suffering from a purulent ophthalmia, gonococchic in origin and extremely contagious, which made his eyes water continuously. Many of the Indians suffered from this complaint, threatened by permanent blindness, and Connolly had seen them treating their eyes with water in which a certain type of fragrant bark had been dissolved.

Ryker's casual, off-hand authority over the Indians puzzled Connolly. Slumped back in his chair against the mahogany dresser, one hand touching the ormolu clock, most of the time he and Pereira indulged in a lachrymose back-chat. Then, oblivious of any danger, Ryker would amble out into the dusty campong, push his way blurrily through the Indians and drum up a party to collect fire wood for the water still, jerking them bodily to their feet as they squatted about their huts. What interested Connolly was the Indians' reaction to this type of treatment. They seemed to be restrained, not by any belief in his strength of personality or primitive kingship, but by a grudging acceptance that for the time being at any rate, Ryker possessed the whip hand over them all. Obviously Ryker served certain useful roles for them as an inter-mediary with the Mission, but this alone would not explain the sources of his power. Beyond certain more or less defined limits— the perimeter of the campong—his authority was minimal.

A hint of explanation came on the second morning of their visit, when Connolly accidentally lost himself in the forest.

After breakfast Connolly sat under the awning on the deck of the patrol launch, gazing out over the brown, jelly-like surface of the river. The campong was silent. During the night the Indians had disappeared into the bush. Like lemmings they were appar-ently prone to these sudden irresistible urges. Occasionally the nomadic call would be strong enough to carry them 200 miles away; at other times they would set off in high spirits and then lose interest after a few miles, returning dispiritedly to the cam-pong in small groups.

Deciding to make the most of their absence, Connolly shouldered the monitoring equipment and climbed onto the pier. A few dying fires smoked plaintively among the huts, and abandoned utensils and smashed pottery lay about in the red dust. In the distance the morning haze over the forest had lifted, and Connolly could see what appeared to be a low hill—a shallow rise no more than a hundred feet in height—which rose off the flat floor of the jungle a quarter of a mile away.

On his right, among the huts, someone moved. An old man sat alone among the refuse of pottery shards and raffia baskets, cross-legged under a small make-shift awning. Barely distinguishable from the dust, his moribund figure seemed to contain the whole futility of the Amazon forest.

Still musing on Ryker's motives for isolating himself in the jungle, Connolly made his way towards the distant rise.

Ryker's behaviour the previous evening had been curious. Shortly after dusk, when the sunset sank into the western forest, bathing the jungle in an immense ultramarine and golden light, the day-long chatter and movement of the Indians ceased abruptly. Connolly had been glad of the silence—the endless thwacks of the rattan canes and grating of the stone mills in which they mixed the Government-issue meal had become tiresom. Pereira made several cautious visits to the edge of the campong, and each time reported that the Indians were sitting in a huge circle outside their huts, watching Ryker's bungalow. The latter was lounging on his veranda in the moonlight, chin in hand, one boot up on the rail, morosely surveying the assembled tribe.

"They've got their spears and ceremonial feathers," Pereira whispered. "For a moment I almost believed they were preparing an attack."

After waiting half an hour, Connolly climbed up on to the pier, found the Indians squatting in their dark silent circle, Ryker glaring down at them. Only the witch-doctor's son made any attempt to approach Connolly, sidling tentatively through the shadows, a piece of what appeared to be blue obsidian in his hand, some talisman of his father's that had lost its potency.

Uneasily, Connolly returned to the launch. Shortly after 3 a.m. they were wakened in their bunks by a tremendous whoop, reached the deck to hear the stampede of feet through the dust, the hissing of overturned fires and cooking pots. Apparently leading the pack, Ryker, emitting a series of re-echoed 'Harooh's!' disappeared into the bush. Within a minute the campong was empty.

"What game is Ryker playing?" Pereira muttered as they stood on the creaking jetty in the dusty moonlight. "This must be the focus of his authority over the Nambas." Baffled, they went back to their bunks.

Reaching the margins of the rise, Connolly strolled through a small orchard which had returned to nature, hearing in his mind the exultant roar of Ryker's voice as it had cleaved the midnight jungle. Idly he picked a few of the barely ripe guavas and vividly coloured cajus with their astringent delicately flavoured juice. After spitting away the pith, he searched for a way out of the orchard, but within a few minutes realized that he was lost.

⎺A continuous mound when seen from the distance, the rise was in fact a nexus of small hillocks that formed the residue of a one-time system of ox-bow lakes, and the basins between the slopes were still treacherous with deep mire. Connolly rested his equipment at the foot of a tree. Withdrawing his pistol, he fired two shots into the air in the hope of attracting Ryker and Pereira. He sat down to await his rescue, taking the opportunity to unlatch his monitors and wipe the dials.

After ten minutes no one had appeared. Feeling slightly demoralized, and frightened that the Indians might return and find him, Connolly shouldered his equipment and set off towards the north-west, in the approximate direction of the campong. The ground rose before him. Suddenly, as he turned behind a palisade of wild magnolia trees, he stepped into an open clearing on the crest of the hill.

Squatting on their heels against the tree-trunks and among the tall grass was what seemed to be the entire tribe of the Nambikwaras. They were facing him, their expressions immobile and watchful, eyes like white beads among the sheaves. Presumably they had been sitting in the clearing, only fifty yards away, when he fired his shots, and Connolly had the uncanny feeling that they had been waiting for him to make his entrance exactly at the point he had chosen.

Hesitating, Connolly tightened his grip on the radio monitor. The Indians' faces were like burnished teak, their shoulders painted with a delicate mosaic of earth colours. Noticing the spears held among the grass, Connolly started to walk on across the clearing towards a breach in the palisade of trees.

For a dozen steps the Indians remained motionless. Then, with a chorus of yells, they leapt forward from the grass and surrounded Connolly in a jabbering pack. None of them were more than five feet tall, but their plump agile bodies buffeted him about, almost knocking him off his feet. Eventually the tumult steadied itself, and two or three of the leaders stepped from the cordon and began to scrutinize Connolly more closely, pinching and fingering him with curious positional movements of the thumb and forefinger, like connoisseurs examining some interesting taxidermic object.

Finally, with a series of high-pitched whines and grunts, the Indians moved off towards the centre of the clearing, propelling Connolly in front of them with sharp·slaps on his legs and shoulders, like drovers goading on a large pig. They were all jabbering furiously to each other, some hacking at the grass with their machetes, gathering bundles of leaves in their arms.

Tripping over something in the grass, Connolly stumbled onto his knees. The catch slipped from the lid of the monitor, and as he stood up, fumbling with the heavy cabinet, the revolver slipped from his holster and was lost under his feet in the rush.

Giving way to his panic, he began to shout over the bobbing heads around him, to his surprise heard one of the Indians beside him bellow to the others. Instantly, as the refrain was taken up, the crowd stopped and re-formed its cordon around him. Gasping, Connolly steadied himself, and started to search the trampled grass for his revolver, when he realized that the Indians were now staring, not at himself, but at the exposed counters of the monitor. The six meters were swinging wildly after the stampede across the clearing, and the Indians craned forward, their machetes and spears lowered, gaping at the bobbing needles.

Then there was a roar from the edge of the clearing, and a huge wild-faced man in a straw hat, a shot-gun held like a crow-bar in his hands, stormed in among the Indians, driving them back. Dragging the monitor from his neck, Connolly felt the steadying hand of Captain Pereira take his elbow.

"Lieutenant, Lieutenant," Pereira murmured reprovingly as they recovered the pistol and made their way back to the campong, the uproar behind them fading among the undergrowth, "we were nearly in time to say grace."

Later that afternoon Connolly sat back in a canvas chair on the deck of the launch. About half the Indians had returned, and were wandering about the huts in a desultory manner, kicking at the fires. Ryker, his authority re-asserted, had returned to his bungalow.

"I thought you said they weren't cannibal," Connolly reminded Pereira.

The Captain snapped his fingers, as if thinking about something more important. "No, they're not. Stop worrying, Lieutenant, you're not going to end up in a pot." When Connolly demurred he swung crisply on his heel. He had sharpened up his uniform, and wore his pistol belt and Sam Browne at their regulation position, his peaked cap jutting low over his eyes. Evidently Connolly's close escape had confirmed some private suspicion. "Look, they're not cannibal in the dietary sense of the term, as used by the Food & Agriculture Organization in its classification of aboriginal peoples. They won't stalk and hunt human game in preference for any other. But—" here the Captain stared fixedly at Connolly "—in certain circumstances, after a fertility ceremonial, for example, they will eat human flesh. Like all members of primitive communities which are small numerically, the Nambikwara never bury their dead. Instead, they eat them, as a means of conserving the loss and to perpetuate the corporeal identity of the departed. Now do you understand?"

Connolly grimaced. "I'm glad to know now that I was about to be perpetuated."

Pereira looked out at the campong. "Actually they would never eat a white man, to avoid defiling the tribe." He paused. "At least, so I've always believed. It's strange, something seems to have...."

Listen, Lieutenant," he explained, "I can't quite piece it together, but I'm convinced we should stay here for a few days longer. Various elements make me suspicious, I'm sure Ryker is hiding something. That mound where you were lost is a sort of sacred tumulus, the way the Indians were looking at your instrument made me certain that they'd seen something like it before—perhaps a panel with many flickering dials...?"

"The *Goliath* 7?" Connolly shook his head sceptically. He listened to the undertow of the river drumming dimly against the keel of the launch. "I doubt it, Captain. I'd like to believe you, but for some reason it doesn't seem very likely."

"I agree. Some other explanation is preferable. But what? The Indians were squatting on that hill, waiting for someone to arrive. What else could your monitor have reminded them of?"

"Ryker's clock?" Connolly suggested. "They may regard it as a sort of ju-ju object, like a magical toy."

"No," Pereira said categorically. "These Indians are highly pragmatic, they're not impressed by useless toys. For them to be deterred from killing you means that the equipment you carried possessed some very real, down-to-earth power. Look, suppose the capsule did land here and was secretly buried by Ryker, and that in some way the clocks help him to identify its whereabouts—" here Pereira shrugged hopefully "—it's just possible."

"Hardly," Connolly said. "Besides, Ryker couldn't have buried the capsule himself, and if Colonel Spender had lived through re-entry Ryker would have helped him."

"I'm not so sure," Pereira said pensively. "It would probably strike our friend Mr. Ryker as very funny for a man to travel all the way to the Moon and back just to be killed by savages. Much too good a joke to pass over."

"What religious beliefs do the Indians have?" Connolly asked.

"No religion in the formalized sense of a creed and dogma. They eat their dead so they don't need to invent an after-life in an attempt to re-animate them. In general they subscribe to one of the so-called cargo cults. As I said, they're very material. That's why they're so lazy. Some time in the future they expect a magic galleon or giant bird to arrive carrying an everlasting cornucopia of worldly goods, so they just sit about waiting for the great day. Ryker encourages them in this idea. It's very dangerous—in some Melanesian islands the tribes with cargo cults have degenerated completely. They lie around all day on the beaches, waiting for the W.H.O. flying boat, or ..." His voice trailed off.

Connolly nodded and supplied the unspoken thought. " Or—a space capsule? "

Despite Pereira's growing if muddled conviction that something associated with the missing space-craft was to be found in the area, Connolly was still sceptical. His close escape had left him feeling curiously calm and emotionless, and he looked back on his possible death with fatalistic detachment, identifying it with the total ebb and flow of life in the Amazon forests, with its myriad unremembered deaths, and with the endless vistas of dead trees leaning across the jungle paths radiating from the campong. After only two days the jungle had begun to invest his mind with its own logic, and the possibility of the space-craft landing there seemed more and more remote. The two elements belonged to different systems of natural order, and he found it increasingly difficult to visualize them overlapping. In addition there was a deeper reason for his scepticism, underlined by Ryker's reference to the 'real' reasons for the space-flights. The implication was that the entire space programme was a symptom of some inner unconscious malaise afflicting mankind, and in particular the western technocracies, and that the space craft and satellites had been launched because their flights satisfied certain buried compulsions and desires. By contrast, in the jungle, where the unconscious was manifest and exposed, there was no need for these insane projections, and the likelihood of the Amazonas playing any part in the success or failure of the space flight became, by a sort of psychological parallax, increasingly blurred and distant, the missing capsule itself a fragment of a huge disintegrating fantasy.

However he agreed to Pereira's request to borrow the monitors and follow Ryker and the Indians on their midnight romp through the forest.

31

Once again, after dusk, the same ritual silence descended over the campong, and the Indians took up their positions in the doors of their huts. Like some morose exiled princeling, Ryker sat sprawled on his veranda, one eye on the clock through the window behind him. In the moonlight the scores of moist dark eyes never wavered as they watched him.

At last, half an hour later, Ryker galvanized his great body into life, with a series of tremendous whoops raced off across the campong, leading the stampede into the bush. Away in the distance, faintly outlined by the quarter moon, the shallow hump of the tribal tumulus rose over the black canopy of the jungle. Pereira waited until the last heel beats had subsided, then climbed onto the pier and disappeared among the shadows.

Far away Connolly could hear the faint cries of Ryker's pack as they made off through the bush, the sounds of machetes slashing at the undergrowth. An ember on the opposite side of the campong flared in the low wind, illuminating the abandoned old man, presumably the former witch doctor, whom he had seen that morning. Beside him was another slimmer figure, the limpid-eyed youth who had followed Connolly about.

A door stirred on Ryker's veranda, providing Connolly with a distant image of the white moonlit back of the river reflected in the mirrors of the mahogany dresser. Connolly watched the door jump lightly against the latch, then walked quietly across the pier to the wooden steps.

A few empty tobacco tins lay about on the shelves around the room, and a stack of empty bottles cluttered one corner behind the door. The ormolu clock had been locked away in the mahogany dresser. After testing the doors, which had been secured with a stout padlock, Connolly noticed a dog-eared paper-backed book lying on the dresser beside a half-empty carton of cartridges.

On a faded red ground, the small black lettering on the cover was barely decipherable, blurred by the sweat from Ryker's fingers. At first glance it appeared to be a set of logarithm tables. Each of the eighty or so pages was covered with column after column of finely printed numerals and tabular material.

Curious, Connolly carried the manual over to the doorway. The title page was more explicit.

A Question of Re-entry

ECHO III
CONSOLIDATED TABLES OF
CELESTIAL TRAVERSES

1965-1980

Published by the National Astronautics and Space Adminis-
stration, Washington, D.C., 1965. Part XV. Longitude 40-80
West, Latitude 10 North-35 South (South American Sub-
Continent) Price 35c.

His interest quickening, Connolly turned the pages. The
manual fell open at the section headed: Lat. 5 South, Long, 60
West. He remembered that this was the approximate position of
Campos Buros. Tabulated by year, month and day, the columns
of figures listed the elevations and compass bearings for sightings
of the Echo III satellite, the latest of the huge aluminium spheres
which had been orbiting the earth since Echo I was launched in
1959. Rough pencil lines had been drawn through all the entries
up to the year 1968. At this point the markings became individual,
each minuscule entry crossed off with a small blunt stroke. The
pages were grey with the blurred graphite.

Guided by this careful patchwork of cross-hatching, Connolly
found the latest entry: March 17, 1978. The time and sighting
were. 1-22 *a.m. Elevation 43 degrees WNW, Capella-Eridanus.*
Below it was the entry for the next day, an hour later, its orienta-
tions differing slightly.

Ruefully shaking his head in admiration of Ryker's cleverness,
Connolly looked at his watch. It was about 1.20, two minutes until
the next traverse. He glanced at the sky, picking out the constellation Eridanus, from which the satellite would emerge.

So this explained Ryker's hold over the Indians! What more
impressive means had a down-and-out white man of intimidating
and astonishing a tribe of primitive savages? Armed with nothing
more than a set of tables and a reliable clock, he could virtually
pin-point the appearance of the satellite at the first second of its
visible traverse. The Indians would naturally be awed and be-
wildered by this phantom charioteer of the midnight sky, steadily

pursuing its cosmic round, like a beacon traversing the profoundest deeps of their own minds. Any powers which Ryker cared to invest in the satellite would seem confirmed by his ability to control the time and place of its arrival.

Connolly realized now how the old alarm clock had told the correct time—by using his tables Ryker had read the exact time off the sky each night. A more accurate clock presumably freed him from the need to spend unnecessary time waiting for the satellite's arrival; he would now be able to set off for the tumulus only a few minutes beforehand.

Walking along the pier he began to search the sky. Away in the distance a low cry sounded into the midnight air, diffusing like a wraith over the jungle. Beside him, sitting on the bows of the launch, Connolly heard the helmsman grunt and point at the sky above the opposite bank. Following the up-raised arm, he quickly found the speeding dot of light. It was moving directly towards the tumulus. Steadily the satellite crossed the sky, winking intermittently as it passed behind lanes of high-altitude cirrus, the conscripted ship of the Nambikwaras' cargo cult.

It was about to disappear among the stars in the south-east when a faint shuffling sound distracted Connolly. He looked down to find the moist-eyed youth, the son of the witch doctor, standing only a few feet away from him, regarding him dolefully.

"Hello, boy," Connolly greeted him. He pointed at the vanishing satellite. "See the star?"

The youth made a barely perceptible nod. He hesitated for a moment, his running eyes glowing like drowned moons, then stepped forward and touched Connolly's wrist-watch, tapping the dial with his horny finger nail.

Puzzled, Connolly held it up for him to inspect. The youth watched the second hand sweep around the dial, an expression of rapt and ecstatic concentration of his face. Nodding vigorously, he pointed to the sky.

Connolly grinned. "So you understand? You've rumbled old man Ryker, have you?" He nodded encouragingly to the youth, who was tapping the watch eagerly, apparently in an effort to conjure up a second satellite. Connolly began to laugh. "Sorry, boy." He slapped the manual. "What you really need is this pack of jokers."

Connolly began to walk back to the bungalow, when the youth darted forward impulsively and blocked his way, thin legs spread in an aggressive stance. Then, with immense ceremony, he drew from behind his back a round painted object with a glass face that Connolly remembered he had seen him carrying before.

"That looks interesting." Connolly bent down to examine the object, caught a glimpse in the thin light of a luminous instrument before the youth snatched it away.

"Wait a minute, boy. Let's have another look at that."

After a pause the pantomime was repeated, but the youth was reluctant to allow Connolly more than the briefest inspection. Again Connolly saw a calibrated dial and a wavering indicator. Then the youth stepped forward and touched Connolly's wrist.

Quickly Connolly unstrapped the metal chain. He tossed the watch to the youth, who instantly dropped the instrument, his barter achieved, and after a delighted yodel turned and darted off among the trees.

Bending down, careful not to touch the instrument with his hands, Connolly examined the dial. The metal housing around it was badly torn and scratched, as if the instrument had been pried from some control panel with a crude implement. But the glass face and the dial beneath it were still intact. Across the centre was the legend:

LUNAR ALTIMETER

Miles: 100

GOLIATH 7

General Electric Corporation,
Schenectedy

Picking up the instrument, Connolly cradled it in his hands. The pressure seals were broken, and the gyro bath floated freely on its air cushion. Like a graceful bird the indicator needle glided up and down the scale.

35

The pier creaked under approaching footsteps. Connolly looked
up at the perspiring figure of Captain Pereira, cap in one hand,
monitor dangling from the other.

" My dear Lieutenant! " he panted, " Wait till I tell you, what a
farce, it's fantastic! Do you know what Ryker's doing?—it's so
simple it seems unbelievable that no one's thought of it before.
It's nothing short of the most magnificent practical *joke*! " Gasping, he sat down on the bale of skins leaning against the gangway.
" I'll give you a clue: Narcissus."

" Echo," Connolly replied flatly, still staring at the instrument
in his hands.

" You spotted it? Clever boy! " Pereira wiped his cap-band.
" How did you guess? It wasn't that obvious." He took the
manual Connolly handed him. " What the—? Ah, I see, this
makes it even more clear. Of course." He slapped his knee with
the manual. " You found this in his room? I take my hat off to
Ryker," he continued as Connolly set the altimeter down on the
pier and steadied it carefully. " Let's face it, it's something of a
pretty clever trick. Can you imagine it, he comes here, finds a tribe
with a strong cargo cult, opens his little manual and says ' Presto,
the great white bird will be arriving: *NOW*! ' "

Connolly nodded, then stood up, wiping his hands on a strip of
rattan. When Pereira's laughter had subsided he pointed down to
the glowing face of the altimeter at their feet. " Captain, something else arrived," he said quietly. " Never mind Ryker and the
satellite. This cargo actually landed."

As Pereira knelt down and inspected the altimeter, whistling
sharply to himself, Connolly walked over to the edge of the pier
and looked out across the great back of the silent river at the giant
trees which hung over the water, like forlorn mutes at some
cataclysmic funeral, their thin silver voices carried away on the
dead tide.

Half an hour before they set off the next morning, Connolly
waited on the deck for Captain Pereira to conclude his interroga-
tion of Ryker. The empty campong, deserted again by the Indians, basked in the heat, a single plume of smoke curling into
the sky. The old witch doctor and his son had disappeared, per-

haps to try their skill with a neighbouring tribe, but the loss of his watch was unregretted by Connolly. Down below, safely stowed away among his baggage, was the altimeter, carefully sterilized and sealed. On the table in front of him, no more than two feet from the pistol in his belt, lay Ryker's manual.

For some reason he did not want to see Ryker, despite his contempt for him, and when Pereira emerged from the bungalow he was relieved to see that he was alone. Connolly had decided that he would not return with the search parties when they came to find the capsule; Pereira would serve adequately as a guide.

"Well?"

The Captain smiled wanly. "Oh, he admitted it, of course." He sat down on the rail, and pointed to the manual. "After all, he had no choice. Without that his existence here would be untenable."

"He admitted that Colonel Spender landed here?"

Pereira nodded. "Not in so many words, but effectively. The capsule is buried somewhere here—under the tumulus, I would guess. The Indians got hold of Colonel Spender, Ryker claims he could do nothing to help him."

"That's a lie. He saved me in the bush when the Indians thought I had landed."

With a shrug Pereira said: "Your positions were slightly different. Besides, my impression is that Spender was dying anyway, Ryker says the parachute was badly burnt. He probably accepted a *fait accompli*, simply decided to do nothing and hush the whole thing up, incorporating the landing into the cargo cult. Very useful too. He'd been tricking the Indians with the Echo satellite, but sooner or later they would have become impatient. After the *Goliath* crashed, of course, they were prepared to go on watching the Echo and waiting for the next landing forever." A faint smile touched his lips. "It goes without saying that he regards the episode as something of a macabre joke. On you and the whole civilized world."

A door slammed on the veranda, and Ryker stepped out into the sunlight. Bare-chested and hatless, he strode towards the launch.

"Connolly," he called down, "you've got my box of tricks there!"

Connolly reached forward and fingered the manual, the butt of his pistol tapping the table edge. He looked up at Ryker, at his big golden frame bathed in the morning light. Despite his still belligerent tone, a subtle change had come over Ryker. The ironic gleam in his eye had gone, and the inner core of wariness and suspicion which had warped the man and exiled him from the world was now visible. Connolly realized that, curiously, their respective roles had been reversed. He remembered Pereira reminding him that the Indians were at equilibrium with their environment, accepting its constraints and never seeking to dominate the towering arbors of the forest, in a sense of externalization of their own unconscious psyches. Ryker had upset that equilibrium, and by using the Echo satellite had brought the 20th century and its psychopathic projections into the heart of the Amazonian deep, transforming the Indians into a community of superstitious and materialistic sightseers, their whole culture oriented around the mythical god of the puppet star. It was Connolly who now accepted the jungle for what it was, seeing himself and the abortive space-flight in this fresh perspective.

Pereira gestured to the helmsman, and with a muffled roar the engine started. The launch pulled lightly against its lines.

"Connolly!" Ryker's voice was shriller now, his bellicose shout overlayed by a higher note. For a moment the two men looked at each other, and in the eyes above him Connolly glimpsed the helpless isolation of Ryker, his futile attempt to identify himself with the forest.

Picking up the manual, Connolly leaned forward and tossed it through the air on to the pier. Ryker tried to catch it, then knelt down and picked it up before it slipped through the springing poles. Still kneeling, he watched as the lines were cast off and the launch surged ahead.

They moved out into the channel and plunged through the bowers of spray into the heavier swells of the open current.

As they reached a sheltering bend and the figure of Ryker

faded for the last time among the creepers and sunlight, Connolly turned to Pereira. "Captain—what actually happened to Colonel Spender? You said the Indians wouldn't eat a white man."

"They eat their gods," Pereira said.

THE DROWNED GIANT

ON the morning after the storm the body of a drowned giant was washed ashore on the beach five miles to the north-west of the city. The first news of its arrival was brought by a nearby farmer and subsequently confirmed by the local newspaper reporters and the police. Despite this the majority of people, myself among them, remained sceptical, but the return of more and more eye-witnesses attesting to the vast size of the giant was finally too much for our curiosity. The library where my colleagues and I were carrying out our research was almost deserted when we set off for the coast shortly after two o'clock, and throughout the day people continued to leave their offices and shops as accounts of the giant circulated around the city.

By the time we reached the dunes above the beach a substantial crowd had gathered, and we could see the body lying in the shallow water two hundred yards away. At first the estimates of its size seemed greatly exaggerated. It was then at low tide, and almost all the giant's body was exposed, but he appeared to be a little larger than a basking shark. He lay on his back with his arms at his sides, in an attitude of repose, as if asleep on the mirror of wet sand, the reflection of his blanched skin fading as the water receded. In the clear sunlight his body glistened like the white plumage of a sea-bird.

Puzzled by this spectacle, and dissatisfied with the matter-of-fact explanations of the crowd, my friends and I stepped down from the dunes on to the shingle. Everyone seemed reluctant to approach the giant, but half an hour later two fishermen in wading boots walked out across the sand. As their diminutive figures neared the recumbent body a sudden hubbub of conversation broke out among the spectators. The two men were completely dwarfed by the giant. Although his heels were partly submerged in the sand, the feet rose to at least twice the fishermen's height, and we immediately realized that this drowned leviathan had the mass and dimensions of the largest sperm whale.

Three fishing smacks had arrived on the scene and with keels raised remained a quarter of a mile off-shore, the crews watching from the bows. Their discretion deterred the spectators on the shore from wading out across the sand. Impatiently everyone stepped down from the dunes and waited on the shingle slopes, eager for a closer view. Around the margins of the figure the sand had been washed away, forming a hollow, as if the giant had fallen out of the sky. The two fishermen were standing between the immense plinths of the feet, waving to us like tourists among the columns of some water-lapped temple on the Nile. For a moment I feared that the giant was merely asleep and might suddenly stir and clap his heels together, but his glazed eyes stared skywards, unaware of the miniscule replicas of himself between his feet.

The fishermen then began a circuit of the corpse, strolling past the long white flanks of the legs. After a pause to examine the fingers of the supine hand, they disappeared from sight between the arm and chest, then re-emerged to survey the head, shielding their eyes as they gazed up at its Graecian profile. The shallow forehead, straight high-bridged nose and curling lips reminded me of a Roman copy of Praxiteles, and the elegantly formed cartouches of the nostrils emphasized the resemblance to monumental sculpture.

Abruptly there was a shout from the crowd, and a hundred arms pointed towards the sea. With a start I saw that one of the fishermen had climbed on to the giant's chest and was now strolling about and signalling to the shore. There was a roar of surprise and triumph from the crowd, lost in a rushing avalanche of shingle as everyone surged forward across the sand.

As we approached the recumbent figure, which was lying in a pool of water the size of a field, our excited chatter fell away again, subdued by the huge physical dimensions of this moribund colossus. He was stretched out at a slight angle to the shore, his legs carried nearer the beach, and this foreshortening had disguised his true length. Despite the two fishermen standing on his abdomen, the crowd formed itself into a wide circle, groups of three or four people tentatively advancing towards the hands and feet.

My companions and I walked around the sea-ward side of the giant, whose hips and thorax towered above us like the hull of a stranded ship. His pearl-coloured skin, distended by immersion in salt water, masked the contours of the enormous muscles and tendons. We passed below the left knee, which was flexed slightly, threads of damp sea-weed clinging to its sides. Draped loosely across the midriff, and preserving a tenuous propriety, was a shawl of heavy open-weaved material, bleached to a pale yellow by the water. A strong odour of brine came from the garment as it steamed in the sun, mingled with the sweet but potent scent of the giant's skin.

We stopped by his shoulder and gazed up at the motionless profile. The lips were parted slightly, the open eye cloudy and occluded, as if injected with some blue milky liquid, but the delicate arches of the nostrils and eyebrows invested the face with an ornate charm that belied the brutish power of the chest and shoulders.

The ear was suspended in mid-air over our heads like a sculptured doorway. As I raised my hand to touch the pendulous lobe someone appeared over the edge of the forehead and shouted down at me. Startled by this apparition, I stepped back, and then saw that a group of youths had climbed up on to the face and were jostling each other in and out of the orbits.

People were now clambering all over the giant, whose reclining arms provided a double stairway. From the palms they walked along the forearms to the elbow and then crawled over the distended belly of the biceps to the flat promenade of the pectoral muscles which covered the upper half of the smooth hairless chest. From here they climbed up on to the face, hand over hand along the lips and nose, or forayed down the abdomen to meet others who had straddled the ankles and were patrolling the twin columns of the thighs.

The Drowned Giant

We continued our circuit through the crowd, and stopped to examine the outstretched right hand. A small pool of water lay in the palm, like the residue of another world, now being kicked away by the people ascending the arm. I tried to read the palm-lines that grooved the skin, searching for some clue to the giant's character, but the distension of the tissues had almost obliterated them, carrying away all trace of the giant's identity and his last tragic predicament. The huge muscles and wrist-bones of the hand seemed to deny any sensitivity to their owner, but the delicate flexion of the fingers and the well-tended nails, each cut symmetrically to within six inches of the quick, argued a certain refinement of temperament, illustrated in the Graecian features of the face, on which the townsfolk were now sitting like flies.

One youth was even standing, arms wavering at his sides, on the very tip of the nose, shouting down at his companions, but the face of the giant still retained its massive composure.

Returning to the shore, we sat down on the shingle, and watched the continuous stream of people arriving from the city. Some six or seven fishing boats had collected off-shore, and their crews waded in through the shallow water for a closer look at this enormous storm-catch. Later a party of police appeared and made a half-hearted attempt to cordon off the beach, but after walking up to the recumbent figure any such thoughts left their minds, and they went off together with bemused backward glances.

An hour later there were a thousand people present on the beach, at least two hundred of them standing or sitting on the giant, crowded along his arms and legs or circulating in a ceaseless melée across his chest and stomach. A large gang of youths occupied the head, toppling each other off the cheeks and sliding down the smooth planes of the jaw. Two or three straddled the nose, and another crawled into one of the nostrils, from which he emitted barking noises like a dog.

That afternoon the police returned, and cleared a way through the crowd for a party of scientific experts—authorities on gross anatomy and marine biology—from the university. The gang of youths and most of the people on the giant climbed down, leaving behind a few hardy spirits perched on the tips of the toes and on the forehead. The experts strode around the giant, heads nodding in vigorous consultation, preceded by the policemen who pushed back the press of spectators. When they reached the outstretched hand the senior officer offered to assist them up on to the palm, but the experts hastily demurred.

After they returned to the shore, the crowd once more climbed on to the giant, and was in full possession when we left at five o'clock, covering the arms and legs like a dense flock of gulls sitting on the corpse of a large fish.

I next visited the beach three days later. My friends at the library had returned to their work, and delegated to me the task of keeping the giant under observation and preparing a report. Perhaps they sensed my particular interest in the case, and it was certainly true that I was eager to return to the beach. There was nothing necrophilic about this, for to all intents the giant was still alive for me, indeed more alive than many of the people watching him. What I found so fascinating was partly his immense scale, the huge volumes of space occupied by his arms and legs, which seemed to confirm the identity of my own miniature limbs, but above all the mere categorical fact of his existence. Whatever else in our lives might be open to doubt, the giant, dead or alive, existed in an absolute sense, providing a glimpse into a world of similar absolutes of which we spectators on the beach were such imperfect and puny copies.

When I arrived at the beach the crowd was considerably smaller, and some two or three hundred people sat on the shingle, picnicking and watching the groups of visitors who walked out across the sand. The successive tides had carried the giant nearer the shore, swinging his head and shoulders towards the beach, so that he seemed doubly to gain in size, his huge body dwarfing the fishing boats beached beside his feet. The uneven contours of the beach had pushed his spine into a slight arch, expanding his chest and tilting back the head, forcing him into a more expressly heroic posture. The combined effects of sea-water and the tumefaction of the tissues had given the face a sleeker and less youthful look. Although the vast proportions of the features made it impossible to assess the age and character of the giant, on my previous visit his classically modelled mouth and nose suggested that he had been a young man of discreet and modest temper. Now, however, he appeared to be at least in early middle age. The puffy cheeks, thicker nose and temples and narrowing eyes gave him a look of well-fed maturity that even now hinted at a growing corruption to come.

This accelerated post-mortem development of the giant's character, as if the latent elements of his personality had gained sufficient momentum during his life to discharge themselves in a brief final resumé, continued to fascinate me. It marked the beginning of the giant's surrender to that all-demanding system of time in which the rest of humanity finds itself, and of which, like the million twisted ripples of a fragmented whirlpool, our finite lives are the concluding products. I took up my position on the shingle directly opposite the giant's head, from where I could see the new arrivals and the children clambering over the legs and arms.

Among the morning's visitors were a number of men in leather jackets and cloth caps, who peered up critically at the giant with a professional eye, pacing out his dimensions and making rough calculations in the sand with spars of driftwood. I assumed them to be from the public works department and other municipal bodies, no doubt wondering how to dispose of this gargantuan piece of jetsam.

Several rather more smartly attired individuals, circus proprietors and the like, also appeared on the scene, and strolled slowly around the giant, hands in the pockets of their long overcoats, saying nothing to one another. Evidently its bulk was too great even for their matchless enterprise. After they had gone the children continued to run up and down the arms and legs, and the youths wrestled with each other over the supine face, the damp sand from their feet covering the white skin.

The following day I deliberately postponed my visit until the late afternoon, and when I arrived there were fewer than fifty or sixty people sitting on the shingle. The giant had been carried still closer to the shore, and was now little more than seventy-five yards away, his feet crushing the palisade of a rotting breakwater. The slope of the firmer sand tilted his body towards the sea, and the bruised face was averted in an almost conscious gesture. I sat down on a large metal winch which had been shackled to a concrete caisson above the shingle, and looked down at the recumbent figure.

His blanched skin had now lost its pearly translucence and was spattered with dirty sand which replaced that washed away by the night tide. Clumps of sea-weed filled the intervals between the fingers and a collection of litter and cuttle-bones lay in the crevices below the hips and knees. But despite this, and the continuous thickening of his features, the giant still retained his magnificent Homeric stature. The enormous breadth of the shoulders, and the huge columns of the arms and legs, still carried the figure into another dimension, and the giant seemed a more authentic image of one of the drowned Argonauts or heroes of the Odyssey than the conventional human-sized portrait previously in my mind.

I stepped down on to the sand, and walked between the pools of water towards the giant. Two small boys were sitting in the well of the ear, and at the far end a solitary youth stood perched high on one of the toes, surveying me as I approached. As I had hoped when delaying my visit, no one else paid any attention to me, and the people on the shore remained huddled beneath their coats.

The giant's supine right hand was covered with broken shells and sand, in which a score of footprints were visible. The rounded bulk of the hip towered above me, cutting off all sight of the sea. The sweetly acrid odour I had noticed before was now more pungent, and through the opaque skin I could see the serpentine coils of congealed blood-vessels. However repellent it seemed, this ceaseless metamorphosis, a visible life in death, alone permitted me to set foot on the corpse.

Using the jutting thumb as a stair-rail, I climbed up on to the palm and began my ascent. The skin was harder than I expected, barely yielding to my weight. Quickly I walked up the sloping forearm and the bulging balloon of the biceps. The face of the drowned giant loomed to my right, the cavernous nostrils and huge flanks of the cheeks like the cone of some freakish volcano.

Safely rounding the shoulder, I stepped out on to the broad promenade of the chest, across which the bony ridges of the rib-cage lay like huge rafters. The white skin was dappled by the darkening bruises of countless foot-prints, in which the patterns of individual heel-marks were clearly visible. Someone had built a small sandcastle on the centre of the sternum, and I climbed on to this partly demolished structure to give myself a better view of the face.

The two children had now scaled the ear and were pulling themselves into the right orbit, whose blue globe, completely occluded by some milk-coloured fluid, gazed sightlessly past their miniature forms. Seen obliquely from below, the face was devoid of all grace and repose, the drawn mouth and raised chin propped up by its gigantic slings of muscles resembling the torn prow of a colossal wreck. For the first time I became aware of the extremity of this last physical agony of the giant, no less painful for his unawareness of the collapsing musculature and tissues . The absolute isolation of the ruined figure, cast like an abandoned ship upon the empty shore, almost out of sound of the waves, transformed his face into a mask of exhaustion and helplessness.

As I stepped forward, my foot sank into a trough of soft tissue, and a gust of fetid gas blew through an aperture between the ribs. Retreating from the fouled air, which hung like a cloud over my head, I turned towards the sea to clear my lungs. To my surprise I saw that the giant's left hand had been amputated.

I stared with bewilderment at the blackening stump, while the solitary youth reclining on his aerial perch a hundred feet away surveyed me with a sanguinary eye.

This was only the first of a sequence of depradations. I spent the following two days in the library, for some reason reluctant to visit the shore, aware that I had probably witnessed the approaching end of a magnificent illusion. When I next crossed the dunes and set foot on the shingle the giant was little more than twenty yards away, and with this close proximity to the rough pebbles all traces had vanished of the magic which once surrounded his distant wave-washed form. Despite his immense size, the bruises and dirt that covered his body made him appear merely human in scale, his vast dimensions only increasing his vulnerability.

His right hand and foot had been removed, dragged up the slope and trundled away by cart. After questioning the small

47

group of people huddled by the breakwater, I gathered that a fertilizer company and a cattle food manufacturer were responsible.

The giant's remaining foot rose into the air, a steel hawzer fixed to the large toe, evidently in preparation for the following day. The surrounding beach had been disturbed by a score of workmen, and deep ruts marked the ground where the hands and foot had been hauled away. A dark brackish fluid leaked from the stumps, and stained the sand and the white cones of the cuttlefish. As I walked down the shingle I noticed that a number of jocular slogans, swastikas and other signs had been cut into the grey skin, as if the mutilation of this motionless colossus had released a sudden flood of repressed spite. The lobe of one of the ears was pierced by a spear of timber, and a small fire had burnt out in the centre of the chest, blackening the surrounding skin. The fine wood ash was still being scattered by the wind.

A foul smell enveloped the cadaver, the undisguisable signature of putrefaction, which had at last driven away the usual gathering of youths. I returned to the shingle and climbed up on to the winch. The giant's swollen cheeks had now almost closed his eyes, drawing the lips back in a monumental gape. The once straight Graecian nose had been twisted and flattened, stamped into the ballooning face by countless heels.

When I visited the beach the following day I found, almost with relief, that the head had been removed.

Some weeks elapsed before I made my next journey to the beach, and by then the human likeness I had noticed earlier had vanished again. On close inspection the recumbent thorax and abdomen were unmistakeably manlike, but as each of the limbs was chopped off, first at the knee and elbow, and then at shoulder and thigh, the carcass resembled that of any headless sea-animal —whale or whale-shark. With this loss of identity, and the few traces of personality that had clung tenuously to the figure, the interest of the spectators expired, and the foreshore was deserted except for an elderly beachcomber and the watchman sitting in the doorway of the contractor's hut.

A loose wooden scaffolding had been erected around the carcass, from which a dozen ladders swung in the wind, and the surrounding sand was littered with coils of rope, long metal-handled knives and grappling irons, the pebbles oily with blood and pieces of bone and skin.

I nodded to the watchman, who regarded me dourly over his brazier of burning coke. The whole area was pervaded by the pungent smell of huge squares of blubber being simmered in a vat behind the hut.

Both the thigh-bones had been removed, with the assistance of a small crane draped in the gauze-like fabric which had once covered the waist of the giant, and the open sockets gaped like barn doors. The upper arms, collar bones and pudenda had likewise been dispatched. What remained of the skin over the thorax and abdomen had been marked out in parallel strips with a tar brush, and the first five or six sections had been pared away from the midriff, revealing the great arch of the rib-cage.

As I left a flock of gulls wheeled down from the sky and alighted on the beach, picking at the stained sand with ferocious cries.

Several months later, when the news of his arrival had been generally forgotten, various pieces of the body of the dismembered giant began to reappear all over the city. Most of these were bones, which the fertilizer manufacturers had found too difficult to crush, and their massive size, and the huge tendons and discs of cartilage attached to their joints, immediately identified them. For some reason, these disembodied fragments seemed better to convey the essence of the giant's original magnificence than the bloated appendages that had been subsequently amputated. As I looked across the road at the premises of the largest wholesale merchants in the meat market, I recognized the two enormous thighbones on either side of the doorway. They towered over the porters' heads like the threatening megaliths of some primitive druidical religion, and I had a sudden vision of the giant climbing to his knees upon these bare bones and striding away through the streets of the city, picking up the scattered fragments of himself on his return journey to the sea.

A few days later I saw the left humerus lying in the entrance to one of the shipyards (its twin for several years lay on the mud among the piles below the harbour's principal commercial wharf). In the same week the mummified right hand was exhibited on a carnival float during the annual pageant of the guilds.

The lower jaw, typically, found its way to the museum of natural history. The remainder of the skull has disappeared, but is probably still lurking in the waste grounds or private gardens of the city—quite recently, while sailing down the river, I noticed two ribs of the giant forming a decorative arch in a waterside garden, possibly confused with the jaw-bones of a whale. A large square of tanned and tattooed skin, the size of an indian blanket, forms a backcloth to the dolls and masks in a novelty shop near the amusement park, and I have no doubt that elsewhere in the city, in the hotels or golf clubs, the mummified nose or ears of the giant hang from the wall above a fireplace. As for the immense pizzle, this ends its days in the freak museum of a circus which travels up and down the north-west. This monumental apparatus, stunning in its proportions and sometime potency, occupies a complete booth to itself. The irony is that it is wrongly identified as that of a whale, and indeed most people, even those who first saw him cast up on the shore after the storm, now remember the giant, if at all, as a large sea beast.

The remainder of the skeleton, stripped of all flesh, still rests on the sea shore, the clutter of bleached ribs like the timbers of a derelict ship. The contractor's hut, the crane and the scaffolding have been removed, and the sand being driven into the bay along the coast has buried the pelvis and backbone. In the winter the high curved bones are deserted, battered by the breaking waves, but in the summer they provide an excellent perch for the sea-wearying gulls.

END·GAME

AFTER his trial they gave Constantin a villa, an allowance and an executioner. The villa was small and high-walled, and had obviously been used for the purpose before. The allowance was adequate to Constantin's needs—he was never permitted to go out and his meals were prepared for him by a police orderly. The executioner was his own. Most of the time they sat on the enclosed veranda overlooking the narrow stone garden, playing chess with a set of large well-worn pieces.

The executioner's name was Malek. Officially he was Constantin's supervisor, and responsible for maintaining the villa's tenuous contact with the outside world, now hidden from sight beyond the steep walls, and for taking the brief telephone call that came promptly at nine o'clock every morning. However, his real role was no secret between them. A powerful, doughy-faced man with an anonymous expression, Malek at first intensely irritated Constantin, who had been used to dealing with more subtle sets of responses. Malek followed him around the villa, never interfering —unless Constantin tried to bribe the orderly for a prohibited newspaper, when Malek merely gestured with a slight turn of one of his large hands, face registering no disapproval, but cutting off the attempt as irrevocably as a bulkhead—nor making any suggestions as to how Constantin should spend his time. Like a large bear, he sat motionlessly in the lounge in one of the faded armchairs, watching Constantin.

Ater a week Constantin tired of reading the old novels in the bottom shelf of the bookcase—somewhere among the grey well-thumbed pages he had hoped to find a message from one of his predecessors—and invited Malek to play chess. The set of chipped mahogany pieces reposed on one of the empty shelves of the bookcase, the only item of decoration or recreational equipment in the villa. Apart from the books and the chess set the small six-roomed house was completely devoid of ornament. There were no curtains or picture rails, bedside tables or standard lamps, and the only electrical fittings were the lights recessed behind thick opaque bowls into the ceilings. Obviously the chess set and the row of novels had been provided deliberately, each representing one of the alternative pastimes available to the temporary tenants of the villa. Men of a phlegmatic or philosophical temperament, resigned to the inevitability of their fate, would chose to read the novels, sinking backwards into a self-anaesthetized trance as they waded through the turgid prose of those nineteenth-century romances.

On the other hand, men of a more volatile and extrovert disposition would obviously prefer to play chess, unable to resist the opportunity to exercise their Machiavellian talents for positional manoeuvre to the last. The games of chess would help to maintain their unconscious optimism and, more subtly, sublimate or divert any attempts at escape.

When Constantin suggested that they play chess Malek promptly agreed, and so they spent the next long month as the late summer turned to autumn. Constantin was glad he had chosen chess; the game brought him into immediate personal involvement with Malek, and like all condemned men he had soon developed a powerful emotional transference on to what effectively was the only person left in his life.

At present it was neither negative nor positive; but a relationship of acute dependence—already Malek's notional personality was becoming overlaid by the associations of all the anonymous but nonetheless potent figures of authority whom Constantin could remember since his earliest childhood: his own father, the priest at the seminary he had seen hanged after the revolution, the first senior commissars, the party secretaries at the ministry of foreign affairs and, ultimately, the members of the central committee themselves. Here, where the anonymous faces had crystallized into those of closely observed colleagues and rivals, the process seemed to come full circle, so that he himself was identified with those shadowy personas who had authorized his death and were now represented by Malek.

Constantin had also, of course, become dominated by another obsession, the need to know: *when*? In the weeks after the trial and sentence he had remained in a curiously euphoric state, too stunned to realize that the dimension of time still existed for him, he had already died *a posteriori*. But gradually the will to live, and his old determination and ruthlessness, which had served him so well for thirty years, reasserted themselves, and he realized that a small hope still remained to him. How long exactly in terms of time he could only guess, but if he could master Malek his survival became a real possibility.

The question remained: When?

Fortunately he could be completely frank with Malek. The first point he established immediately.

"Malek," he asked on the tenth move one morning, when he had completed his development and was relaxing for a moment. "Tell me, do you know—when?"

Malek looked up from the board, his large almost bovine eyes gazing blandly at Constantin. "Yes, Mr. Constantin, I know when." His voice was deep and functional, as expressionless as a weighing machine's.

Constantin sat back reflectively. Outside the glass panes of the veranda the rain fell steadily on the solitary fir tree which had maintained a precarious purchase among the stones under the wall. A few miles to the south-west of the villa were the outskirts of the small port, one of the dismal so-called 'coastal resorts' where junior ministry men and party hacks were sent for their bi-annual holidays. The weather, however, seemed peculiarly inclement, the sun never shining through the morose clouds, and for a moment, before he checked himself, Constantin felt glad to be within the comparative warmth of the villa.

"Let me get this straight," he said to Malek. "You don't merely know in a general sense—for example, after receiving an instruction from so-and-so—but you know *specifically* when?"

"Exactly." Malek moved his queen out of the game. His chess was sound but without flair or a personal style, suggesting that he had improved merely by practice—most of his opponents, Constantin realized with sardonic amusement, would have been players of a high class.

"You know the *day* and the *hour* and the *minute*," Constantin pressed. Malek nodded slowly, most of his attention upon the game, and Constantin rested his smooth sharp chin in one hand, watching his opponent. "It could be within the next ten seconds, or again, it might not be for ten years?"

"As you say." Malek gestured at the board. "Your move."

Constantin waved this aside. "I know, but don't let's rush it. These games are played on many levels, Malek. People who talk about three-dimensional chess obviously know nothing about the present form." Occasionally he made these openings in the hope of loosening Malek's tongue, but conversation with him seemed to be impossible.

Abruptly he sat forward across the board, his eyes searching Malek's. "You alone know the date, Malek, and as you have said, it might not be for ten years—or twenty. Do you think you can keep such a secret to yourself for so long?"

Malek made no attempt to answer this, and waited for Constantin to resume play. Now and then his eyes inspected the corners of the veranda, or glanced at the stone garden outside. From the kitchen came the occasional sounds of the orderly's boots scraping the floor as he lounged by the telephone on the deal table.

As he scrutinized the board Constantin wondered how he could provoke any response whatever from Malek; the man had shown no reaction at the mention of ten years, although the period was ludicrously far ahead. In all probability their real game would be a short one. The indeterminate date of the execution, which imbued the procedure with such a bizarre flavour, was not intended to add an element of torture or suspense to the condemned's last days, but simply to obscure and confuse the very fact of his exit. If a definite date were known in advance there might be a last-minute rally of sympathy, an attempt to review the sentence and perhaps apportion the blame elsewhere, and the

unconscious if not conscious sense of complicity in the condemned man's crimes might well provoke an agonized reappraisal
and, after the execution of the sentence, a submerged sense of
guilt upon which opportunists and intriguers could play to
advantage.

By means of the present system, however, all these dangers and
unpleasant side-effects were obviated, the accused was removed
from his place in the hierarchy when the opposition to him was at
its zenith and conveniently handed over to the judiciary, and
thence to one of the courts of star chamber whose proceedings
were always held in camera and whose verdicts were never
announced.

As far as his former colleagues were concerned, he had disappeared into the endless corridor world of the bureaucratic
purgatories, his case permanently on file but never irrevocably
closed. Above all, the fact of his guilt was never established and
confirmed. As Constantin was aware, he himself had been con-
victed upon a technicality in the margins of the main indictment
against him, a mere procedural device, like a bad twist in the plot
of a story, designed solely to bring the investigation to a close.
Although he knew the real nature of his crime, Constantin had
never been formally notified of his guilt; in fact the court had
gone out of its way to avoid preferring any serious charges
against him whatever.

This ironic inversion of the classical Kafkaesque situation, by
which, instead of admitting his guilt to a non-existent crime, he
was forced to connive in a farce maintaining his innocence of
offences he knew full well he had committed, was preserved in his
present situation at the execution villa.

The psychological basis was more obscure but in some way far
more threatening, the executioner beckoning his victim towards
him with a beguiling smile, reassuring him that all was forgiven.
Here he played upon, not those unconscious feelings of anxiety
and guilt, but that innate conviction of individual survival, that
obsessive preoccupation with personal immortality which is
merely a disguised form of the universal fear of the image of
one's own death. It was this assurance that all was well, and the

absence of any charges of guilt or responsibility, which had made so orderly the queues into the gas chambers.

At present the paradoxical face of this diabolical device was worn by Malek, his lumpy amorphous features and neutral but ambiguous attitude making him seem less a separate personality than the personification of the apparat of the state. Perhaps the sardonic title of 'supervisor' was nearer the truth than had seemed at first sight, and that Malek's role was simply to officiate, or at the most serve as moderator, at a trial by ordeal in which Constantin was his own accused, prosecutor and judge.

However, he reflected as he examined the board, aware of Malek's bulky presence across the pieces, this would imply that they had completely misjudged his own personality, with its buoyancy and almost gallic verve and panache. He, of all people, would be the last to take his own life in an orgy of self-confessed guilt. Not for him the neurotic suicide so loved of the Slav. As long as there were a way out he would cheerfully shoulder any burden of guilt, tolerant of his own weaknesses, ready to shrug them off with a quip. This insouciance had always been his strongest ally.

His eyes searched the board, roving down the open files of the queens and bishops, as if the answer to the pressing enigma were to be found in these polished corridors.

When? His own estimate was two months. Almost certainly, (and he had no fear here that he was rationalizing) it would not be within the next two or three days, nor even the next fortnight. Haste was always unseemly, quite apart from violating the whole purpose of the exercise. Two months would see him safely into limbo, and be sufficiently long for the suspense to break him down and reveal any secret allies, sufficiently brief to fit his particular crime.

Two months? Not as long as he might have wished. As he translated his queen's bishop into play Constantin began to map out his strategy for defeating Malek. The first task, obviously, was to discover when Malek was to carry out the execution, partly to give him peace of mind, but also to allow him to adjust the context of his escape. A physical leap to freedom over the wall would be pointless. Contacts had to be established, pressure brought to bear at various sensitive points in the hierarchy, paving the way for a reconsideration of his case. All this would take time.

His thoughts were interrupted by the sharp movement of Malek's left hand across the board, followed by a gutteral grunt. Surprised by the speed and economy with which Malek had moved his piece as much by the fact that he himself was in check, Constantin sat forward and examined his position with more care. He glanced with grudging respect at Malek, who had sat back as impassively as ever, the knight he had deftly taken on the edge of the table in front of him. His eyes watched Constantin with their usual untroubled calm, like those of an immensely patient governess, his great shoulders hidden within the bulky suiting. But for a moment, when he had leaned across the board, Constantin had seen the powerful extension and flexion of his shoulder musculature.

Don't look so smug, my dear Malek, Constantin said to himself with a wry smile. At least I know now that you are left-handed. Malek had taken the knight with one hand, hooking the piece between the thick knuckles of his ring and centre fingers, and then substituting his queen with a smart tap, a movement not easily performed in the centre of the crowded board. Useful though the confirmation was—Constantin had noticed Malek apparently trying to conceal his left-handedness during their meals and when opening and closing the windows—he found this sinistral aspect of Malek's personality curiously disturbing, an indication that there would be nothing predictable about his opponent, or the ensuing struggle of wits between them. Even Malek's apparent lack of sharp intelligence was belied by the astuteness of his last move.

Constantin was playing white, and had chosen the Queen's Gambit, assuming that the fluid situation invariably resulting from the opening would be to his advantage and allow him to get on with the more serious task of planning his escape. But Malek had avoided any possible errors, steadily consolidating his position, and had even managed to launch a counter-gambit, offering a knight-to-bishop exchange would would soon undermine Constantin's position if he accepted.

" A good move, Malek," he commented. "But perhaps a little risky in the long run." Declining the exchange, he lamely blocked the checking queen with a pawn.

Malek stared stolidly at the board, his heavy policeman's face, with its almost square frame from one jaw angle to the other, betraying no sign of thought. His approach, Constantin reflected as he watched his opponent, would be that of the pragmatist, judging always by immediate capability rather than by any concealed intentions. As if confirming this diagnosis, Malek simply returned his queen to her former square, unwilling or unable to exploit the advantage he had gained and satisfied by the captured piece.

Bored by the lower key on to which the game had descended, and the prospect of similar games ahead, Constantin castled his king to safety. For some reason, obviously irrational, he assumed that Malek would not kill him in the middle of a game, particularly if he, Malek, were winning. He recognized that this was an unconscious reason for wanting to play chess in the first place, and had no doubt motivated the many others who had also sat with Malek on the veranda, listening to the late summer rain. Suppressing a sudden pang of fear, Constantin examined Malek's powerful hands protruding from his cuffs like two joints of meat. If Malek wanted to, he could probably kill Constantin with his bare hands.

That raised a second question, almost as fascinating as the first.

"Malek, another point." Constantin sat back, searching in his pockets for imaginary cigarettes (none were allowed him). "Forgive my curiosity, but I am an interested party, as it were—" He flashed Malek his brightest smile, a characteristically incisive thrust modulated by ironic self-deprecation which had been so successful with his secretaries and at ministry receptions, but the assay at humour failed to move Malek. "Tell me, do you know ... how——? " Searching for some euphemism, he repeated: " Do you know how you are going to...? " and then gave up the attempt, cursing Malek to himself for lacking the social grace to rescue him from his awkwardness.

Malek's chin rose slightly, a minimal nod. He showed no signs of being bored or irritated by Constantin's laboured catechism, or of having noticed his embarrassment.

"What is it, then?" Constantin pressed, recovering himself. "Pistol, pill or—" with a harsh laugh he pointed through the window "—do you set up a guillotine in the rain? I'd like to know."

Malek looked down at the chess-board, his features more glutinous and dough-like than ever. Flatly, he said: "It has been decided."

Constantin snorted. "What on earth does *that* mean?" he snapped belligerently. "Is it painless?"

For once Malek smiled, a thin smeer of amusement hung fleetingly around his mouth. "Have you ever killed anything, Mr. Constantin?" he asked quietly. "Yourself, personally, I mean."

"Touché," Constantin granted. He laughed deliberately, trying to dispel the tension. "A perfect reply." To himself he said: I mustn't let curiosity get the upper hand, the man was laughing at me.

"Of course," he went on, "death is always painful. I merely wondered whether, in the legal sense of the term, it would be humane. But I can see that you are a professional, Malek, and the question answers itself. A great relief, believe me. There are so many sadists about, perverts and the like—" again he watched carefully to see if the implied sneer provoked Malek "—that one can't be too grateful for a clean curtain fall. It's good to know. I can devote these last days to putting my affairs in order and coming to terms with the world. If only I knew how long there was left I could make my preparations accordingly. One can't be forever saying one's last prayers. You see my point?"

Colourlessly, Malek said: "The Prosecutor-General advised you to make your final arrangements immediately after the trial."

"But what does that mean?" Constantin asked, pitching his voice a calculated octave higher. "I'm a human being, not a book-keeper's ledger that can be totted up and left to await the auditor's pleasure. I wonder if you realize, Malek, the courage this situation demands from me? It's easy for you to sit there——"

Abruptly Malek stood up, sending a shiver of terror through Constantin. With a glance at the sealed windows, he moved around the chess table towards the lounge. "We will postpone the game," he said. Nodding to Constantin, he went off towards the kitchen where the orderly was preparing lunch.

Constantin listened to his shoes squeaking faintly across the unpolished floor, then irritably cleared the pieces off the board and sat back with the black king in his hand. At least he had provoked Malek into leaving him. Thinking this over, he wondered whether to throw caution to the winds and begin to make life intolerable for Malek—it would be easy to pursue him around the villa, arguing hysterically and badgering him with neurotic questions. Sooner or later Malek would snap back, and might give away something of his intentions. Alternatively, Constantin could try to freeze him out, treating him with contempt as the hired killer he was, refusing to share a room or his meals with him and insisting on his rights as a former member of the central committee. The method might well be successful. Almost certainly Malek was telling the truth when he said he knew the exact day and minute of Constantin's execution. The order would have been given to him and he would have no discretion to advance or delay the date to suit himself. Malek would be reluctant to report Constantin for difficult behaviour—the reflection on himself was too obvious and his present post was not one from which he could graciously retire—and in addition not even the Police-President would be able to vary the execution date now that it had been set without convening several meetings. There was then the danger of re-opening Constantin's case. He was not without his allies, or at least those who were prepared to use him for their own advantage.

But despite these considerations, the whole business of play-acting lacked appeal for Constantin. His approach was more serpentine. Besides, if he provoked Malek, uncertainties were introduced, of which there were already far too many.

He noticed the supervisor enter the lounge and sit down quietly in one of the grey armchairs, his face, half-hidden in the shadows, turned towards Constantin. He seemed indifferent to the normal pressures of boredom and fatigue (luckily for himself, Constantin reflected—an impatient man would have pulled the trigger on the morning of the second day), and content to sit about in the armchairs, watching Constantin as the grey rain fell outside and the damp leaves gathered against the walls. The difficulties of establishing a relationship with Malek—and some sort of relationship was essential before Constantin could begin to think of escape— seemed insuperable, only the games of chess offering an opportunity.

Placing the black king on his own king's square, Constantin called out: "Malek, I'm ready for another game, if you are."

Malek pushed himself out of the chair with his long arms, and then took his place across the board. For a moment he scrutinized Constantin with a level glance, as if ascertaining that there would be no further outbursts of temper, and then began to set up the white pieces, apparently prepared to ignore the fact that Constantin had cleared the previous game before its completion.

He opened with a stolid Ruy Lopez, an over-analysed and uninteresting attack, but a dozen moves later, when they broke off for lunch, he had already forced Constantin to castle on the Queen's side and had established a powerful position in the centre.

As they took their lunch together at the card table behind the sofa in the lounge, Constantin reflected upon this curious element which had been introduced into his relationship with Malek. While trying to check any tendency to magnify an insignificant triviality into a major symbol, he realised that Malek's proficiency at chess, and his ability to produce powerful combinations out of pedestrian openings, was symptomatic of his concealed power over Constantin.

The drab villa in the thin autumn rain, the faded furniture and unimaginative food they were now mechanically consuming, the whole grey limbo with its slender telephone connection with the outside world were, like his chess, exact extensions of Malek's personality, yet permeated with secret passages and doors. The unexpected thrived in such an ambience. At any moment, as he shaved, the mirror might retract to reveal the flaming muzzle of a machine pistol, or the slightly bitter flavour of the soup they were drinking might be other than that of lentils.

These thoughts preoccupied him as the afternoon light began to fade in the east, the white rectangle of the garden wall illuminated against this dim backdrop like a huge tabula rasa. Excusing himself from the chess game, Constantin feigned a headache and retired to his room upstairs.

The door between his room and Malek's had been removed, and as he lay on the bed he was conscious of the supervisor sitting in his chair with his back to the window. Perhaps it was Malek's presence which prevented him from gaining any real rest, and when he rose several hours later and returned to the veranda he felt tired and possessed by a deepening sense of foreboding.

With an effort he rallied his spirits, and by concentrating his whole attention on the game was able to extract what appeared to be a drawn position. Although the game was adjourned without comment from either player, Malek seemed to concede by his manner that he had lost his advantage, lingering for a perceptible moment over the board when Constantin rose from the table.

The lesson of all this was not lost to Constantin the following day. He was fully aware that the games of chess were not only taxing his energies but providing Malek with a greater hold upon himself than he upon Malek. Although the pieces stood where they had left them the previous evening, Constantin did not suggest that they resume play. Malek made no move towards the board, apparently indifferent to whether the game was finished or not. Most of the time he sat next to Constantin by the single radiator in the lounge, occasionally going off to confer with the orderly in the kitchen. As usual the telephone rang briefly each morning, but otherwise there were no callers or visitors to the villa. To all intents it remained suspended in a perfect vacuum.

It was this unvarying nature of their daily routines which Constantin found particularly depressing. Intermittently over the next few days he played chess with Malek, invariably finding himself in a losing position, but the focus of his attention was elsewhere, upon the enigma cloaked by Malek's expressionless face. Around him a thousand invisible clocks raced onwards towards their beckoning zeros, a soundless thunder like the drumming of apocalyptic hoof-irons.

His mood of foreboding had given way to one of mounting fear, all the more terrifying because, despite Malek's real role, it

seemed completely sourceless. He found himself unable to con-
centrate for more than a few minutes upon any task, left his
meals unfinished and fidgeted helplessly by the veranda window.
The slightest movement by Malek would make his nerves thrill
with anguish; if the supervisor left his customary seat in the
lounge to speak to the orderly Constantin would find himself
almost paralysed by the tension, helplessly counting the seconds
until Malek returned. Once, during one of their meals, Malek
started to ask him for the salt and Constantin almost choked to
death.

The ironic humour of this near-fatality reminded Constantin
that almost half of his two-month sentence had elapsed. But his
crude attempts to obtain a pencil from the orderly and later, failing this, to mark the letters in a page torn from one of the novels
were intercepted by Malek, and he realized that short of defeating
the two policemen in single-handed combat he had no means of
escaping his ever more imminent fate.

Latterly he had noticed that Malek's movements and general
activity around the villa seemed to have quickened. He still sat for
long periods in the armchair, observing Constantin, but his formerly impassive presence was graced by gestures and inclinations of
the head that seemed to reflect a heightened cerebral activity, as if
he were preparing himself for some long-awaited denouement.
Even the heavy musculature of his face seemed to have relaxed
and grown sleeker, his sharp mobile eyes, like those of an experienced senior inspector of police, roving constantly about the rooms.

Despite his efforts, however, Constantin was unable to galvanize
himself into any defensive action. He could see clearly that Malek
and himself had entered a new phase in their relationship, and
that at any moment their outwardly formal and polite behaviour
would degenerate into a gasping ugly violence, but he was nonetheless immobilized by his own state of terror. The days passed in
a blur of uneaten meals and abandoned chess games, their very
identity blotting out any sense of time or progression, the watching figure of Malek always before him.

Every morning, when he woke after two or three hours of sleep to find his consciousness still intact, a discovery almost painful in its relief and poignancy, he would be immediately aware of Malek standing in the next room, then waiting discreetly in the hallway as Constantin shaved in the bathroom (also without its door) following him downstairs to breakfast, his careful reflective tread like that of a hangman descending from his gallows.

After breakfast Constantin would challenge Malek to a game of chess, but after a few moves would begin to play wildly, throwing pieces forwards to be decimated by Malek. At times the supervisor would glance curiously at Constantin, as if wondering whether his charge had lost his reason, and then continue to play his careful exact game, invariably winning or drawing. Dimly Constantin perceived that by losing to Malek he had also surrendered to him psychologically, but the games had now become simply a means of passing the unending days.

Six weeks after they had first begun to play chess, Constantin more by luck than skill succeeded in an extravagant pawn gambit and forced Malek to sacrifice both his centre and any possibility of castling. Roused from his state of numb anxiety by the temporary victory, Constantin sat forward over the board, irritably waving away the orderly who announced from the door of the lounge that he would serve lunch.

" Tell him to wait, Malek. I mustn't lose my concentration at this point, I've very nearly won the game."

" Well ..." Malek glanced at his watch, then over his shoulder at the orderly, who, however, had turned on his heel and returned to the kitchen. He started to stand up. " It can wait. He's bringing the——"

" No! " Constantin snapped. " Just give me five minutes, Malek. Damn it, one adjourns on a move, not half-way through it."

" Very well." Malek hesitated, after a further glance at his watch. He climbed to his feet. " I will tell him."

Constantin concentrated on the board, ignoring the supervisor's retreating figure, the scent of victory clearing his mind. But thirty seconds later he sat up with a start, his heart almost seizing inside his chest.

Malek had gone upstairs! Constantin distinctly remembered him saying he would tell the orderly to delay lunch, but instead he had walked straight up to his bedroom. Not only was it extremely unusual for Constantin to be left unobserved when the orderly was otherwise occupied, but the latter had still not brought in their first luncheon course.

Steadying the table, Constantin stood up, his eyes searching the open doorways in front and behind him. Almost certainly the orderly's announcement of lunch was a signal, and Malek had found a convenient pretext for going upstairs to prepare his execution weapon.

Faced at last by the nemesis he had so long dreaded, Constantin listened for the sounds of Malek's feet descending the staircase. A profound silence enclosed the villa, broken only by the fall of one of the chess pieces to the tiled floor. Outside the sun shone intermittently in the garden, illuminating the broken flagstones of the ornamental pathway and the bare face of the walls. A few stunted weeds flowered among the rubble, their pale colours blanched by the sunlight, and Constantin was suddenly filled by an overwhelming need to escape into the open air for the few last moments before he died. The east wall, lit by the sun's rays, was marked by a faint series of horizontal grooves, the remnants perhaps of a fire escape ladder, and the slender possibility of using these as hand-holds made the enclosed garden, a perfect killing ground, preferable to the frantic claustrophobic nexus of the villa.

Above him, Malek's measured tread moved across the ceiling to the head of the staircase. He paused there and then began to descend the stairs, his steps chosen with a precise and careful rhythm.

Helplessly, Constantin searched the veranda for something that would serve as a weapon. The french windows on to the garden were locked, and a slotted pinion outside secured the left-hand member of the pair to the edge of the sill. If this were raised there was a chance that the windows could be forced outwards.

Scattering the chess pieces onto the floor with a sweep of his hand, Constantin seized the board and folded it together, then stepped over to the window and drove the heavy wooden box through the bottom pane. The report of the bursting glass echoed like a gun shot through the villa. Kneeling down, he pushed his hand through the aperture and tried to lift the pinion, jerking it up and down in its rusty socket. When it failed to clear the sill he forced his head through the broken window and began to heave against it helplessly with his thin shoulders, the fragments of broken glass falling on to his neck.

Behind him a chair was kicked back, and he felt two powerful hands seize his shoulders and pull him away from the window. He struck out hysterically with the chess box, and then was flung head-first to the tiled floor.

His convalescence from this episode was to last most of the following week. For the first three days he remained in bed, recovering his physical identity, waiting for the sprained muscles of his hands and shoulders to repair themselves. When he felt sufficiently strong to leave his bed he went down to the lounge and sat at one end of the sofa, his back to the windows and the thin autumn light.

Malek still remained in attendance, and the orderly prepared his meals as before. Neither of them made any comment upon Constantin's outburst of hysteria, or indeed betrayed any signs that it had taken place, but Constantin realized that he had crossed an important rubicon. His whole relationship with Malek had experienced a profound change. The fear of his own imminent death, and the tantalising mystery of its precise date which had so obsessed him, had been replaced by a calm acceptance that the judicial processes inaugurated by his trial would take their course and that Malek and the orderly were merely the local agents of this distant apparat. In a sense his sentence and present tenuous existence at the villa were a microcosm of life itself, with its inherent but unfeared uncertainties, its inevitable quietus to be made on a date never known in advance. Seeing his role at the villa in this light Constantin no longer felt afraid at the prospect of his own extinction, fully aware that a change in the political wind could win him a free pardon.

In addition, he realized that Malek, far from being his executioner, a purely formal role, was in fact an intermediary between himself and the hierarchy, and in an important sense a potential ally of Constantin's. As he reformed his defence against the indictment preferred against him at the trial—he knew he had been far too willing to accept the *fait accompli* of his own guilt—he calculated the various ways in which Malek would be able to assist him. There was no doubt in his mind that he had misjudged Malek. With his sharp intelligence and commanding presence, the supervisor was very far from being a hatchet-faced killer—this original impression had been the result of some cloudiness in Constantin's perceptions, an unfortunate myopia which had cost him two precious months in his task of arranging a re-trial.

Comfortably swathed in his dressing-gown, he sat at the card-table in the lounge (they had abandoned the veranda with the colder weather, and a patch of brown paper over the window reminded him of that first circle of purgatory) concentrating on the game of chess. Malek sat opposite him, hands clasped on one knee, his thumbs occasionally circling as he pondered a move. Although no less reticent than he had ever been, his manner seemed to indicate that he understood and confirmed Constantin's reappraisal of the situation. He still followed Constantin around the villa, but his attentions were noticeable more perfunctory, as if he realized that Constantin would not try again to escape.

From the start, Constantin was completely frank with Malek.

"I am convinced, Malek, that the Prosecutor-General was misdirected by the Justice Department, and that the whole basis of the trial was a false one. All but one of the indictments were never formally presented, so I had no opportunity to defend myself. You understand that, Malek? The selection of the capital penalty for one count was purely arbitrary."

Malek nodded, moving a piece. "So you have explained, Mr. Constantin. I am afraid I do not have a legalistic turn of mind."

"There's no need for you to," Constantin assured him. "The point is obvious. I hope it may be possible to appeal against the

67

court's decision and ask for a re-trial." Constantin gestured with a piece. "I criticize myself for accepting the indictments so readily. In effect I made no attempt to defend myself. If only I had done so I am convinced I should have been found innocent."

Malek murmured non-committally, and gestured towards the board. Constantin resumed play. Most of the games he consistently lost to Malek, but this no longer troubled him and, if anything, only served to reinforce the bonds between them.

Constantin had decided not to ask the supervisor to inform the Justice Department of his request for a re-trial until he had convinced Malek that his case left substantial room for doubt. A premature application would meet with an automatic negative from Malek, whatever his private sympathies. Conversely, once Malek was firmly on his side he would be prepared to risk his reputation with his seniors, and indeed his championing of Constantin's cause would be convincing proof in itself of the latter's innocence.

As Constantin soon found from his one-sided discussions with Malek, arguing over the legal technicalities of the trial, with their infinitely subtle nuances and implications, was an unprofitable method of enlisting Malek's support and he realized that he would have to do so by sheer impress of personality, by his manner, bearing and general conduct, and above all by his confidence of his innocence in the face of the penalty which might at any moment be imposed upon him. Curiously, this latter pose was not as difficult to maintain as might have been expected; Constantin already felt a surge of conviction in his eventual escape from the villa. Sooner or later Malek would recognize the authenticity of this inner confidence.

To begin with, however, the supervisor remained his usual phlegmatic self. Constantin talked away at him from morning to evening, every third word affirming the probability of his being found 'innocent', but Malek merely nodded with a faint smile and continued to play his errorless chess.

"Malek, I don't want you to think that I challenge the competence of the court to try the charges against me, or that I hold it in disrespect," he said to the supervisor as they played their usual morning board some two weeks after the incident on the veranda. "Far from it. But the court must make its decisions within the context of the evidence presented by the prosecutor. And even then, the greatest imponderable remains—the role of the accused. In my case I was, to all intents, not present at the trial, so my innocence is established by *force majeure*. Don't you agree, Malek?"

Malek's eyes searched the pieces on the board, his lips pursing thinly. "I'm afraid this is above my head, Mr. Constantin. Naturally I accept the authority of the court without question."

"But so do I, Malek. I've made that plain. The real question is simply whether the verdict was justified in the light of the new circumstances I am describing."

Malek shrugged, apparently more interested in the end-game before them. "I recommend you to accept the verdict, Mr. Constantin. For your peace of mind, you understand."

Constantin looked away with a gesture of impatience. "I don't agree, Malek. Besides, a great deal is at stake." He glanced up at the windows which were drumming in the cold autumn wind. The casements were slightly loose, and the air lanced around them. The villa was poorly heated, only the single radiator in the lounge warming the three rooms downstairs. Already Constantin dreaded the winter. His hands and feet were perpetually cold and he could find no means of warming them.

"Malek, is there any chance of obtaining another heater?" he asked. "It's none too warm in here. I have a feeling it's going to be a particularly cold winter."

Malek looked up from the board, his bland grey eyes regarding Constantin with a flicker of curiosity, as if this last remark were one of the few he had heard from Constantin's lips which contained any overtones whatever.

"It is cold," he agreed at last. "I will see if I can borrow a heater. This villa is closed for most of the year."

Constantin pestered him for news of the heater during the following week—partly because the success of his request would have symbolized Malek's first concession to him—but it failed to materialize. After one palpably lame excuse Malek merely ignored his further reminders. Outside, in the garden, the leaves whirled about the stones in a vortex of chilling air, and overhead the low clouds raced seaward. The two men in the lounge hunched over their chess-board by the radiator, hands buried in their pockets between moves.

Perhaps it was this darkening weather which made Constantin impatient of Malek's slowness in seeing the point of his argument, and he made his first suggestions that Malek should transmit a formal request for a re-trial to his superiors at the Department of Justice.

"You speak to someone on the telephone every morning, Malek," he pointed out when Malek demurred. "There's no difficulty involved. If you're afraid of compromising yourself—though I would have thought that a small price to pay in view of what is at stake—the orderly can pass on a message."

"It's not feasible, Mr. Constantin." Malek seemed at last to be tiring of the subject. "I suggest that you——"

"Malek!" Constantin stood up and paced around the lounge. "Don't you realize that you must? You're literally my only means of contact, if you refuse I'm absolutely powerless, there's no hope of getting a reprieve!"

"The trial has already taken place, Mr. Constantin," Malek pointed out patiently.

"It was a mis-trial! Don't you understand, Malek, I accepted that I was guilty when in fact I was completely innocent!"

Malek looked up from the board, his eyebrows lifting. "*Completely* innocent. Mr. Constantin?"

Constantin snapped his fingers. "Well, virtually innocent. At least in terms of the indictment and trial."

"But that is merely a technical difference, Mr. Constantin. The Department of Justice is concerned with absolutes."

"Quite right, Malek. I agree entirely." Constantin nodded approvingly at the supervisor and privately noted his quizzical expression, the first time Malek had displayed a taste for irony.

He was to notice this fresh leit-motiv recurringly during the

70

next days; whenever he raised the subject of his request for a re-trial Malek would counter with one of his deceptively naive queries, trying to establish some minor tangential point, almost as if he were leading Constantin on to a fuller admission. At first Constantin assumed that the supervisor was fishing for informa· tion about other members of the hierarchy which he wished to use for his own purposes, but the few titbits he offered were ignored by Malek, and it dawned upon him that Malek was genuinely interested in establishing the sincerity of Constantin's conviction of his own innocence.

He showed no signs, however, of being prepared to contact his superiors at the Department of Justice, and Constantin's impatience continued to mount. He now used their morning and afternoon chess sessions as an opportunity to hold forth at length on the subject of the shortcomings of the judicial system, using his own case as an illustration, and hammered away at the theme of his innocence, even hinting that Malek might find himself held responsible if by any mischance he was not granted a reprieve.

"The position I find myself in is really most extraordinary," he told Malek almost exactly two months after his arrival at the villa. "Everyone else is satisfied with the court's verdict, and yet I alone know that I am innocent. I feel very like someone who is about to be buried alive."

Malek managed a thin smile across the chess pieces. "Of course, Mr. Constantin, it is possible to convince oneself of anything, given a sufficient incentive."

"But Malek, I assure you," Constantin insisted, ignoring the board and concentrating his whole attention upon the supervisor, "this is no death-cell repentance. Believe me, I know. I have examined the entire case from a thousand perspectives, questioned every possible motive. There is no doubt in my mind. I may once have been prepared to accept the possibility of my guilt, but I realize now that I was entirely mistaken—experience encourages us to take too great a responsibility for ourselves, when we fall short of our ideals we become critical of ourselves and ready to assume that we are at fault. How dangerous that can be,

Malek, I now know. Only the truly innocent man can really understand the meaning of guilt."

Constantin stopped and sat back, a slight weariness overtaking him in the cold room. Malek was nodding slowly, a thin and not altogether unsympathetic smile on his lips as if he understood everything Constantin had said. Then he moved a piece, and with a murmured 'excuse me' left his seat and went out of the room.

Drawing the lapels of the dressing gown around his chest, Constatin studied the board with a desultory eye. He noticed that Malek's move appeared to be the first bad one he had made in all their games together, but he felt too tired to make the most of his opportunity. His brief speech to Malek, confirming all he believed, now left nothing more to be said. From now on whatever happened was up to Malek.

"Mr. Constantin."

He turned in his chair and, to his surprise, saw the supervisor standing in the doorway, wearing his long grey overcoat.

"Malek——?" For a moment Constantin felt his heart gallop, and then controlled himself. "Malek, you've agreed at last, you're going to take me to the Department?"

Malek shook his head, his eyes staring sombrely at Constantin. "Not exactly. I thought we might look at the garden, Mr. Constantin. A breath of fresh air, it will do you good."

"Of course, Malek, it's kind of you." Constantin rose a little unsteadily to his feet, and tightened the cord of his dressing gown. "Pardon my wild hopes." He tried to smile at Malek, but the supervisor stood by the door, hands in his overcoat pockets, his eyes lowered fractionally from Constantin's face.

They went out on to the veranda towards the french windows. Outside the cold morning air whirled in frantic circles around the small stone yard, the leaves spiralling upwards into the dark sky. To Constantin there seemed little point in going out into the garden, but Malek stood behind him, one hand on the latch.

"Malek." Something made him turn and face the supervisor.

"You do understand what I mean, when I say I am absolutely innocent. I *know* that."

"Of course, Mr. Constantin." The supervisor's face was relaxed and almost genial. "I understand. When you know you are innocent, then you are guilty."

His hand opened the veranda door on to the whirling leaves.

THE ILLUMINATED MAN

By day fantastic birds flew through the petrified forest, and jewelled alligators glittered like heraldic salamanders on the banks of the crystalline rivers. By night the illuminated man raced among the trees, his arms like golden cartwheels, his head like a spectral crown....

DURING the last year, since the news of what is now variously known as the Hubble Effect, the Rostov-Lysenko Syndrome and the LePage Amplification Synchronoclasmique first gained world-wide attention, there have been so many conflicting reports from the three focal areas in Florida, Byelorussia and Madagascar that I feel it necessary to preface my own account of the phenomenon with the assurance that it is entirely based upon first-hand experience. All the events I describe were witnessed by myself during the recent, almost tragic visit to the Florida Everglades arranged by the United States government for the scientific attaches in Washington. The only facts I was not able to verify are the details of Charles Foster Marquand's life which I obtained from Captain Shelley, the late chief of police at Maynard, and although he was a biassed and untrustworthy witness I feel that in this single case he was almost certainly accurate.

How much longer remains before all of us, wherever we are, become expert authorities upon the exact nature of the Hubble Effect is still open to conjecture. As I write, here within the safety and peace of the garden of the British Embassy at Puerto Rico, I see a report in today's *New York Times* that the whole of the Florida peninsula, with the exception of a single highway to Tampa, has been closed and that to date some three million of the state's inhabitants have been resettled in other parts of the United States. But apart from the estimated losses in real estate values and hotel revenues (" Oh, Miami," I cannot help saying to myself, " you city of a thousand cathedrals to the rainbow sun ") the news of this extraordinary human migration seems to have prompted little comment. Such is mankind's innate optimism, our conviction that we can survive any deluge or cataclysm, that we unconsciously dismiss the momentous events in Florida with a shrug, confident that some means will be found to avert the crisis when it comes.

And yet it now seems obvious that the real crisis is long past. Tucked away on a back page of the same *New York Times* is a short report of the sighting of another 'double galaxy' by observers at the Hubble Institute on Mount Palomar. The news is summarised in less than a dozen lines and without comment, although the implication is inescapable that yet another focal area has been set up somewhere on the earth's surface, perhaps in the temple-filled jungles of Cambodia or the haunted amber forests of the Chilean highland. But it is only a year since the Mount Palomar astronomers identified the first double galaxy in the constellation Andromeda, the great oblate diadem that is probably the most beautiful object in the universe, the island galaxy of M 31.

Although these sightings by now seem commonplace, and at least half a dozen 'double constellations' can be picked from the night sky on any evening of the week, four months ago when the party of scientific attaches landed at Miami Airport on a conducted tour of the stricken area there was still widespread ignorance of what the Hubble Effect (as the phenomenon had been christened in the Western Hemisphere and the English-speaking world) actually involved. Apart from a handful of forestry workers and biologists from the U.S. Department of Agriculture, few qualified observers had witnessed the phenomenon and there were implausible stories in the newspapers of the forest 'crystallising' and everything 'turning into coloured glass'.

One unfortunate consequence of the Hubble Effect is that it is virtually impossible to photograph anything transformed by it. As any reader of scientific journals knows, glassware is extremely difficult to reproduce, and even blocks of the highest screen on the best quality art papers—let alone the coarse blocks used on newsprint—have failed to reproduce the brilliant multi-facetted lattices of the Hubble Effect, with their myriads of interior prisms, as anything more than a vague blur like half-melted snow.

Perhaps in retaliation, the newspapers had begun to suggest that the secrecy which surrounded the affected area in the Everglades—then no more than three or four acres of forest to the north-east of Maynard—was being deliberately imposed by the administration, and a clamour was raised about the rights of inspection and the unseen horrors concealed from the public. It so happened that the focal area discovered by Professor Auguste LePage in Madagascar—in the Matarre Valley, far into the hinterland of the island—was about 150 miles from the nearest road-head and totally inaccessible, while the Soviet authorities had clamped a security cordon as tight as Los Alamos's around their own affected area in the Pripet Marshes of Byelorussia, where a legion of scientific workers under the leadership of the metabiologist Lysenko (all, incidentally, chasing a complete red herring) was analysing every facet of the inexplicable phenomenon.

Before any political capital could be made from this campaign, the Department of Agriculture in Washington announced that all facilities for inspection would be gladly provided, and the invitation to the scientific attaches proceeded as part of the programme of technical missions and tours.

As we drove westwards from Miami Airport it was immediately obvious that in a sense the newspapers had been right, and that there was far more to the Hubble Effect than the official handouts had let us believe. The highway to Maynard had been closed to general traffic, and our bus twice overtook military convoys within twenty miles of Miami. In addition, as if to remind us of the celestial origin of the phenomenon, the news of yet another manifestation came through on the radio bulletins.

"There's an Associated Press report from New Delhi," George Schneider, the West German attache, came aft to tell us. "This time there are millions of reliable witnesses. Apparently it should have been plainly visible in the Western Hemisphere last night. Did none of you see it?"

Paul Mathieu, our French confrere, pulled a droll face. "Last night I was looking at the moon, my dear George, not the Echo satellite. It sounds ominous, but if Venus now has two lamps, so much the better."

Involuntarily we looked out through the windows, searching above the roadside pines for any glimpse of the Echo satellite. According to the AP reports its luminosity had increased by at least ten-fold, transforming the thin pinpoint of light which had burrowed across the night sky for so many faithful years into a brilliant luminary outshone only by the moon. All over Asia, from the refugee camps on the shores of the Jordan to the crowded tenements of Shanghai, it was being observed at the very moment we were making our fifty-mile drive to Maynard.

"Perhaps the balloon is breaking up," I suggested in a lame effort to revive our spirits. "The fragments of aluminium paint will be highly reflective and form a local cloud like a gigantic mirror. It's probably nothing to do with the Hubble Effect."

"I'm sorry, James. I wish we could believe that." Sidney Reston, of the State Department, who was acting as our courier, interrupted his conversation with the U.S. Army major in charge of the bus to sit down with us. "But it looks as if they're very much connected. All the other satellites aloft are showing the same increased albedo, seems more and more like a case of 'Hubble bubble, double trouble'."

This absurd jingle echoed in my ears as we neared the eastern fringes of Big Cypress Swamp. Five miles from Maynard we left the highway and turned on to a rough track which ran through the date palms towards the Opotoka River. The surface of the road had been churned by scores of tracked vehicles, and a substantial military camp had been set up among the great oaks, the lines of tents hidden by the grey festoons of the spanish moss. Large piles of collapsible metal fencing were being unloaded from the trucks, and I noticed a squad of men painting a number of huge black signs with a vivid luminous paint.

"Are we going on manoeuvres, major?" the Swedish member of our party complained as the dust filled the cabin. "We wished to see the forest near Maynard. Why have we left the highway?"

"The highway is closed," the major replied evenly. "You'll be

77

taken on a tour of the site, I assure you, gentlemen. The only safe approach is by river."

"*Safe* approach?" I repeated to Reston. "I say, what is this, Sidney?"

"Just the army, James," he assured me. "You know what they're like in emergencies. If a tree moves they declare war on it." With a shake of his head he peered out at the activity around us. "But I admit I can't see why they have to proclaim martial law."

Reaching the bank of the river, where half a dozen amphibious vehicles were moored by a floating quay, we debarked from the bus and were taken into a large quonset used for briefing visitors. Here we found some fifty or sixty other notables —senior members of government laboratories, public health officials and science journalists—who had been brought by bus from Miami earlier that morning. The atmosphere of light-hearted banter barely concealed a growing uneasiness, but the elaborate precautions of the military still seemed ludicrously exaggerated. After an interval for coffee we were officially welcomed and issued with our instructions for the day. These warned us in particular to remain strictly within the marked perimeters, not to attempt to obtain any of the 'contaminated material', and above all never to linger at any one spot but always to remain in rapid motion.

Needless to say, the pantomime humour of all this was lost on none of us and we were in high spirits when we set off down the river in three of the landing craft, the green walls of the forest slipping past on either side. I noticed immediately the quieter mood, by contrast, of the passenger beside me. A slimly built man of about forty, he was wearing a white tropical suit which emphasized the thin rim of dark beard framing his face. His black hair was brushed low over a bony forehead, and with the jaundiced gaze in his small liquid eyes gave him the appearance of a moody D. H. Lawrence. I made one or two attempts to talk to him, but he smiled briefly and looked away across the water. I assumed that he was one of the research chemists or biologists.

Two miles downstream we met a small convoy of motor launches harnessed together behind a landing craft. All of them

were crammed with cargo, their decks and cabin roofs loaded
with household possessions of every sort, baby carriages and
mattresses, washing machines and bundles of linen, so that there
were only a few precarious inches of freeboard amidships.
Solemn-faced children sat with suitcases on their knees above the
freight, and they and their parents gazed at us stonily as we
passed.

Now it is a curious thing, but one seldom sees on the faces of
Americans the expression of wan resignation all too familiar to
the traveller elsewhere in the world, that sense of cowed helplessness before natural or political disaster seen in the eyes of refu-
gees from Caporetto to Korea, and its unmistakeable stamp upon
the families moving past us abruptly put an end to our light-
hearted mood. As the last of the craft pushed slowly through the
disturbed water we all turned and watched it silently, aware that
in a sense it carried ourselves.

"What *is* going on?" I said to the bearded man. "They look as
if they're evacuating the town!"

He laughed crisply, finding an unintended irony in my remark.
"Agreed—it's pretty pointless! But I guess they'll come back in
due course."

Irritated by this elliptical comment delivered in a curt off-hand
voice—he had looked away again, engrossed upon some more
interesting inner topic—I turned and joined my colleagues.

"But why is the Russian approach so different?" George
Schneider was asking. "Is the Hubble Effect the same as this
Lysenko Syndrome? Perhaps it is a different phenomenon?"

One of the Department of Agriculture biologists, a grey-haired
man carrying his jacket over one arm, shook his head. "No,
they're almost certainly identical. Lysenko as usual is wasting the
Soviets' time. He maintains that crop yields are increased because
there's an increase in tissue weight. But the Hubble Effect is much
closer to a cancer as far as we can see—and about as curable—a
proliferation of the sub-atomic identity of all matter. It's almost as
if a sequence of displaced but identical images were being produced by refraction through a prism, but with the element of time
replacing the role of light." As it transpired, these were prophetic
words.

79

We were rounding a bend as the river widened in its approach towards Maynard, and the water around the two landing craft ahead was touched by a curious roseate sheen, as if reflecting a distant sunset or the flames of some vast silent conflagration. The sky, however, remained a bland limpid blue, devoid of all cloud. Then we passed below a small bridge, where the river opened into a wide basin a quarter of a mile in diameter.

With a simultaneous gasp of surprise we all craned forward, staring at the line of jungle facing the white-framed buildings of the town. Instantly I realized that the descriptions of the forest 'crystallizing' and 'turning into coloured glass' were exactly truthful. The long arc of trees hanging over the water dripped and glittered with myriads of prisms, the trunks and fronds of the date palms sheathed by bars of livid yellow and carmine light that bled away across the surface of the water, so that the whole scene seemed to be reproduced by an over-active technicolor process. The entire length of the opposite shore glittered with this blurred chiaroscuro, the overlapping bands of colour increasing the density of the vegetation, so that it was impossible to see more than a few feet between the front line of trunks.

The sky was clear and motionless, the hot sunlight shining uninterruptedly upon this magnetic shore, but now and then a stir of wind would cross the water and the trees erupted into cascades of rippling colour that lanced away into the air around us. Then, slowly, the coruscation subsided and the images of the individual trunks, each sheathed in its brilliant armour of light, reappeared, their dipping foliage loaded with deliquescing jewels.

Everyone in our craft was gaping at this spectacle, the vivid crystal light dappling our faces and clothes, and even my bearded companion was moved by astonishment. Clasping the seat in front of him, he leaned across the rail, the white fabric of his suit transformed into a brilliant palimpsest.

Our craft moved in a wide arc towards the quay, where a score of power cruisers were being loaded by the townsfolk, and we came within some fifty yards of the prismatic jungle, the hatch-work of coloured bars across our clothes transforming us into a boatload of harlequins. There was a spontaneous round of laughter, more in relief than amusement. Then several arms pointed to the water-line, where we saw that the process had not affected the vegetation alone. Extending outwards for two or three yards from the bank were the long splinters of what appeared to be crystallizing water, the angular facets emitting a blue prismatic light washed by the wake from our craft. These splinters were growing in the water like crystals in a chemical solution, accreting more and more material to themselves, so that along the bank there was a congested mass of rhomboidal spears like the lengthening barbs of a reef.

Surprised by the extent of the phenomenon—I had expected, perhaps under the influence of the Lysenko theories, little more than an unusual plant disease, such as tobacco mosaic—I gazed up at the overhanging trees. Unmistakeably each was still alive, its leaves and boughs filled with sap, and yet at the same time each was encased in a mass of crystalline tissue like an immense glacé fruit. Everywhere the branches and fronds were encrusted by the same translucent lattice, through which the sunlight was refracted into rainbows of colour.

A hubbub of speculation broke out in our craft, during which only myself and the bearded man remained silent. For some reason I suddenly felt less concerned to find a so-called 'scientific' explanation for the strange phenomenon we had seen. The beauty of the spectacle had stirred my memory, and a thousand images of childhood, forgotten for nearly forty years, now filled my mind, recalling the paradisal world of one's earliest years when everything seems illuminated by that prismatic light described so exactly by Wordsworth in his recollections of childhood. Since the death of my wife and three-year-old daughter in a car accident ten years earlier I had deliberately repressed such feelings, and the vivid magical shore before us seemed to glow like the brief spring of my marriage.

But the presence of so many soldiers and military vehicles, and the wan-faced townsfolk evacuating their homes, ensured that the little enclave of the transfigured forest—by comparison the remainder of the Everglades basin seemed a drab accumulation of peat, muck and marls—would soon be obliterated, the crystal trees dismembered and carried away to a hundred antiseptic laboratories.

At the front of the landing craft the first passengers began to debark. A hand touched my arm, and the white-suited man, apparently aware of my mood, pointed with a smile at the sleeve of his suit, as if encouraging me. To my astonishment a faint multicoloured dappling still remained, despite the shadows of the people getting to their feet around us, as if the light from the forest had contaminated the fabric and set off the process anew. "What on——? Wait! " I called. " Your suit! "

But before I could speak to him he stood up and hurried down the gangway, the last pale shimmer from his suit disappearing along the crowded quay.

Our party was divided into several smaller groups, each accompanied by two NCO's, and we moved off past the queue of cars and trucks loaded with the townsfolk's possessions. The families waited their turn patiently, flagged on by the local police, eyeing us without interest. The streets were almost deserted, and these were the last people to go—the houses were empty, shutters sealed across the windows, and soldiers paced in pairs past the closed banks and stores. The sidestreets were packed with abandoned cars, confirming that the river was the only route of escape from the town.

As we walked along the main street, the glowing jungle visible two hundred yards away down the intersections on our left, a police car swerved into the street and came to a halt in front of a us. Two men stepped out, a tall blond-haired police captain and a Presbyterian minister carrying a small suitcase and a parcel of books. The latter was about thirty-five, with a high scholar's forehead and tired eyes. He seemed uncertain which way to go, and waited as the police captain strode briskly around the car.

" You'll need your embarkation card, Dr. Thomas." The captain handed a coloured ticket to the minister, and then fished a set of keys attached to a mahogany peg from his pocket. " I took these from the door. You must have left them in the lock."

The priest hesitated, uncertain whether to take the keys. " I left them there deliberately, captain. Someone may want to take refuge in the church."

" I doubt it, Doctor. Wouldn't help them, anyway." The captain waved briefly. " See you in Miami."

Acknowledging the salute, the priest stared at the keys in his palm, then slipped them reluctantly into his cassock. As he walked past us towards the wharf his moist eyes searched our faces with a troubled gaze, as if he suspected that a member of his congregation might be hiding in our midst.

The police captain appeared equally fatigued, and began a sharp dialogue with the officer in charge of our parties. His words were lost in the general conversation, but he pointed impatiently beyond the roof-tops with a wide sweep of one arm, as if indicating the approach of a storm. Although of strong physique, there was something weak and self-centred about his long fleshy face and pale blue eyes, and obviously his one remaining ambition, having emptied the town of its inhabitants, was to clear out at the first opportunity.

I turned to the corporal lounging by a fire hydrant and pointed to the glowing vegetation which seemed to follow us, skirting the perimeter of the town. "Why is everyone leaving, corporal? Surely it's not infectious—there's no danger from close contact?"

The corporal glanced laconically over his shoulder at the crystalline foliage glittering in the meridian sunlight. "It's not infectious. Unless you stay in there too long. When it cut the road both sides of town I guess most people decided it was time to pull out."

"Both sides?" George Schneider echoed. "How big is the affected area, corporal? We were told three or four acres."

The soldier shook his head dourly. "More like three or four hundred. Or thousand, even." He pointed to the helicopter circling the forest a mile or so away, soaring up and down over the date palms, apparently spraying them with some chemical. "Reaches right over there, towards Lake Okeechobee."

"But you have it under control," George said. "You're cutting it back all right?"

"Wouldn't like to say," the corporal replied cryptically. He indicated the blond policeman remonstrating with the supervising officer. "Captain Shelley tried a flame thrower on it a couple of days ago. Didn't help any."

The policeman's objections over-ruled—he slammed the door of his car and drove off in dudgeon—we set off once more and at

83

the next intersection approached the forest which stood back on either side of the road a quarter of a mile away. The vegetation was sparser, the sawgrass growing in clumps among the sandy soil on the verges, and a mobile laboratory had been set up in a trailer, 'U.S. Department of Agriculture' stencilled on its side. A platoon of soldiers was wandering about, taking cuttings from the palmettos and date palms, which they carefully placed like fragments of stained glass on a series of trestle tables. The main body of the forest curved around us, circling the northern perimeter of the town, and we immediately saw that the corporal had been correct in his estimate of the affected area's extent. Parallel with us one block to the north was the main Maynard—Miami highway, cut off by the glowing forest on both the eastern and western approaches to the town.

Splitting up into two's and three's, we crossed the verge and began to wander among the glacé ferns which rose from the brittle ground. The sandy surface seemed curiously hard and annealed, small spurs of fused sand protruding from the newly formed crust.

Examining the specimens collected on the tables, I touched the smooth glass-like material that sheathed the leaves and branches, following the contours of the original like a displaced image in a defective mirror. Everything appeared to have been dipped in a vat of molten glass, which had then set into a skin fractured by slender veins.

A few yards from the trailer two technicians were spinning several encrusted branches in a centrifuge. There was a continuous glimmer and sparkle as splinters of light glanced out of the bowl and vanished into the inspection area, and as far as the perimeter fence, running like a serrated white bandage around the prismatic wound of the forest, people turned to watch.

When the centrifuge stopped we peered into the bowl, where a handful of limp branches, their blanched leaves clinging damply to the metal bottom, lay stripped of their glacé sheaths. Below the bowl, however, the liquor receptacle remained dry and empty.

Twenty yards from the forest a second helicopter prepared for take-off, its drooping blades rotating like blunted scythes, the down-draught sending up a shower of light from the disturbed vegetation. With an abrupt lurch it made a laboured ascent, swinging sideways through the air, and then moved away across the forest roof, its churning blades apparently gaining little purchase on the air. There was a confused shout of 'Fire!' from the soldiers below, and we could see clearly the vivid discharge of light which radiated from the blades like St. Elmo's fire. Then, with an agonized roar like the bellow of a stricken animal, the aircraft slid backwards through the air and plunged towards the forest canopy a hundred feet below, the two pilots plainly visible at their controls. Sirens sounded from the staff cars parked around the inspection area, and there was a concerted rush towards the forest as the helicopter disappeared from sight.

As we raced along the road we felt its impact with the ground, and a sudden pulse of light drummed through the trees. The road led towards the point of the crash, a few houses looming at intervals at the ends of empty drives.

"The blades must have crystallized while it was standing near the trees," George Schneider shouted as we climbed over the perimeter fence. "You could see the crystals melting, like the branches in the centrifuge, but not quickly enough. Let's hope the pilots are all right."

Several soldiers ran ahead of us, waving us back, but we ignored them and hurried on through the trees. After fifty yards we were well within the body of the forest, and had entered an enchanted world, the spanish moss investing the great oaks with brilliant jewelled trellises. The air was markedly cooler, as if everything were sheathed in ice, but a ceaseless play of radiant light poured through the stained-glass canopy overhead, turning the roof of the forest into a continuous three-dimensional kaleidoscope.

The process of crystallization was here far more advanced. The white fences along the road were so heavily encrusted that they formed an unbroken palisade, the frost at least a foot thick on either side of the palings. The few houses between the trees glistened like wedding cakes, their plain white roofs and chimneys transformed into exotic minarets and baroque domes. On a lawn of green glass spurs a child's toy, perhaps once a red tricycle with yellow wheels, glittered like a Fabergé gem, the wheels starred into brilliant jasper crowns. Lying there, it reminded me of my daughter's toys scattered on the lawn after my return from the hospital. They had glowed for a last time with the same prismatic light.

The soldiers were still ahead of me, but George and Paul Mathieu had fallen behind. Leaning against the frosted white fencing, they were plucking the soles of their shoes. By now it was obvious why the Miami-Maynard highway had been closed. The surface of the road was pierced by a continuous carpet of needles, spurs of glass and quartz as much as six inches high, reflecting the coloured light through the leaves above. The spurs tore at my shoes, forcing me to move hand over hand along the verge of the road, where a section of heavier fencing marked the approach to a distant mansion.

Behind me a siren whined, and the police car I had seen earlier plunged along the road, its heavy tyres cutting through the crystal surface. Twenty yards ahead it rocked to a halt, its engine stalled, and the police captain jumped out. With an angry shout he waved me back down the road, now a tunnel of yellow light formed by the interlocking canopies overhead.

" Get back! There's another wave coming! " He ran after the soldiers a hundred yards away, his boots crushing the crystal carpet.

Wondering why he sould be so keen to clear the forest, I rested for a moment by the police car. A noticeable change had come over the forest, as if dusk had begun to fall prematurely from the sky. Everywhere the glacé sheaths which enveloped the trees and vegetation had become duller and more opaque, and the crystal floor underfoot was grey and occluded, turning the needles into spurs of basalt. The panoply of coloured light had vanished, and a dim amber gloom moved across the trees, shadowing the sequinned lawns.

Simultaneoulsy it had become colder. Leaving the car, I started to make my way down the road—Paul Mathieu and a soldier, hands shielding their faces, were disappearing around a bend— but the icy air blocked my path like a refrigerated wall. Turning up the collar of my tropical suit, I retreated to the car, wondering whether to take refuge inside it. The cold deepened, numbing my face like a spray of acetone, and my hands felt brittle and flesh-less. Somewhere I heard the hollow shout of the police captain, and caught a glimpse of someone running at full speed through the ice-grey trees.

On the right-hand side of the road the darkness completely enveloped the forest, masking the outlines of the trees, and then extended in a sudden sweep across the roadway. My eyes smarted with pain, and I brushed away the small crystals of ice which had formed over my eyeballs. Everywhere a heavy frost was forming, accelerating the process of crystallization. The spurs in the road-way were now over a foot in height, like the spines of a giant porcupine, and the lattices between the tree-trunks were thicker and more translucent, so that the original trunks seemed to shrink into a mottled thread within them. The interlocking leaves formed a continuous mosaic, the crystal elements thickening and overlaying each other. For the first time I suddenly visualized the possibility of the entire forest freezing solidly into a huge col-oured glacier, with myself trapped within its interstices.

The windows of the car and the black body were now sheathed in an ice-like film. Intending to open the door so that I could switch on the heater, I reached for the handle, but my fingers were burned by the intense cold.

" You there! Come on! This way! "

Behind me, the voice echoed down the drive. As the darkness and cold deepened, I saw the police captain waving to me from the colonnade of the mansion. The lawn between us seemed to belong to a less sombre zone. The grass still retained its vivid liquid sparkle and the white eaves of the house were etched clearly against the surrounding darkness, as if this enclave were preserved like an island in the eye of a hurricane.

I ran up the drive towards the house, and with relief found that the air was at least ten degrees warmer. The sunlight shone through the leafy canopy with uninterrupted brilliance. Reaching the portico, I searched for the police captain, but he had run off into the forest again. Uncertain whether to follow him, I watched the approaching wall of darkness slowly cross the lawn, the glit-tering foliage overhead sinking into its pall. The police car was now encrusted by a thick layer of frozen glass, its windshield blossoming into a thousand fleur-de-lis crystals.

Quickly making my way around the house as the zone of safety moved off through the forest, I crossed the remains of an old vegetable garden, where seed-plants of green glass three feet high rose into the air like exquisite ornamented sculptures. I reached the forest again and waited there as the zone hesitated and veered off, trying to remain within the centre of its focus. I seemed to have entered a subterranean cavern, where jewelled rocks loomed from the spectral gloom like huge marine plants, the sprays of crystal sawgrass like fountains frozen in time.

For the next hour I raced helplessly through the forest, my sense of direction lost, driven by the swerving walls of the zone of safety as it twisted like a benign tornado among the trees. Several times I crossed the road, where the great spurs were almost waist high, forced to clamber over the brittle stems. Once, as I rested against the trunk of a bifurcated oak, an immense multi-coloured bird erupted from a bough over my head and flew off with a wild screech, an aureole of molten light cascading from its red and yellow wings, like the birth-flames of phoenix.

At last the strange whirlpool subsided and a pale light filtered through the stained glass canopy, transfiguring everything with its iridescence. Again the forest was a place of rainbows, the deep carmine light glowing from the jewelled grottos. I walked along a narrow road which wound towards a great white house standing like a classical pavilion on a rise in the centre of the forest. Transformed by the crystal frost, it appeared to be an intact fragment of Versailles or Fontainebleau, its ornate pilasters and sculptured friezes spilling from the wide roof which overtopped the forest. From the upper floors I would be able to see the distant water towers at Maynard, or at least trace the serpentine progress of the river.

The road narrowed, declining the slope which led up to the house, but its annealed crust, like half-fused quartz, offered a more comfortable surface than the crystal teeth of the lawn. Suddenly I came across what was unmistakeably a jewelled rowing boat sat solidly into the roadway, a chain of lapis lazuli mooring it to the verge. Then I realized that I was walking along a small tributary of the river. A thin stream of water still ran below the solid crust, and evidently this vestigial motion alone prevented it from erupting into the exotic spur-like forms of the forest floor.

As I paused by the boat, feeling the huge topaz and amethyst stones encrusted along its sides, a grotesque four-legged creature half-embedded in the surface lurched forwards through the crust, the loosened pieces of the lattice attached to its snout and shoulders shaking like a transparent cuirass. Its jaws mouthed the air silently as it struggled on its hooked legs, unable to clamber more than a few feet from the hollow trough in its own outline now filling with a thin trickle of water. Invested by the glittering sparkle of light that poured from its body, the alligator resembled some fabulous armourial beast. It lunged towards me again, and I kicked its snout, scattering the crystals which choked its mouth.

Leaving it to subside once more into a frozen posture, I climbed the bank and limped across the lawn to the mansion, whose fairy towers loomed above the trees. Although out of breath and very nearly exhausted I had a curious premonition, of intense hope and longing, as if I were some fugitive Adam chancing upon a forgotten gateway to the forbidden paradise.

From an upstairs window, the bearded man in the white suit watched me, a shot-gun under his arm.

Now that ample evidence of the Hubble Effect is available to scientific observers throughout the world, there is general agreement upon its origins and the few temporary measures that can be taken to reverse its progress. Under pressure of necessity during my flight through the phantasmagoric forests of the Everglades I had discovered the principal remedy—to remain in rapid motion—but I still assumed that some accelerated genetic mutation was responsible, even though such inanimate objects as cars and metal fencing were equally affected. However, by now even the Lysenkoists have grudgingly accepted the explanation given by workers at the Hubble Institute, that the random transfigurations throughout the world are a reflection of distant cosmic processes of enormous scope and dimensions, first glimpsed in the Andromeda spiral.

We know now that it is time ('Time with the Midas touch,' as

Charles Marquand described it) which is responsible for the transformation. The recent discovery of anti-matter in the universe inevitably involves the conception of anti-time as the fourth side of this negatively charged continuum. Where anti-particle and particle collide they not only destroy their own physical identities, but their opposing time-values eliminate each other, subtracting from the universe another quantum from its total store of time. It is random discharges of this type, set off by the creation of anti-galaxies in space, which have led to the depletion of the time-store available to the materials of our own solar system.

Just as a supersaturated solution will discharge itself into a crystalline mass, so the supersaturation of matter in a continuum of depleted time leads to its appearance in a parallel spatial matrix. As more and more time 'leaks' away, the process of supersaturation continues, the original atoms and molecules producing spatial replicas of themselves, substance without mass, in an attempt to increase their foothold upon existence. The process is theoretically without end, and eventually it is possible for a single atom to produce an infinite number of duplicates of itself and so fill the entire universe, from which simultaneously all time has expired, an ultimate macrocosmic zero beyond the wildest dreams of Plato and Democritus.

As I lay back on one of the glass-embroidered chesterfields in a bedroom upstairs, the bearded man in the white suit explained something of this to me in his sharp intermittent voice. He still stood by the open window, peering down at the lawn and the crystal stream where the alligator and the jewelled boat lay embalmed. As the broken panes annealed themselves he drove the butt of his shot-gun through them. His thin beard gave him a fevered and haunted aspect, emphasized by the white frost forming on the shoulders and lapels of his suit. For some reason he spoke to me as if to an old friend.

"It was obvious years ago, B——. Look at the viruses with their crystalline structure, neither animate nor inanimate, and their immunity to time." He swept a hand along the sill and picked up a cluster of the vitreous grains, then scattered them across the floor like smashed marbles. "You and I will be like them soon, and the rest of the world. Neither living nor dead!"

He broke off to raise his shot-gun, his dark eyes searching between the trees. "We must move on," he announced, leaving the window. "When did you last see Captain Shelley?"

"The police captain?" I sat up weakly, my feet slipping on the floor. Several plate glass windows appeared to have been fractured and then fused together above the carpet. The ornate Persian patterns swam below the surface like the floor of some perfumed pool in the Arabian Nights. "Just after we ran to search for the helicopter. Why are you afraid of him?"

"He's a venomous man," he replied briefly. "As cunning as a pig."

We made our way down the crystal stairway. Everything in the house was covered by the same glacé sheath, embellished by exquisite curlicues and helixes. In the wide lounges the ornate Louis XV furniture had been transformed into huge pieces of opalescent candy, whose countless reflections glowed like giant chimeras in the cut-glass walls. As we disappeared through the trees towards the stream my companion shouted exultantly, as much to the forest as to myself: "We're running out of time, B——, running out of time!"

Always he was on the look-out for the police captain. Which of them was searching for the other I could not discover, nor the subject of their blood-feud. I had vounteered my name to him, but he brushed aside the introduction. I guessed that he had sensed some spark of kinship as we sat together in the landing craft, and that he was a man who would plunge his entire sympathy or hostility upon such a chance encounter. He told me nothing of himself. Shot-gun cradled under his arm, he moved rapidly along the fossilized stream, his movements neat and deliberate, while I limped behind. Now and then we passed a jewelled power cruiser embedded in the crust, or a petrified alligator would rear upwards and grimace at us noiselessly, its crystal-line skin glowing with a thousand prisms as it shifted in a fault of coloured glass.

Everywhere there was the same fantastic corona of light, transfiguring and identifying all objects. The forest was an endless labyrinth of glass caves, sealed off from the remainder of the world, (which, as far as I knew, by now might be similarly affected), lit by subterranean lamps burning below the surface of the rocks.

"Can't we get back to Maynard?" I shouted after him, my voice echoing among the vaults. "We're going deeper into the forest."

"The town is cut off, my dear B——. Don't worry, I'll take you there in due course." He leapt nimbly over a fissure in the surface of the river. Below the mass of dissolving crystals a thin stream of fluid rilled down a buried channel.

For several hours, led by this strange white-suited figure with his morose preoccupied gaze, we moved through the forest, sometimes in complete circles as if my companion were familiarizing himself with the topography of that jewelled twilight world. When I sat down to rest on one of the vitrified trunks and brushed away the crystals now forming on the soles of my shoes, despite our constant movement—the air was always icy, the dark shadows perpetually closing and unfolding around us—he would wait impatiently, watching me with ruminative eyes as if deciding whether to abandon me to the forest.

At last we reached the fringes of a small clearing, bounded on three sides by the fractured dancing floor of a river bend, where a high-gabled summer house pushed its roof towards the sky through a break in the overhead canopy. From the single spire a slender web of opaque strands extended to the surrounding trees, like a diaphanous veil, investing the glass garden and the crystalline summer house with a pale marble sheen, almost sepulchural in its intensity. As if reinforcing this impression, the windows on to the veranda running around the house were now encrusted with elaborate scroll-like designs, like the ornamented stone casements of a tomb.

Waving me back, my companion approached the fringes of the garden, his shot-gun raised before him. He darted from tree to tree, pausing for any sign of movement, then crossed the frozen surface of the river with a feline step. High above him, its wings pinioned by the glass canopy, a golden oriole flexed slowly in the afternoon light, liquid ripples of its aura circling outwards like the rays of a miniature sun.

"Marquand!"

A shot roared into the clearing, its report echoing around the glass trees, and the blond-haired police captain raced towards the summer house, a revolver in his hand. As he fired again the crystal trellises of the spanish moss shattered and frosted, collapsing around me like a house of mirrors. Leaping down from the veranda, the bearded man made off like a hare across the river, bent almost double as he darted over the faults in the surface.

The rapidity with which all this had happened left me standing helplessly by the edge of the clearing, my ears ringing with the two explosions. I searched the forest for any signs of my companion, and then the police captain, standing on the veranda, gestured me towards him with his pistol.

"Come here!" When I tentatively approached he came down the steps, scrutinizing me suspiciously. "What are you doing around here? Aren't you one of the visiting party?"

I explained that I had been trapped after the crash of the helicopter. "Can you take me back to the army post? I've been wandering around the forest all day."

A morose frown twisted his long face. "The Army's a long way off. The forest's changing all the time." He pointed across the river. "What about Marquand? Where did you meet him?"

"The bearded man? He was taking shelter in a house near the river. Why did you shoot at him? Is he a criminal?"

Shelley nodded after a pause. His manner was somehow furtive and shifty. "Worse than that. He's a madman, completely crazy." He started to walk up the steps, apparently prepared to let me make my own way into the forest. "You'd better be careful, there's no knowing what the forest is going to do. Keep moving but circle around on yourself, or you'll get lost."

"Wait a minute!" I called after him. "Can't I rest here? I need a map—perhaps you have a spare one?"

"A map? What good's a map now?" He hesitated as my arms fell limply to my sides. "All right, you can come in for five minutes." This concession to humanity was obviously torn from him.

The summer house consisted of a single circular room and a small kitchen at the rear. Heavy shutters had been placed against the windows, now locked to the casements by the interstitial crystals, and the only light entered through the door.

Shelley holstered his pistol and turned the door handle gently. Through the frosted panes were the dim outlines of a high four-poster bed, presumably stolen from one of the nearby mansions. Gilded cupids played about the mahogany canopy, pipes to their lips, and four naked carytids with upraised arms formed the corner posts.

"Mrs. Shelley," the captain explained in a low voice. "She's not too well."

For a moment we gazed down at the occupant of the bed, who lay back on a large satin bolster, a febrile hand on the silk counterpane. At first I thought I was looking at an elderly woman, probably the captain's mother, and then realized that in fact she was little more than a child, a young woman in her early twenties. Her long platinum hair lay like a white shawl over her shoulders, her thin high-cheeked face raised to the scanty light. Once she might have had a nervous porcelain beauty, but her wasted skin and the fading glow of light in her half-closed eyes gave her the appearance of someone preternaturally aged, reminding me of my own wife in the last minutes before her death.

"Shelley." Her voice cracked faintly in the amber gloom. "Shelley, it's getting cold again. Can't you light a fire?"

"The wood won't burn, Emerelda. It's all turned into glass." The captain stood at the foot of the bed, his peaked hat held in his hands, peering down solicitously as if he were on duty. He unzipped his leather jacket. "I brought you these. They'll help you."

He leaned forwards, hiding something from me, and spilled several handfuls of red and blue gem-stones across the counterpane. Rubies and sapphires of many sizes, they glittered in the thin light with a feverish heat.

"Shelley, thank you...." The girl's free hand scuttled across the counterpane to the stones. Her child-like face had become almost vulpine with greed. Seizing a handful, she brought them up to her neck and pressed them tightly against her skin, where the bruises formed like fingerprints. Their contact seemed to revive her and she stirred slowly, several of the jewels slipping to the floor.

"What were you shooting at, Shelley?" she asked after an interval. "There was a gun going off, it gave me a headache."

"Just an alligator, Emerelda. There are some smart alligators around here, I have to watch them. You get some rest now."

"But, Shelley, I need more of these, you only brought me a few today...." Her hand, like a claw, searched the counterpane. Then she turned away from us and seemed to subside into sleep, the jewels lying like scarabs on the white skin of her breast.

Captain Shelley nudged me and we stepped quietly into the kitchen. The small cubicle was almost empty, a disconnected refrigerator standing on the cold stove. Shelley opened the door and began to empty the remainder of the jewels on to the shelves, where they lay like cherries among the half-dozen cans. A light frost covered the enamel exterior of the refrigerator, as everything else in the kitchen, but the inner walls remained unaffected.

"Who is she?" I asked as Shelley pried the lid off a can. "Shouldn't you try to get her away from here?"

Shelley stared at me with his ambiguous expression. He seemed always to be concealing something, his blue eyes fractionally lowered from my own. "She's my wife," he said with a curious emphasis, as if unsure of the fact. "Emerelda. She's safer here, as long as I watch out for Marquand."

"Why should he want to hurt her? He seemed sane enough to me."

"He's a maniac!" Shelley said with sudden force. "He spent six months in a straight-jacket. He wants to take Emerelda and live in his crazy house in the middle of the swamp." As an afterthought, he added: "She was married to Marquand."

As we ate, forking the cold meat straight from the can, he told me of the strange melancholy architect, Charles Foster Marquand, who had designed several of the largest hotels in Miami and then two years earlier abruptly abandoned his work in disgust. He had married Emerelda, after bribing her parents, within a few hours of seeing her in an amusement park, and then carried her away to a grotesque folly he had built among the sharks and alligators in the swamp. According to Shelley he never spoke to Emerelda after the marriage ceremony, and prevented her from leaving the house or seeing anyone except a blind negro servant. Apparently he saw his bride in a sort of Pre-Raphaelite dream, caged within his house like the lost spirit of his imagination. When she finally escaped, with Captain Shelley's assistance, he had gone beserk and spent some time as a voluntary patient at an asylum. Now he had returned with the sole ambition of returning with Emerelda to his house in the swamps, and Shelley was convinced, perhaps sincerely, that his morbid and lunatic presence was responsible for Emerelda's lingering malaise.

At dusk I left them, barricaded together in the white sepulchre of the summer house, and set off in the direction of the river which Shelley said was half a mile away, hoping to follow it to Maynard. With luck an army unit would be stationed at the nearest margins of the affected zone, and the soldiers would be able to retrace my steps and rescue the police captain and his dying wife.

Shelley's lack of hospitality did not surprise me. In turning me out into the forest he was using me as a decoy, confident that Marquand would immediately try to reach me for news of his former wife. As I made my way through the dark crystal grottos I listened for his footsteps, but the glass sheaths of the trees sung and crackled with a thousand voices as the forest cooled in the darkness. Above, through the lattices between the trees, I could see the great fractured bowl of the moon. Around me, in the vitreous walls, the reflected stars glittered like myriads of fireflies.

At this time I noticed that my own clothes had begun to glow in the dark, the fine frost that covered my suit spangled by the starlight. Spurs of crystal grew from the dial of my wrist-watch, imprisoning the hands within a medallion of moonstone.

At midnight I reached the river, a causeway of frozen gas that might have soared high across the Milky Way. Forced to leave it when the surface broke into a succession of giant cataracts, I approached the outskirts of Maynard, passing the mobile laboratory used by the Department of Agriculture. The trailer, and the tables and the equipment scattered around it had been enveloped by the intense frost, and the branches in the centrifuge had blossomed again into brilliant jewelled sprays. I picked up a discarded helmet, now a glass porcupine, and drove it through a window of the trailer.

In the darkness the white-roofed houses of the town gleamed like the funerary temples of a necropolis, their cornices ornamented with countless spires and gargoyles, linked together across the roads by the expanding tracery. A frozen wind moved through the streets, which were waist-high forests of fossil spurs, the abandoned cars embedded within them like armoured saurians on an ancient ocean floor.

Everywhere the process of transformation was accelerating. My feet were encased in huge crystal slippers. It was these long spurs which enabled me to walk along the street, but soon they would fuse together and lock me to the ground.

The eastern entrance to the town was sealed by the forest and the erupting roadway. Limping westwards again, in the hope of returning to Captain Shelley, I passed a small section of the sidewalk that remained clear of all growth, below the broken window of a jewellery store. Handfuls of looted stones were scattered across the pavement, ruby and emerald rings, topaz brooches and pendants, intermingled with countless smaller stones and industrial diamonds that glittered coldly in the starlight.

As I stood among the stones I noticed that the crystal outgrowths from my shoes were dissolving and melting, like icicles exposed to sudden heat. Pieces of the crust fell away and slowly deliquesced, vanishing without trace into the air.

Then I realized why Captain Shelley had brought the jewels to his wife, and why she had seized upon them so eagerly. By some optical or electromagnetic freak, the intense focus of light within the stones simultaneously produced a compression of time, so that the discharge of light from the surfaces reversed the process of crystallization. (Perhaps it is this gift of time which accounts for the eternal appeal of precious gems, as well as of all baroque painting and architecture? Their intricate crests and cartouches, occupying more than their own volume of space, so contain a greater ambient time, providing that unmistakeable premonition of immortality sensed within St. Peter's or the palace at Nymphenburg. By contrast the architecture of the 20th century, characteristically one of rectangular unornamented facades, of simple

97

Euclidean space and time, is that of the New World, confident of its firm footing in the future and indifferent to those pangs of mortality which haunt the mind of old Europe.)

Quickly I knelt down and filled my pockets with the stones, cramming them into my shirt and cuffs. I sat back against the store front, the semi-circle of smooth pavement like a miniature patio, at whose edges the crystal undergrowth glittered like a spectral garden. Pressed to my cold skin, the hard faces of the jewels seemed to warm me, and within a few seconds I fell into an exhausted sleep.

I woke into brilliant sunshine in a street of temples, a thousand rainbows spangling the gilded air with a blaze of prismatic colours. Shielding my eyes, I lay back and looked up at the rooftops, their gold tiles apparently inlaid with thousands of coloured gems, like the temple quarter of Bangkok.

A hand pulled roughly at my shoulder. Trying to sit up, I found that the semicircle of clear sidewalk had vanished, and my body lay sprawled on a bed of sprouting needles. The growth had been most rapid in the entrance to the store, and my right arm was encased in a mass of crystalline spurs, three or four inches long, that reached almost to my shoulder. My hand was sheathed in a huge frozen gauntlet of prismatic crystals, almost too heavy to lift, my fingers outlined by a rainbow of colours.

Overwhelmed by panic, I managed to drag myself on to my knees, and found the bearded man in the white suit crouching behind me, his shot-gun in his hands.

" Marquand! " With a cry, I raised my jewelled arm. " For God's sake! "

My voice distracted him from his scrutiny of the light-filled street. His lean face with its small bright eyes was transfigured by strange colours that mottled his skin and drew out the livid blues and violets of his beard. His suit radiated a thousand bands of colour.

He moved towards me but before he could speak there was a roar of gunfire and the glass sheet encrusted to the doorway shattered into a shower of crystals. Marquand flinched and hid behind me, then pulled me backwards through the window. As another shot was fired down the street we stumbled past the looted counters into an office where the door of a safe stood open on to a jumble of metal cash boxes. Marquand snapped back the lids on to the empty trays, and then began to scoop together the few jewels scattered across the floor.

Stuffing them into my empty pockets, he pulled me through a window into the rear alley, and from there into the adjacent street, transformed by the overhead lattices into a tunnel of crimson and vermilion light. We stopped at the first turning, and he beckoned to the glistening forest fifty yards away.

" Run, run! Anywhere through the forest, it's all you can do! "

He pushed me forwards with the butt of his shotgun, whose breach was now encrusted by a mass of silver crystals, like a medieval flintlock. I raised my arm helplessly. In the sunlight the jewelled spurs coruscated like a swarm of coloured fireflies. "My arm, Marquand! It's reached my shoulder! "

" Run! Nothing else can help you! " His illuminated face flickered angrily. "Don't waste the stones, they won't last you forever! "

Forcing myself to run, I set off towards the forest, where I entered the first of the caves of light. I whirled my arm like a clumsy propeller, and felt the crystals recede slightly. By luck I soon reached a tributary of the river, and hurled myself like a wild man along its petrified surface.

For many hours, or days, I raced through the forest I can no longer remember, for all sense of time deserted me. If I stopped for more than a minute the crystal bands would seize my neck and shoulder, and I ran past the trees for hour after hour, only pausing when I slumped exhausted on the glass beaches. Then I pressed the jewels to my face, warding off the glacé sheath. But their power slowly faded, and as their facets blunted they turned into nodes of unpolished silica.

Once, as I ran through the darkness, my arm whirling before me, I passed the summer house where Captain Shelley kept guard over his dying wife, and heard him fire at me from the veranda.

At last, late one afternoon, when the deepening ruby light of dusk settled through the forest, I entered a small clearing where the deep sounds of an organ reverberated among the trees. In the centre was a small church, its gilt spire fused to the surrounding trees.

Raising my jewelled arm, I drove back the oak doors and entered the nave. Above me, refracted by the stained glass windows, a brilliant glow of light poured down upon the altar. Listening to the surging music, I leaned against the altar rail and extended my arm to the gold cross set with rubies and emeralds. Immediately the sheath slipped and dissolved like a melting sleeve of ice. As the crystals deliquesced the light poured from my arm like an overflowing fountain.

Turning his head to watch me, the priest sat at the organ, his firm hands drawing from the pipes their great unbroken music, which soared away, interweaved by countless overtones, through the panels of the windows towards the dismembered sun.

> *Life, like a dome of many-coloured glass,*
> *Stains the white radiance of eternity.*

For the next week I stayed with him, as the last crystal spurs dissolved from the tissues of my arm. All day I knelt beside him, working the bellows of the organ with my arm as the Pelestrina and Bach echoed around us. At dusk, when the sun sank in a thousand fragments into the western night, he would break off and stand on the porch, looking out at the spectral trees.

I remembered him as Dr. Thomas, the priest Captain Shelley had driven to the harbour. His slim scholar's face and calm eyes, their serenity belied by the nervous movements of his hands, like the false calm of someone recovering from an attack of fever, would gaze at me as we ate our small supper on a foot-stool beside the altar, sheltered from the cold all-embalming wind by the jewels in the cross. At first I thought he regarded my survival as an example of the Almighty's intervention, and I made some token expression of gratitude. At this he smiled ambiguously.

Why he had returned I did not try to guess. By now his church was surrounded on all sides by the crystal trellises, as if overtopped by the mouth of an immense glacier.

One morning he found a blind snake, its eyes transformed into enormous jewels, searching hesitantly at the door of the porch, and carried it in his hands to the altar. He watched it with a wry smile when, its sight returned, it slid away noiselessly among the pews.

On another day I woke to the early morning light and found him, alone, celebrating the Eucharist. He stopped, half-embarrassed, and over breakfast confided: "You probably wonder what I was doing, but it seemed an appropriate moment to test the validity of the sacrament." He gestured at the prismatic colours pouring through the stained glass windows, whose original scriptural scenes had been transformed into paintings of bewildering abstract beauty. "It may sound heretical to say so, but the body of Christ is with us everywhere here—in each prism and rainbow, in the ten thousand faces of the sun." He raised his thin hands, jewelled by the light ."So you see, I fear that the church, like its symbol—" here he pointed to the cross "—may have outlived its function."

I searched for an answer. "I'm sorry. Perhaps if you left here——"

"No!" he insisted, annoyed by my obtuseness. "Can't you understand? Once I was a true apostate—I knew God existed but could not believe in him. Now," he laughed bitterly, "events have overtaken me."

With a gesture he led me down the nave to the open porch, and pointed up to the dome-shaped lattice of crystal beams which reached from the rim of the forest like the buttresses of an immense cupola of diamond and glass. Embedded at various points were the almost motionless forms of birds with out-stretched wings, golden orioles and scarlet macaws, shedding brilliant pools of light. The bands of liquid colour rippled outwards through the forest, the reflections of the melting plumage enveloping us in endless concentric patterns. The overlapping arcs hung in the air like the votive windows of a city of cathedrals. Everywhere around us I could see countless smaller birds, butterflies and insects, joining their miniature haloes to the coronation of the forest.

He took my arm. "Here in this forest everything is transfigured and illuminated, joined together in the last marriage of time and space."

Towards the end, when we stood side by side with our backs to the altar, as the aisle transformed itself into an occluding tunnel of glass pillars, his conviction seemed to fail him. With an expression almost of panic he watched the keys of the organ manuals frosting like the coins of a bursting coffer, and I knew that he was searching for some means of escape.

Then at last he rallied, seized the cross from the altar and pressed it into my arms, with a sudden anger born of absolute certainty dragged me roughly to the porch and propelled me to one of the narrowing vaults.

"Go! Get away from here! Find the river!'

When I hesitated, the heavy sceptre weighing upon my arms, he shouted fiercely: "Tell them I ordered you to take it! "

I last saw him standing arms outstretched to the approaching walls, in the posture of the illuminated birds, his eyes filled with wonder and relief at the first circles of light conjured from his upraised palms.

Struggling with the huge golden incubus of the cross, I made my way towards the river, my tottering figure reflected in the hanging mirrors of the spanish moss like a lost Simon of Cyrene pictured in a medieval manuscript.

I was still sheltering behind it when I reached Captain Shelley's summer house. The door was open, and I looked down at the bed in the centre of a huge fractured jewel, in whose frosted depths, like swimmers asleep on the bottom of an enchanted pool, Emerelda and her husband lay together. The Captain's eyes were closed, and the delicate petals of a blood-red rose blossomed from the hole in his breast like an exquisite marine plant. Beside him Emerelda slept serenely, the unseen motion of her heart sheathing her body in a faint amber glow, the palest residue of life.

Something glittered in the dusk behind me. I turned to see a brilliant chimera, a man with incandescent arms and chest, race past among the trees, a cascade of particles diffusing in the air behind him. I flinched back behind the cross, but he vanished as suddenly as he had appeared, whirling himself away among the crystal vaults. As his luminous wake faded I heard his voice echoing across the frosted air, the plaintive words jewelled and ornamented like everything else in that transmogrified world. "𝕰𝖒𝖊𝖗𝖊𝖑𝖉𝖆 . . . ! 𝕰𝖒𝖊𝖗𝖊𝖑𝖉𝖆 . . . !"

Here on this calm island of Puerto Rico, in the garden of the British Embassy these few months later, the strange events of that phantasmagoric forest seem a dozen worlds away. Yet in fact I am no more than 1,000 miles from Florida as the crow (or should I say, the gryphon) flies, and already there have been numerous other outbreaks at many times this distance from the three focal areas. Somewhere I have seen a report that at the present rate of progress at least a third of the earth's surface will be affected by the end of the next decade, and a score of the world's capital cities petrified beneath layers of prismatic crystal, as Miami has already been—some reporters have described the abandoned resort as a city of a thousand cathedral spires, like a vision of St. John the Divine.

To tell the truth, however, the prospect causes me little worry. It is obvious to me now that the origins of the Hubble Effect are more than physical. When I stumbled out of the forest into an army cordon ten miles from Maynard two days after seeing the helpless phantom that had once been Charles Marquand, the gold cross clutched in my arms, I was determined never to visit the Everglades again. By one of those ludicrous inversions of logic, I found myself, far from acclaimed as a hero, standing summary trial before a military court and charged with looting. The gold cross had apparently been stripped of its jewels, and in vain did I protest that these vanished stones had been the price of my survival. At last I was rescued by the embassy in Washington under the plea of diplomatic immunity, but my suggestion that a patrol equipped with jewelled crosses should enter the forest and attempt to save the priest and Charles Marquand met with little success. Despite my protests I was sent to San Juan to recuperate.

The intention of my superiors was that I should be cut off from all memory of my experience—perhaps they sensed some small but significant change in me. Each night, however, the fractured disc of the Echo satellite passes overhead, illuminating the midnight sky like a silver chandelier. And I am convinced that the sun itself has begun to effloresce. At sunset, when its disc is veiled by the crimson dust, it seems to be crossed by a distinctive lattice-work, a vast portcullis which will one day spread outwards to the planets and the stars, halting them in their courses.

I know now that I shall return to the Everglades. As the example of that brave apostate priest who gave the cross to me illustrates, there is an immense reward to be found in that frozen forest. There in the Everglades the transfiguration of all living and inanimate forms occurs before our eyes, the gift of immortality a direct consequence of the surrender by each of us of our own physical and temporal identity. However apostate we may be in this world, there perforce we become apostles of the prismatic sun.

So, when my convalescence is complete and I return to Washington, I shall seize an opportunity to visit the Florida peninsula again with one of the many scientific expeditions. It should not be too difficult to arrange my escape and then I shall return to the solitary church in that enchanted world, where by day fantastic birds fly through the petrified forest and jewelled alligators glitter like heraldic salamanders on the banks of the crystalline rivers, and where by night the illuminated man races among the trees, his arms like golden cartwheels and his head like a spectral crown.

THE REPTILE ENCLOSURE

"THEY remind me of the Gadarene swine," Mildred Pelham remarked.

Interrupting his scrutiny of the crowded beach below the cafeteria terrace, Roger Pelham glanced at his wife. "Why do you say that?"

Mildred continued to read for a few moments, and then lowered her book. "Well, don't they?" she asked rhetorically ."They look like pigs."

Pelham smiled weakly at this mild but characteristic display of misanthropy. He peered down at his own white knees protruding from his shorts and at his wife's plump arms and shoulders. "I suppose we all do," he temporized. However, there was little chance of Mildred's remark being overheard and resented. They were sitting at a corner table, with their backs to the hundreds of ice-cream eaters and cola-drinkers crammed elbow to elbow on the terrace. The dull hubbub of voices was overlayed by the endless commentaries broadcast over the transistor radios propped among the bottles, and by the distant sounds of the fairground behind the dunes.

A short drop below the terrace was the beach, covered by a mass of reclining figures which stretched from the water's edge up to the roadway behind the cafeteria and then away over the dunes. Not a single grain of sand was visible. Even at the tide-line, where a little slack water swilled weakly at a debris of old cigarette packets and other trash, a huddle of small children clung to the skirt of the beach, hiding the grey sand.

Gazing down at the beach again, Pelham realized that his wife's ungenerous judgment was no more than the truth. Everywhere bare haunches and shoulders jutted into the air, limbs lay in serpentine coils. Despite the sunlight and the considerable period of time they had spent on the beach, many of the people were still white-skinned, or at most a boiled pink, restlessly shifting in their little holes in a hopeless attempt to be comfortable.

Usually this spectacle of jostling, over-exposed flesh, with its unsavoury bouquet of stale suntan lotion and sweat—looking along the beach as it swept out to the distant cape, Pelham could almost see the festering corona, sustained in the air by the babble of ten thousand transistor radios, reverberating like a swarm of flies—would have sent him hurtling along the first inland highway at seventy miles an hour. But for some reason Pelham's usual private distaste for the general public had evaporated. He felt strangely exhilarated by the presence of so many people (he had calculated that he could see over 50 thousand along the five-mile stretch of beach) and found himself unable to leave the terrace, although it was now 3 o'clock and neither he nor Mildred had eaten since breakfast. Once their corner seats were surrendered they would never regain them.

To himself he mused: "The ice-cream eaters on Echo beach...." He played with the empty glass in front of him. Shreds of synthetic orange pulp clung to the sides, and a fly buzzed half-heartedly from one to another. The sea was flat and calm, an opaque grey disc, but a mile away a low surface mist lay over the water like vapour on a vat.

"You look hot, Roger. Why don't you go in for a swim?"

"I may. You know, it's a curious thing, but of all the people here, not one is swimming."

Mildred nodded in a bored way. A large passive woman, she seemed content merely to sit in the sunlight and read. Yet it was she who had first suggested that they drive out to the coast, and for once had suppressed her usual grumbles when they ran into the first heavy traffic jams and were forced to abandon the car and complete the remaining two miles on foot. Pelham had not seen her walk like that for ten years.

"It is rather strange," she said. "But it's not particularly warm."

"I don't agree." Pelham was about to continue when he suddenly

stood up and looked over the rail at the beach. Half way down the
slope, parallel with the promenade, a continuous stream of people
moved slowly along an informal right-of-way, shouldering past
each other with fresh bottles of cola, lotion and ice-cream.

"Roger, what's the matter?"

"Nothing....I thought I saw Sherrington." Pelham searched
the beach, the moment of recognition lost.

"You're always seeing Sherrington. That's the fourth time
alone this afternoon. Do stop worrying."

"I'm not worrying. I can't be certain, but I felt I saw him
then."

Reluctantly, Pelham sat down, edging his chair fractionally
closer to the rail. Depite his mood of lethargy and vacuous boredom, an indefinable but distinct feeling of restlessness had preoccupied him all day. In some way associated with Sherrington's
presence on the beach, this uneasiness had been increasing
steadily. The chances of Sherrington—with whom he shared an
office in the Physiology Department at the University—actually
choosing this section of the beach were remote, and Pelham was
not even sure why he was so convinced that Sherrington was there
at all. Perhaps these illusory glimpses—all the more unlikely in
view of Sherrington's black beard and high severe face, his
stooped long-legged walk—were simply projections of this under-
lying tension and his own peculiar dependence upon Sherrington.

However, this sense of uneasiness was not confined to himself.
Although Mildred seemed immune, most of the people on the
beach appeared to share this mood with Pelham. As the day
progressed the continuous hubbub gave way to more sporadic
chatter. Occasionally the noise would fall away altogether, and
the great concourse, like an immense crowd waiting for the long-
delayed start of some public spectacle, would sit up and stir impatiently. To Pelham, watching carefully from his vantage point
over the beach, these ripples of restless activity, as everyone
swayed forward in long undulations, were plainly indicated by the
metallic glimmer of the thousands of portable radios moving in
an oscillating wave. Each successive spasm, recurring at roughly
half-hour intervals, seemed to take the crowd slightly nearer the
sea.

Directly below the concrete edge of the terrace, among the mass of reclining figures, a large family group had formed a private enclosure. To one side of this, literally within reach of Pelham, the adolescent members of the family had dug their own nest, their sprawling angular bodies, in their damp abbreviated swimming suits, entwined in and out of each other like some curious annular animal. Well within earshot, despite the continuous background of noise from the beach and the distant fair-grounds, Pelham listened to their inane talk, following the thread of the radio commentaries as they switched aimlessly from one station to the next.

"They're about to launch another satellite," he told Mildred. "*Echo XXII.*"

"Why do they bother?" Mildred's flat blue eyes surveyed the distant haze over the water. "I should have thought there were more than enough of them flying about already."

"Well..." For a moment Pelham debated whether to pursue the meagre conversational possibilities of his wife's reply. Although she was married to a lecturer in the School of Physiology, her interest in scientific matters was limited to little more than a blanket condemnation of the entire sphere of activity. His own post at the University she regarded with painful tolerance, despising the untidy office, scruffy students and meaningless laboratory equipment. Pelham had never been able to discover exactly what calling she would have respected. Before their marriage she maintained what he later realized was a polite silence on the subject of his work; after eleven years this attitude had barely changed, although the exigencies of living on his meagre salary had forced her to take an interest in the subtle, complex and infinitely wearying game of promotional snakes and ladders.

As expected, her acerbic tongue had made them few friends, but by a curious paradox Pelham felt that he had benefited from the grudging respect this had brought her. Sometimes her waspish comments, delivered at the overlong sherry parties, always in a loud voice during some conversational silence (for example, she had described the elderly occupant of the Physiology chair as 'that gerontological freak' within some five feet of the Professor's wife) delighted Pelham by their mordant accuracy, but in general there was something frightening about her pitiless lack of sympathy for the rest of the human race. Her large bland face, with its prim, rosebud mouth, reminded Pelham of the description of the Mona Lisa as looking as if she had just dined off her husband. Mildred, however, did not even smile.

"Sherrington has a rather interesting theory about the satellites," Pelham told her. "I'd hoped we might see him so that he could explain it again. I think you'd be amused to hear it, Mildred. He's working on IRM's at present——"

"On what?" The group of people behind them had turned up the volume of their radio and the commentary, of the final countdown at Cape Kennedy, boomed into the air over their heads.

Pelham said: "IRM's—innate releasing mechanisms. I've described them to you before, they're inherited reflexes——" He stopped, watching his wife impatiently.

Mildred had turned on him the dead stare with which she surveyed the remainder of the people on the beach. Testily Pelham snapped: "Mildred, I'm trying to explain Sherrington's theory about the satellites!"

Undeterred, Mildred shook her head. "Roger, it's too noisy here, I can't possibly listen. And to Sherrington's theories less than to anyone else's."

Almost imperceptibly, another wave of restless activity was sweeping along the beach. Perhaps in response to the final digital climax of the commentators at Cape Kennedy, people were sitting up and dusting the coarse sand from each other's backs. Pelham watched the sunlight flickering off the chromium radio sets and diamante sunglasses as the entire beach swayed and surged. The noise had fallen appreciably, letting through the sound of the wurlitzer at the fun-fair. Everywhere there was the same expectant stirring. To Pelham, his eyes half-closed in the glare, the beach seemed like an immense pit of seething white snakes.

Somewhere, a woman's voice shouted. Pelham sat forward, searching the rows of faces masked by sun-glasses. There was a sharp edge to the air, an unpleasant and almost sinister implication of violence hidden below the orderly surface.

Gradually, however, the activity subsided. The great throng

relaxed and reclined again. Greasily, the water lapped at the supine feet of the people lying by the edge of the sea. Propelled by one of the off-shore swells, a little slack air moved over the beach, carrying with it the sweet odour of sweat and sun-tan lotion. Averting his face, Pelham felt a spasm of nausea contract his gullet. Without doubt, he reflected, homo sapiens en masse presented a more unsavoury spectacle than almost any other species of animal. A corral of horses or steers conveyed an impression of powerful nervous grace, but this mass of articulated albino flesh sprawled on the beach resembled the diseased anatomical fantasy of a surrealist painter. Why had all these people congregated there? The weather reports that morning had not been especially propitious. Most of the announcements were devoted to the news of the imminent satellite launching, the last stage of the world-wide communications network which would now provide every square foot of the globe with a straight-line visual contact with one or other of the score of satellites in orbit. Perhaps the final sealing of this inescapable aerial canopy had prompted everyone to seek out the nearest beach and perform a symbolic act of self-exposure as a last gesture of surrender.

Uneasily, Pelham moved about in his chair, suddenly aware of the edge of the metal table cutting into his elbows. The cheap slatted seat was painfully uncomfortable, and his whole body seemed enclosed in an iron maiden of spikes and clamps. Again a curious premonition of some appalling act of violence stirred through his mind, and he looked up at the sky, almost expecting an airliner to plunge from the distant haze and disintegrate on the crowded beach in front of him.

To Mildred he remarked: "It's remarkable how popular sunbathing can become. It was a major social problem in Australia before the second World War."

Mildred's eyes flickered upwards from her book. "There was probably nothing else to do."

"That's just the point. As long as people are prepared to spend their entire time sprawled on a beach there's little hope of ever building up any other pastimes. Sunbathing is anti-social because it's an entirely passive pursuit." He dropped his voice when he noticed the people sitting around him glancing over their shoulders, ears drawn to his high precise diction. "On the other hand, it does bring people together. In the nude, or the near-nude, the shop-girl and the duchess are virtually indistinguishable."

"*Are* they?"

Pelham shrugged. "You know what I mean. But I think the psychological role of the beach is much more interesting. The tide-line is a particularly significant area, a penumbral zone that is both of the sea and above it, forever half-immersed in the great time-womb. If you accept the sea as an image of the unconscious, then this beachward urge might be seen as an attempt to escape from the existential role of ordinary life and return to the universal time-sea——"

"Roger, please!" Mildred looked away wearily. "You sound like Charles Sherrington."

Pelham stared out to sea again. Below him, a radio commentator announced the position and speed of the successfully launched satellite, and its pathway around the globe. Idly, Pelham calculated that it would take some fifteen minutes to reach them, almost exactly at half past three. Of course it would not be visible from the beach, although Sherrington's recent work on the perception of infra-red radiation suggested some of the infra-red light reflected from the sun might be perceived subliminally by their retinas.

Reflecting on the opportunities this offered to a commercial or political demagogue, Pelham listened to the radio on the sand below, when a long white arm reached out and switched it off. The possessor of the arm, a plump white-skinned girl with the face of a placid madonna, her round cheeks framed by ringlets of black hair, rolled over on to her back, disengaging herself from her companions, and for a moment she and Pelham exchanged glances. He assumed that she had deliberately switched off the radio to prevent him hearing the commentary, and then realized that in fact the girl had been listening to his voice and hoped that he would resume his monologue.

Flattered, Pelham studied the girl's round serious face, and her mature but child-like figure stretched out almost as close to him, and as naked, as it would have been had they shared a bed. Her frank, adolescent but curiously tolerant expression barely

changed, and Pelham turned away, unwilling to accept its implications, realizing with a pang the profound extent of his resignation to Mildred, and the now unbreachable insulation this provided against any new or real experience in his life. For ten years
the thousand cautions and compromises accepted each day to
make existence tolerable had steadily secreted their numbing
anodynes, and what remained of his original personality, with all
its possibilities, was embalmed like a specimen in a jar. Once he
would have despised himself for accepting his situation so passively, but he was now beyond any real self-judgment, for no
criteria were valid by which to assess himself, a state of graceless-
ness far more abject than that of the vulgar, stupid herd on the
beach around him.

"Something's in the water." Mildred pointed along the shore.
"Over there."

Pelham followed her raised arm. Two hundred yards away a
small crowd had gathered at the water's edge, the sluggish waves
breaking at their feet as they watched some activity in the
shallows. Many of the people had raised newspapers to shield
their heads, and the older women in the group held their skirts
between their knees.

"I can't see anything." Pelham rubbed his chin, distracted by a
bearded man on the edge of the promenade above him, a face not
Sherrington's but remarkably like it. "There seems to be no
danger, anyway. Some unusual sea-fish may have been cast
ashore."

On the terrace, and below on the beach, everyone was waiting
for something to happen, heads craned forward expectantly. As
the radios were turned down, so that any sounds from the distant
tableau might be heard, a wave of silence passed along the beach
like an immense darkening cloud shutting off the sunlight. The
almost complete absence of noise and movement, after the long
hours of festering motion, seemed strange and uncanny, focusing
an intense atmosphere of self-awareness upon the thousands of
watching figures.

The group by the water's edge remained where they stood, even
the small children staring placidly at whatever held the attention
of their parents. For the first time a narrow section of the beach

was visible, a clutter of radios and beach equipment half-buried in the sand like discarded metallic refuse. Gradually the new arrivals pressing down from the promenade occupied the empty places, a manoeuvre carried out without any reaction from the troupe by the tide-line. To Pelham they seemed like a family of penitent pilgrims who had travelled some enormous distance and were now standing beside their sacred waters, waiting patiently for its revivifying powers to work their magic.

"What *is* going on?" Pelham asked, when after several minutes there was no indication of movement from the water-side group. He noticed that they formed a straight line, following the shore, rather than an arc. "They're not watching anything at all."

The off-shore haze was now only five hundred yards away, obscuring the contours of the huge swells. Completely opaque, the water looked like warm oil, a few wavelets now and then dissolving into greasy bubbles as they expired limply on the sand, intermingled with bits of refuse and old cigarette cartons. Nudging the shore like this, the sea resembled an enormous pelagic beast roused from its depths and blindly groping at the sand.

"Mildred, I'm going down to the water for a moment." Pelham stood up. "There's something curious——" He broke off, pointing to the beach on the other side of the terrace. "Look! There's another group. What on earth——?"

Again, as everyone watched, this second body of spectators formed by the water's edge seventy-five yards from the terrace. Altogether some two hundred people were silently assembling along the shore-line, gazing out across the sea in front of them. Pelham found himself cracking his knuckles, then clasped the rail with both hands, as much to restrain himself from joining them. Only the congestion on the beach held him back.

This time the interest of the crowd passed in a few moments, and the murmur of background noise resumed.

"Heavens knows what they're doing." Mildred turned her back on the group. "There are more of them over there. They must be waiting for something."

Sure enough, half a dozen similar groups were now forming by the water's edge, at almost precise one hundred yard intervals.

Pelham scanned the far ends of the bay for any signs of a motor boat. He glanced at his watch. It was nearly 3:30. "They can't be waiting for anything," he said, trying to control his nervousness. Below the table his feet twitched a restless tattoo, gripping for purchase on the sandy cement. "The only thing expected is the satellite, and no one will see that anyway. There must be something in the water." At the mention of the satellite he remembered Sherrington again. "Mildred, don't you feel——"

Before he could continue the man behind him stood up with a curious lurch, as if hoping to reach the rail, and tipped the sharp edge of his seat into Pelham's back. For a moment, as he struggled to steady the man, Pelham was enveloped in a rancid smell of sweat and stale beer. He saw the glazed focus in the other's eyes, his rough unshaved chin and open mouth like a muzzle, pointing with a sort of impulsive appetite towards the sea.

"The satellite!" Freeing himself Pelham craned upwards at the sky. A pale impassive blue, it was clear of both aircraft and birds—although they had seen gulls twenty miles inland that morning, as if a storm had been anticipated. As the glare stung his eyes, points of retinal light began to arc and swerve across the sky in epileptic orbits. One of these, however, apparently emerging from the western horizon, was moving steadily across the edge of his field of vision, boring dimly towards him

Around them, people began to stand up, and chairs scraped and dragged across the floor. Several bottles toppled from one of the tables and smashed on the concrete.

"Mildred!"

Below them, in a huge disorganized melée extending as far as the eye could see, people were climbing slowly to their feet. The diffused murmur of the beach had given way to a more urgent, harsher sound, echoing overhead from either end of the bay. The whole beach seemed to writhe and stir with activity, the only motionless figures those of the people standing by the water. These now formed a continuous palisade along the shore, shutting off the sea. More and more people joined their ranks, and in places the line was nearly ten deep.

Everyone on the terrace was now standing. The crowds already on the beach were being driven forward by the pressure of new arrivals from the promenade, and the party below their table had been swept a further twenty yards towards the sea.

"Mildred, can you see Sherrington anywhere?" Confirming from her wrist-watch that it was exactly 3:30, Pelham pulled her shoulder, trying to hold her attention. Mildred returned what was almost a vacant stare, an expression of glazed incomprehension. "Mildred! We've got to get away from here!" Hoarsely, he shouted: "Sherrington's convinced we can see some of the infrared light shining from the satellites, they may form a pattern setting off IRM's laid down millions of years ago when other space vehicles were circling the earth. Mildred——!"

Helplessly, they were lifted from their seats and pressed against the rail. A huge concourse of people was moving down the beach, and soon the entire five-mile-long slope was packed with standing figures. No one was talking, and everywhere there was the same expression, self-immersed and preoccupied, like that on the faces of a crowd leaving a stadium. Behind them the great wheel of the fair-ground was rotating slowly, but the gondolas were empty, and Pelham looked back at the deserted fun-fair only a hundred yards from the multitude on the beach, its roundabouts revolving among the empty sideshows.

Quickly he helped Mildred over the edge of the rail, then jumped down on to the sand, hoping to work their way back to the promenade. As they stepped around the corner, however, the crowd advancing down the beach carried them back, tripping over the abandoned radios in the sand.

Still together, they found their footing when the pressure behind them ceased. Steadying himself, Pelham continued: "...Sherrington thinks Cro-Magnon Man was driven frantic by panic, like the Gadarene swine—most of the bone-beds have been found under lake shores. The reflex may be too strong——" He broke off.

The noise had suddenly subsided, as the immense congregation, now packing every available square foot of the beach, stood silently facing the water. Pelham turned towards the sea, where the haze, only fifty yards away, edged in great clouds towards the beach. The forward line of the crowd, their heads bowed slightly, stared passively at the gathering billows. The surface of the water glowed with an intense luminous light, vibrant and spectral, and the air over the beach, grey by comparison, made the lines of motionless figures loom like tombstones.

Obliquely in front of Pelham, twenty yards away in the front rank, stood a tall man with a quiet, meditative expression, his beard and high temples identifying him without doubt.

"Sherrington!" Pelham started to shout. Involuntarily he looked upwards to the sky, and felt a blinding speck of light singe his retinas.

In the background the music of the fun-fair revolved in the empty air.

Then, with a galvanic surge, everyone on the beach began to walk forward into the water.

THE DELTA AT SUNSET

EACH evening, when the dense powdery dusk lay over the creeks and drained mud-basins of the delta, the snakes would come out on to the beaches. Half-asleep on the wicker stretcher-chair below the awning of his tent, Charles Gifford watched their sinuous forms coiling and uncoiling as they wound their way up the slopes. In the opaque blue light the dusk swept like a fading searchlight over the damp beaches, and the interlocked bodies shone with an almost phosphorescent brilliance.

The nearest creeks were three hundred yards from the camp, but for some reason the appearance of the snakes always co-incided with Gifford's recovery from his evening fever. As this receded, carrying with it the familiar diorama of reptilian phantoms, he would sit up in the stretcher-chair and find the snakes crawling across the beaches, almost as if they had materialized from his dreams. Involuntarily he would search the sand around the tent for any signs of their damp skins.

"The strange thing is they always come out at the same time," Gifford said to the Indian head-boy who had emerged from the mess tent and was now covering him with a blanket. "One minute there's nothing there, and the next thousands of them are swarming all over the mud."

"You not cold, sir?" the Indian asked.

"Look at them now, before the light goes. It's really fantastic. There must be a sharply defined threshold——" He tried to lift his pale, bearded face above the hillock formed by the surgical cradle over his foot, and snapped: "All right, all right!"

"Doctor?" The head-boy, a thirty-year-old Indian named Mechippe, continued to straighten the cradle, his limpid eyes, set in a face of veined and weathered teak, watching Gifford.

"I said get out of the damned way!" Leaning weakly on one elbow, Gifford watched the last light fade across the winding causeways of the delta, taking with it a final image of the snakes. Each evening, as the heat mounted with the advancing summer, they came out in greater numbers, as if aware of the lengthening periods of his fever.

"Sir, I get more blanket for you?"

"No, for God's sake." Gifford's thin shoulders shivered in the dusk air, but he ignored the discomfort. He looked down at his inert, corpse-like body below the blanket, examining it with far more detachment than he had felt for the unknown Indians dying in the makeshift WHO field hospital at Taxcol. At least there was a passive repose about the Indians, a sense of the still intact integrity of flesh and spirit, if anything reinforced by the failure of one of the partners. It was this paradigm of fatalism which Gifford would have liked to achieve—even the most wretched native, identifying himself with the irrevocable flux of nature, had bridged a greater span of years than the longest-lived European or American with his obsessive time-consciousness, cramming so-called significant experiences into his life like a glutton. By contrast, Gifford realized, he himself had merely thrown aside his own body, divorcing it like some no longer useful partner in a functional business marriage. So marked a lack of loyalty depressed him.

He tapped his bony loins. "It's not this, Mechippe, that ties us to mortality, but our confounded egos." He smiled slyly at the head-boy. "Louise would appreciate that, don't you think?"

The head-boy was watching a refuse fire being raised behind the mess tent. He looked down sharply at the supine figure on the stretcher-chair, his half-savage eyes glinting like arrow heads in the oily light of the burning brush. "Sir? You want——?"

"Forget it," Gifford told him. "Bring two whiskey sodas. And some more chairs. Where's Mrs. Gifford?"

He glanced up at Mechippe when he failed to reply. Briefly their eyes met, in an instant of absolute clarity. Fifteen years earlier, when Gifford had come to the delta with his first archaeological expedition, Mechippe had been one of the junior camp-followers. Now he was in the late middle age of the Indian, the notches on his cheeks lost in the deep hatchwork of lines and scars, wise in the tent-lore of the visitors.

" Miss' Gifford—resting," he said cryptically. In an attempt to alter the tempo and direction of their dialogue, he added: " I tell Mr. Lowry, then bring whiskies and hot towel, Doctor."

" O.K., Mechippe." Lying back with an ironic smile, Gifford listened to the head-boy's footsteps move away softly through the sand. The muted sounds of the camp stirred around him—the cooling plash of water in the shower stall, the soft interchanges of the Indians, the whining of a desert dog waiting to approach the refuse dump—and he sank downwards into the thin tired body stretched out in front of him like a collection of bones in a carpet bag, rekindling the fading senses of touch and pressure in his limbs.

In the moonlight, the white beaches of the delta glistened like banks of luminous chalk, the snakes festering on the slope like the worshippers of a midnight sun.

Half an hour later they drank their whiskies together in the dark tinted air. Revived by Mechippe's massage, Charles Gifford sat upright in the stretcher-chair, gesturing with his glass. The whisky had momentarily cleared his brain; usually he was reluctant to discuss the snakes in his wife's presence, let alone Lowry's, but the marked increase in their numbers seemed important enough to mention. There was also the mildly malicious pleasure —less amusing now than it had been—of seeing Louise shudder at any mention of the snakes.

" What is so unusual," he explained, " is the way they emerge on to the banks at the same time. There must be a precise level of luminosity, an exact number of photons, to which they all respond—presumably an innate trigger."

Dr. Richard Lowry, Gifford's assistant and since his accident the acting leader of the expedition, watched Gifford uncomfortably from the edge of his canvas chair, rotating his glass below his long nose. He had been placed down-wind from the loose bandages swaddling Gifford's foot (little revenges of this kind, however childish, alone sustained Gifford's interest in the people around him), and carefully averted his face as he asked: "But why the sudden increase in numbers? A month ago there was barely a snake in sight?"

"Dick, *please*!" Louise Gifford turned an expression of martyred weariness on Lowry. "Must we?"

"There's an obvious answer," Gifford said to Lowry. "During the summer the delta drains, and begins to look like the half-empty lagoons that were here 50 million years ago. The giant amphibians had died out, and the small reptiles were the dominant species. These snakes are probably carrying around what is virtually a coded internal landscape, a picture of the Paleocene as sharp as our own memories of New York and London." He turned to his wife, the shadows cast by the distant refuse fire hollowing his cheeks. "What's the matter, Louise? Don't say you can't remember New York and London?"

"I don't know whether I can or not." She pushed a lock of fraying blonde hair off her forehead. "I wish you wouldn't think about the snakes all the time."

"Well, I'm beginning to understand them. I was always baffled by the way they'd appear at the same time. Besides, there's nothing else to do. I don't want to sit here staring at that damned Toltec ruin of yours."

He gestured towards the low ridge of sandstone, its profile illuminated against the white moonlit clouds, which marked the margins of the alluvial bench half a mile from the camp. Before Gifford's accident their chairs had faced the ruined terrace city emerging from the thistles which covered the ridge. But Gifford had tired of staring all day at the crumbling galleries and colonnades where his wife and Lowry worked together. He told Mechippe to dismantle the tent and turn it through ninety degrees, so that he could watch the last light of the sunset fading over the western delta. The burning refuse fires they now faced provided at least a few wisps of motion. Gazing for hours across the endless creeks and mud-banks, whose winding outlines became more and more serpentine as the summer drought persisted and the level of the water table fell, he had one evening discovered the snakes.

"Surely its simply a shortage of dissolved oxygen," Lowry commented. He noticed Gifford regarding him with an expression of critical distaste, and added: "Jung believes the snake is primarily a symbol of the unconscious, and that its appearance always heralds a crisis in the psyche."

"I suppose I accept that," Charles Gifford said. With rather forced laughter he added, shaking his foot in the cradle: "I have to. Don't I, Louise?" Before his wife, who was watching the fires with a distracted expression, could reply he went on: "Though in fact I disagree with Jung. For me the snake is a symbol of transformation. Every evening at sunset the great lagoons of the Paleocene are re-created here, not only for the snakes but for you and I too, if we care to look. Not for nothing is the snake a symbol of wisdom."

Richard Lowry frowned doubtfully into his glass. "I'm not convinced, sir. It was primitive man who had to assimilate events in the external world to his own psyche."

"Absolutely right," Gifford rejoined. "How else is nature meaningful, unless she illustrates some inner experience? The only real landscapes are the internal ones, or the external projections of them, such as this delta." He passed his empty glass to his wife. "Agree, Louise? Though perhaps you take a Freudian view of the snakes?"

This thin jibe, uttered with the cold humour which had become characteristic of Gifford, brought their conversation to a halt. Restlessly, Lowry looked at his watch, eager to be away from Gifford and his pathetic boorishness. Gifford, a cold smirk on his lips, waited for Lowry to catch his eye; by a curious paradox his dislike of his assistant was encouraged by the latter's reluctance to retaliate, rather than by the still ambiguous but crystallizing relationship between Lowry and Louise. Lowry's meticulous neutrality and good manners seemed to Gifford an attempt to preserve a world on which Gifford had turned his back, that world where there were no snakes on the beaches and where events moved on a single plane of time like the blurred projection of a three-dimensional object by a defective camera obscura.

Lowry's politeness was also, of course, an attempt to shield himself and Louise from Gifford's waspish tongue. Like Hamlet taking advantage of his madness to insult and cross-examine anyone at will, Gifford often used the exhausted half-lucid interval after his fever subsided to make his more pointed comments. As he emerged from the penumbral shallows, the looming figures of his wife and assistant still surrounded by the rotating mandalas he saw in his dreams, he would give full rein to his tortured humour. That in this way he was helping his wife and Lowry towards an inevitable climax only encouraged Gifford.

His long farewell to Louise, protracted now for so many years, at last seemed feasible, even if only part of the greater good-bye, the vast leave-taking that Gifford was about to embark upon. The fifteen years of their marriage had been little more than a single frustrated farewell, a search for a means to an end which their own strengths of character had always prevented.

Looking up at Louise's sun-grazed but still handsome profile, at her fading blonde hair swept back off her angular shoulders, Gifford realized that his dislike of her was in no way personal, but merely part of the cordial distaste he felt for almost the entire human race. And even this deeply ingrained misanthropy was only a reflection of his own undying self-contempt. If there were few people whom he had ever liked, there were, equally, few moments during which he had ever liked himself. His entire life as an archaeologist, from his early adolescence when he had first collected fossil ammonites from a nearby limestone outcropping, was an explicit attempt to return to the past and discover the sources of his self-loathing.

" Do you think they'll send an aeroplane? " Louise asked after breakfast the next morning. " There was a noise then. . . ."

" I doubt it," Lowry said. He gazed up at the empty sky. " We didn't ask for one. The landing field at Taxcol is disused. During the summer the harbour drains and everyone moves up-coast."

" There'll be a doctor, surely? Not everyone will have gone? "

" Yes, there's a doctor. There's one permanently attached to the port authority."

" A drunken fool," Gifford interjected. "I refuse to let him touch me with his poxy hands. Forget about the doctor, Louise. Even if someone is prepared to come out here, how do you think he'll manage it? "

" But Charles——"

Gifford gestured irritably at the glistening mudbanks. "The whole delta is draining like a dirty bath, no one is going to risk a stiff dose of malaria just to put a splint on my ankle. Anyway, that boy Mechippe sent is probably still hanging around here somewhere."

"But Mechippe insisted he was reliable." Louise looked down helplessly at her husband propped against the back of the stretcher-chair. "Dick, I wish you could have gone with him. It's only fifty miles. You would have been there by now."

Lowry nodded uneasily. "Well, I didn't think ... I'm sure everything will be all right. How is the leg, sir?"

"Just dandy." Gifford had been staring out across the delta. He noticed Lowry peering down at him with a long puckered face. "What's the matter, Richard? Does the smell offend you?" Suddenly exasperated, he snapped: "Do me a favour and take a walk, dear chap."

"What——?" Lowry stared at him uncertainly. "Of course, Doctor."

Gifford watched Lowry's neatly groomed figure walk away stiffly among the tents. "He's awfully correct, isn't he? But he doesn't know how to take an insult yet. I'll see that he gets plenty of practice."

Louise slowly shook her head. "Do you have to, Charles? Without him we'd be in rather a spot, you know. I don't think you're being very fair."

"*Fair?*" Gifford repeated the word with a grimace. "What are you talking about? For God's sake, Louise."

"All right then," his wife replied patiently. "I don't think you should blame Richard for what's happened."

"I don't. Is that what your dear Dick suggests? Now that this thing is beginning to smell he's trying to throw his guilt back on to me."

"He is not——"

Gifford petulantly thumped the wicker elbow rest. "He damned well is!" He gazed up darkly at his wife, his thin twisted mouth framed by the rim of beard. "Don't worry, my dear, you will too by the time this thing is finished."

"Charles, please...."

"Who cares, anyway?" Gifford lay back weakly for a moment, and then, as he recovered, a curious feeling of light-headed and almost euphoric calm coming over him, began again: "Dr. Richard Lowry. How he loves his doctorate. I wouldn't have had the nerve at his age. A third-rate Ph.D. for work that I did for him, and he styles himself 'Doctor'."

"So do you."

"Don't be a fool. I can remember when at least two Chairs were offered to me."

"But you couldn't degrade yourself by accepting them," his wife commented, a trace of irony in her voice.

"No, I could not," Gifford attested vehemently. "Do you know what Cambridge is like, Louise? It's *packed* with Richard Lowry's! Besides, I had a far better idea. I married a rich wife. She was charming, beautiful, and in a slightly ambiguous way respected my moody brilliance, but above all she was rich."

"How pleasant for you."

"People who marry for money earn it. I really earned mine."

"Thank you, Charles."

Gifford chuckled to himself. "One thing, Louise, you do know how to take an insult. It's a matter of breeding. I'm surprised you aren't more choosey over Lowry."

"Choosey?" Louise laughed awkwardly. "I hadn't realized that I'd chosen him. I think Richard is very obliging and helpful —as you knew when you made him your assistant, by the way."

Gifford began to compose his reply, when a sudden chill enveloped his chest and shoulders. He pulled weakly at the blanket, an immense feeling of fatigue and inertia overtaking him. He looked up glassily at his wife, their bickering conversation forgotten. The sunlight had vanished, and a profound darkness lay over the face of the delta, illuminated for a brief interval by the seething outlines of thousands of snakes. Trying to capture the image in his eyes, he struggled forward against the incubus pressing upon his chest, and then slid backwards into a pit of nausea and giddiness. "Louise . . . !"

Quickly his wife's hands were on his own, her shoulder supporting his head. He vomited emptily, struggling with his contracting musculature like a snake trying to shed its skin. Dimly he heard his wife shout for someone and the cradle topple to the ground, dragging the bedclothes with it.

"Louise," he whispered, "one of these nights. . . . I want you to take me down to the snakes."

Now and then, during the afternoon, when the pain in his foot became acute, he would wake to find Louise sitting beside him. All the while he moved through ceaseless dreams, sinking from one plane of reverie to the next, the great mandalas guiding him downwards, enthroning him upon their luminous dials.

During the next few days the conversations with his wife were less frequent. As his condition deteriorated, Gifford felt able to do little more than stare out across the mud-flats, almost unaware of the movement and arguments around him. His wife and Mechippe formed a tenuous bridge with reality, but the true centre of his attention was the nexus of beaches on to which the snakes emerged in the evenings. This was a zone of complete timelessness, where at last he sensed the simultaneity of all time, the coexistence of all events in his past life.

The snakes now made their appearance half an hour earlier. Once he caught a glimpse of their motionless albino forms exposed on the slopes in the hot noon air. Their chalk-white skins and raised heads, in a reclining posture very like his own, made them seem immeasurably ancient, like the white sphinxes in the funeral corridors to the pharaonic tombs at Karnak.

Although his strength had ebbed markedly, the infection on his foot had spread only a few inches above the ankle, and Louise Gifford realized that her husband's deterioration was a symptom of a profound psychological malaise, the *mal de passage* induced by the potently atmospheric landscape and its evocation of the lagoon-world of the Paleocene. She suggested to Gifford during one of his lucid intervals that they move the camp half a mile across the plain into the shadow of the ridge, near the Toltec terrace city where she and Lowry carried out their archaeological work.

But Gifford had refused, reluctant to leave the snakes on the beach. For some reason he disliked the terrace city. This was not because it was there that he had inflicted on himself the wound which now threatened his life. That this was simply an unfortunate accident devoid of any special symbolism he accepted without qualification. But the enigmatic presence of the terrace city, with its crumbling galleries and internal courts encrusted by the giant thistles and wire moss, seemed a huge man-made artefact which militated against the super-real naturalism of the delta. However, the terrace city, like the delta, was moving backwards in time, the baroque tracery of the serpent deities along the friezes dissolving and being replaced by the intertwined tendrils of the moss-plants, the pseudo-organic forms made by man in the image of nature reverting to their original. Kept at a distance behind him, as a huge backdrop, the ancient Toltec ruin seemed to brood in the dust like a decaying mastodon, a dying mountain whose dark dream of the earth enveloped Gifford with its luminous presence.

"Do you feel well enough to move on?" Louise asked Gifford when they had received no word of Mechippe's messenger after a further week. She gazed down at him critically as he lay in the shade under the awning, his thin body almost invisible among the folds of the blankets and the monstrous tent over his leg, only the arrogant face with its stiffening beard reminding her of his identity. "Perhaps if we met the search party half-way...."

Gifford shook his head, his eyes moving off across the bleached plain to the almost drained channels of the delta. "Which search party? There isn't a boat with a shallow enough draught between here and Taxcol."

"Perhaps they'll send a helicopter. They could see us from the air."

"Helicopter? You've got a bee in your bonnet, Louise. We'll stay here for another week or so."

"But your leg," his wife insisted. "A doctor should——"

"How can I move? Jerked about on a stretcher, I'd be dead within five minutes." He looked up wearily at his wife's pale sunburnt face, waiting for her to go away.

She hovered over him uncertainly. Fifty yards away, Richard Lowry sat in the open air outside his tent, watching her quietly.

Involuntarily, before she could prevent herself, her hand moved to straighten her hair.

" Is Lowry there? " Gifford asked.

" Richard? Yes." Louise hesitated. " We'll be back for lunch. I'll change your dressing then."

As she stepped from his field of vision Gifford lifted his chin slightly to examine the beaches obscured by the morning haze. The baked mud slopes glistened like hot concrete, and only a thin trickle of black fluid leaked slowly along the troughs. Here and there small islands fifty yards in diameter, shaped like perfect hemispheres, rose off the floors of the channels, imparting a curious geometric formality to the landscape. The whole area remained completely motionless, but Gifford lay patiently in his stretcher-chair, waiting for the snakes to come out on to the beaches.

When he noticed Mechippe serving lunch to him he realized that Lowry and Louise had not returned from the site.

" Take it away." He pushed aside the bowl of condensed soup. " Bring me whiskey soda. Double." He glanced sharply at the Indian. " Where's Mrs. Gifford? "

Mechippe steered the soup bowl back on to his tray. " Miss' Gifford coming soon, sir. Sun very hot, she wait till afternoon."

Gifford lay back for a moment, thinking of Louise and Richard Lowry, the image of them together touching the barest residue of emotion. Then he tried to wave away the haze with his hand.

" What's that——? "

" Sir? "

" Damn it, I thought I saw one." He shook his head slowly as the white form he had fleetingly glimpsed vanished among the opalescent slopes. " Too early, though. Where's that whiskey? "

" Coming, sir."

Panting slightly after the exertion of sitting up, Gifford looked around restlessly at the clutter of tents. Diagonally behind him, emerging from the lengthening focus of his eyes, loomed the long ridges of the Toltec city. Somewhere among its spiral galleries and corridors were Louise and Richard Lowry. Looking down from one of the high terraces across the alluvial bench, the distant camp would seem like a few bleached husks, guarded by a dead man propped up in a chair.

"Darling, I'm awfully sorry. We tried to get back but I twisted my heel—" Louise Gifford laughed lightly at this "—rather as you did, now that I come to think of it. Perhaps I'll be joining you here in a day or two. I'm so glad Mechippe looked after you and changed the dressing. How do you feel? You look a lot better."

Gifford nodded drowsily. The afternoon fever had subsided but he felt drained and exhausted, his awareness of his wife's chattering presence only stimulated by the whiskey he had been drinking slowly all day. "It's been a day at the zoo," he said, adding, with tired humour: "At the reptile enclosure."

"You and your snakes. Charles, you are a scream." Louise paced around the stretcher-chair, down-wind of the cradle, then withdrew to the lee-side. She waved to Richard Lowry, who was carrying some specimen trays into his tent. "Dick, I suggest we shower and then join Charles for drinks."

"Great idea," Lowry called back. "How is he?"

"Much better." To Gifford she said: "You don't mind, Charles? It will do you good to talk a little."

Gifford gestured vaguely with his head. When his wife had gone to her tent he focused his eyes carefully on the beaches. There, in the evening light, the snakes festered and writhed, their long forms gliding in and out of each other, the whole darkening horizon locked together by their serpentine embrace. There were now literally tens of thousands of them, reaching beyond the margins of the beach across the open ground towards the camp. During the afternoon, at the height of his fever, he had tried to call to them, but his voice had been too weak.

Later, over their cocktails, Richard Lowry asked: "How do you feel, sir?" When Gifford made no reply he said: "I'm glad to hear the leg is better."

"You know, Dick, I think it's psychological," Louise remarked. "As soon as you and I are out of the way Charles improves." Her eyes caught Richard Lowry's and held them.

Lowry played with his glass, a faintly self-assured smile on his bland face. "What about the messenger? Is there any news?"

"Have you heard anything, Charles? Perhaps someone will fly over in a couple of days."

During this exchange of pleasantries, and those which followed on the subsequent days, Charles Gifford remained silent and withdrawn, sinking more deeply into the interior landscape emerging from the beaches of the delta. His wife and Richard Lowry sat with him in the evenings when they returned from the terrace city, but he was barely aware of their presence. By now they seemed to move in a peripheral world, players in a marginal melodrama. Now and then he would think about them, but the effort seemed to lack point. His wife's involvement with Lowry left him unperturbed; if anything, he felt grateful to Lowry for freeing him from Louise.

Once, two or three days later, when Lowry came to sit by him in the evening, Gifford roused himself and said dryly: "I hear you found treasure in the terrace city." But before Lowry could produce a reply he relapsed again into his vigil.

One night shortly afterwards, when he was woken in the early hours of the morning by a sudden spasm of pain in his foot, he saw his wife and Lowry walking through the powdery blue darkness by the latter's tent. For a fleeting moment their embracing figures were like the snakes coiled together on the beaches.

"Mechippe!"

"Doctor?"

"*Mechippe!*"

"I am here, sir."

"Tonight, Mechippe," Gifford told him, "you sleep in my tent. Understand? I want you near me. Use my bed, if you want. Will you hear if I call?"

"Of course, sir. I hear you." The head-boy's polished ebony face regarded Gifford circumspectly. He now tended Gifford with a care that indicated that the latter, however much a novice, had at last entered the world of absolute values, composed of the delta and the snakes, the brooding presence of the Toltec ruin and his dying leg.

After midnight, Gifford lay quietly in the stretcher-chair, watching the full moon rise over the luminous beaches. Like a

Medusa's crown, thousands of the snakes had climbed the crests of the beaches and were spreading thickly across the margins of the plain, their white backs exposed to the moonlight.

"Mechippe."

The head-boy had been squatting silently in the shadows. "Dr. Gifford?"

Gifford spoke in a low but clear voice. "Crutches. Over there." As the head-boy passed the two carved sticks Gifford tossed aside the blankets. Carefully he withdrew his leg from the cradle, then sat up and lifted it on to the ground. He leaned forward into the crutches and found his balance. The bandaged foot, like a white club, stuck out in front of him. "Now. In the field-desk, right-hand drawer, there's my gun. Bring it to me."

For once the head-boy hesitated. "Gun, sir?"

"Smith & Wesson. It should be loaded, but there's a box of cartridges."

Again the head-boy hesitated, his eyes roving to the two tents spaced in a line away from them, their entrances hooded by the dust canopies. The whole camp lay in silence, the light stirring of the wind muted by the still warm sand and the dark talcum-like air. "Gun," he said. "Yes, sir."

Easing himself slowly to his feet, Gifford paused uncertainly. His head swam with the exertion, but the huge anchor of his left foot held him to the ground. Taking the pistol, he gestured with it towards the delta.

"We're going to see the snakes, Mechippe. You help me. All right?"

Mechippe's eyes flashed in the moonlight. "The snakes, sir?"

"Yes. You take me half way there. Then you can come back. Don't worry, I'll be all right."

Mechippe nodded slowly, his eyes looking out over the delta. "I help you, doctor."

Labouring slowly across the sand, Gifford steadied himself on the head-boy's arm. After a few steps he found his left leg too heavy to lift, and dragged the dead load through the soft sand.

"Christ, it's a long way." They had covered twenty yards. By some optical freak the nearest snakes now seemed to be half a mile away, barely visible between the slight rises. "Let's get on with it."

They plodded on a further ten yards. The open mouth of Lowry's tent was on their left, the white bell of the mosquito net looming in the shadows like a sepulchre. Almost exhausted, Gifford tottered unsteadily, trying to focus his eyes through the tinted air.

There was a sudden flash and roar as the revolver discharged itself, cannoning out of his hand. He felt Mechippe's fingers stiffen on his arm, and heard someone emerge from Lowry's tent, a woman's startled cry of fear. A second figure, this time a man's, appeared and with a backward glance at Gifford darted away like a startled animal among the tents, racing head down towards the terrace city.

Annoyed by these interruptions, Gifford searched blindly for the revolver, struggling with the crutches. But the darkness condensed around him, and the sand came upwards to strike his face.

The next morning, as the tents were dismantled and packed away, Gifford felt too tired to look out across the delta. The snakes never appeared until the early afternoon, and the disappointment of failing to reach them the previous night had drained his energy.

When only his own tent remained of the camp, and the naked shower scaffoldings protruded from the ground like pieces of abstract sculpture marking a futuristic cairn, Louise came over to him.

"It's time for them to pack your tent." Her tone was matter-of-fact but guarded. "The boys are building a stretcher for you. You should be comfortable."

Gifford gestured her away. "I can't go. Leave Mechippe with me and take the others."

"Charles, be practical for once." Louise stood before him, her face composed. "We can't stay here indefinitely, and you need treatment. It's obvious now that Mechippe's boy never reached Taxcol. Our supplies won't last forever."

"They don't have to last forever." Gifford's eyes, almost closed, surveyed the distant horizon like a pair of defective binoculars. "Leave me one month's."

"Charles——"

"For heaven's sake, Louise...." Wearily he let his head loll on the pillow. He noticed Richard Lowry supervising the stowage of the stores, the Indian boys moving around him like willing children. "Why all the hurry? Can't you stay another week?"

"We can't, Charles." She looked her husband straight in the face. "Richard feels he must go. You understand. For your sake."

"My sake?" Gifford shook his head. "I don't give a damn about Lowry. Last night I was going out to look at the snakes."

"Well...." Louise smoothed her bush shirt. "This trip has been such a fiasco, Charles, there are many things that frighten me. I'll tell them to dismantle the tent when you're ready."

"Louise." With a last effort Gifford sat up. In a quiet voice, in order not to embarrass his wife by letting Richard Lowry hear him, he said: "I went out to look at the *snakes*. You do understand that?"

"But Charles!" With a sudden burst of exasperation his wife snapped: "Don't you realize, there are no snakes! Ask Mechippe, ask Richard Lowry or any of the boys! The entire river is as dry as a bone!"

Gifford turned to look at the white beaches of the delta. "You and Lowry go. I'm sorry, Louise, but I couldn't stand the trip."

"You must!" She gestured at the distant hills, at the terrace city and the delta. "There's something wrong with this place, Charles, somehow it's convinced you that...."

Followed by a group of boys, Richard Lowry walked slowly towards them, signalling with his hands to Louise. She hesitated, then on an impulse waved him back and sat down beside Gifford. "Charles, listen. I'll stay with you for another week as you ask, so that you can come to terms with these hallucinations, if you promise me that you'll leave then. Richard can go ahead on his own, he'll meet us in Taxcol with a doctor." She lowered her voice, "Charles, I'm sorry about Richard. I realize now ..."

She leaned forward to see her husband's face. He lay in his seat in front of the solitary tent, the circle of boys watching him patiently from a distance. Ten miles away a solitary cloud drifted over one of the mesas, like a plume of smoke above a dormant but still active volcano.

"Charles." She waited for her husband to speak, hoping that he would reprove and so perhaps even forgive her. But Charles Gifford was thinking only of the snakes on the beaches.

THE TERMINAL BEACH

At night, as he lay asleep on the floor of the ruined bunker, Traven heard the waves breaking along the shore of the lagoon, like the sounds of giant aircraft warming up at the ends of their runways. This memory of the great night raids against the Japanese mainland had filled his first months on the island with images of burning bombers falling through the air around him. Later, with the attacks of beri-beri, the nightmare passed and the waves began to remind him of the deep Atlantic rollers on the beach at Dakar, where he had been born, and of watching from the window in the evenings for his parents to drive home along the corniche road from the airport. Overcome by this long forgotten memory, he woke uncertainly from the bed of old magazines on which he slept and went out to the dunes that screened the lagoon.

Through the cold night air he could see the abandoned Superfortresses lying among the palms beyond the perimeter of the emergency landing field three hundred yards away. Traven walked through the dark sand, already forgetting where the shore lay, although the atoll was little more than half a mile in width. Above him, along the crests of the dunes, the tall palms leaned into the dim air like the symbols of a cryptic alphabet. The landscape of the island was covered by strange ciphers.

Giving up the attempt to find the beach, Traven stumbled into a set of tracks left years earlier by a large caterpillar vehicle. The heat released by the weapons tests had fused the sand, and the double line of fossil imprints, uncovered by the evening air, wound its serpentine way among the hollows like the footfalls of an ancient saurian.

Too weak to walk any further, Traven sat down between the tracks. Hoping that they might lead him to the beach, he began to excavate the wedge-shaped grooves from a drift into which they disappeared. He returned to the bunker shortly before dawn, and slept through the hot silences of the following noon.

The Blocks

As usual on these enervating afternoons, when not even a breath of on-shore breeze disturbed the dust, Traven sat in the shadow of one of the blocks, lost somewhere within the centre of the maze. His back resting against the rough concrete surface, he gazed with a phlegmatic eye down the surrounding aisles and at the line of doors facing him. Each afternoon he left his cell in the abandoned camera bunker among the dunes and walked down into the blocks. For the first half an hour he restricted himself to the perimeter aisle, now and then trying one of the doors with the rusty key in his pocket—found among the litter of smashed bottles and cans in the isthmus of sand separating the testing ground from the air-strip—and then inevitably, with a sort of drugged stride, he set off into the centre of the blocks, breaking into a run and darting in and out of the corridors, as if trying to flush some invisible opponent from his hiding place. Soon he would be completely lost. Whatever his efforts to return to the perimeter, he always found himself once more in the centre.

Eventually he would abandon the task, and sit down in the dust, watching the shadows emerge from their crevices at the foot of the blocks. For some reason he invariably arranged to be trapped when the sun was at zenith—on Eniwetok, the thermo-nuclear noon.

One question in particular intrigued him: "What sort of people would inhabit this minimal concrete city?"

The Synthetic Landscape

"This island is a state of mind," Osborne, one of the scientists working in the old submarine pens, was later to remark to Traven. The truth of this became obvious to Traven within two or three weeks of his arrival. Despite the sand and the few anaemic palms, the entire landscape of the island was synthetic, a man made artifact with all the associations of a vast system of derelict concrete motor-ways. Since the moratorium on atomic tests, the island had been abandoned by the Atomic Energy Commission, and the wilderness of weapons aisles, towers and blockhouses ruled out any attempt to return it to its natural state. (There were also stronger unconscious motives, Traven recognized: if primitive man felt the need to assimilate events in the external world to his own psyche, 20th century man had reversed this process; by this Cartesian yardstick, the island at least *existed*, in a sense true of few other places.)

But apart from a few scientific workers, no one yet felt any wish to visit the former testing ground, and the naval patrol boat anchored in the lagoon had been withdrawn three years before Traven's arrival. Its ruined appearance, and the associations of the island with the period of the Cold War—what Traven had christened 'The Pre-Third'—were profoundly depressing, an Auschwitz of the soul whose mausoleums contained the mass-graves of the still undead. With the Russo-American *détente* this nightmarish chapter of history had been gladly forgotten.

The Pre-Third

> *The actual and potential destructiveness of the atomic bomb plays straight into the hands of the Unconscious. The most cursory study of the dream-life and fantasies of the insane shows that ideas of world-destruction are latent in the unconscious mind ... Nagasaki destroyed by the magic of science is the nearest man has yet approached to the realization of dreams that even during the safe immobility of sleep are accustomed to develop into nightmares of anxiety.*
>
> Glover: 'War, Sadism and Pacifism'

The Pre-Third: the period was characterized in Traven's mind above all by its moral and psychological inversions, by its sense of the whole of history, and in particular of the immediate future —the two decades, 1945-65—suspended from the quivering volcano's lip of World War III. Even the death of his wife and six-year-old son in a motor accident seemed only part of this immense synthesis of the historical and psychic zero, the frantic highways where each morning they met their deaths the advance causeways to the global armageddon.

Third Beach

He had come ashore at midnight, after a hazardous search for an opening in the reef. The small motor-boat he had hired from an Australian pearl-diver at Charlotte Island subsided into the shallows, its hull torn by the sharp coral. Exhausted, Traven walked through the darkness among the dunes, where the dim outlines of bunkers and concrete towers loomed between the palms.

He woke the next morning into bright sunlight, lying half-way down the slope of a wide concrete beach. This ringed an empty reservoir or target basin some two hundred feet in diameter, part of a system of artificial lakes built down the centre of the atoll. Leaves and dust choked the exit grilles, and a pool of warm water two feet deep lay below him, reflecting a distant line of palms.

Traven sat up and took stock of himself. This brief inventory, which merely confirmed his physical identity, was limited to little more than his thin body in its frayed cotton garments. In the context of the surrounding terrain, however, even this collection of tatters seemed to possess a unique vitality. The desolation and emptiness of the island, and the absence of any local fauna, were emphasized by the huge sculptural forms of the target basins set into its surface. Separated from each other by narrow isthmuses, the lakes stretched away along the curve of the atoll. On either side, sometimes shaded by the few palms that had gained a precarious purchase in the cracked cement, were roadways, camera towers and isolated blockhouses, together forming a continuous concrete cap upon the island, a functional, megalithic architecture as grey and minatory (and apparently as ancient, in its projection into, and from, time future) as any of Assyria and Babylon.

The series of weapons tests had fused the sand in layers, and the pseudo-geological strata condensed the brief epochs, microseconds in duration, of thermonuclear time. Typically the island inverted the geologist's maxim, ' The key to the past lies in the present.' Here, the key to the present lay in the future. This island was a fossil of time future, its bunkers and blockhouses illustrating the principle that the fossil record of life was one of armour and the exoskeleton.

Traven knelt in the warm. pool, and splashed his shirt and trousers. The reflection revealed the watery image of gaunt shoulders and bearded face. He had come to the island with no supplies other than a small bar of chocolate, assuming that in some way the island would provide its own sustenance. Perhaps, too, he had identified the need for food with a forward motion in time, and that with his return to the past, or at most into a zone of non-time, this need would be eliminated. The privations of the previous six months, during his journey across the Pacific, had already reduced his always thin body to that of a migrant beggar, held together by little more than the preoccupied gaze in his eye. Yet this emaciation, by stripping away the superfluities of the flesh, revealed an inner sinewy toughness, an economy and directness of movement.

For several hours Traven wandered about, inspecting one bunker after another for a convenient place to sleep. He crossed the remains of a small landing field, next to a dump where a dozen B-29s lay across one another like dead reptile birds.

The Corpses

Once he entered a small street of metal shacks, containing a cafeteria, recreation rooms and shower stalls. A wrecked juke-box lay half-buried in the sand behind the cafeteria, its selection of records still in their rack.

Further along, flung into a small target lake fifty yards from the shacks, were the bodies of what at first he thought were the former inhabitants of this ghost town—a dozen life-size plastic models. Their half-melted faces, contorted into bleary grimaces, gazed up at him from the jumble of legs and torsoes.

On either side of him, muffled by the dunes, came the sounds of waves, the great rollers on the seaward side breaking over the reefs, and on to the beaches within the lagoon. However, he avoided the sea, hesitating before any rise or dune that might take him within its sight. Everywhere the camera towers offered him a convenient aerial view of the confused topography of the island, but he avoided their rusting ladders.

Traven soon realized that however random the blockhouses and towers might seem, their common focus dominated the landscape and gave to it a unique perspective. As he noticed when he sat down to rest in the window slit of one of the bunkers, all these observation posts occupied positions on a series of concentric perimeters, moving in tightening arcs towards the inmost sanctuary. This ultimate circle, below ground zero, remained hidden beyond a line of dunes a quarter of a mile to the west.

The Terminal Bunker

After sleeping for a few nights in the open, Traven returned to the concrete beach where he had woken on his first morning on the island, and made his home—if the term could be applied to that damp crumbling hovel—in a camera bunker fifty yards from the target lakes. The dark chamber between the thick canted walls, tomb-like though it might seem, gave him a sense of physical reassurance. Outside, the sand drifted against the sides, half-burying the narrow doorway, as if crystallizing the immense epoch of time that had elapsed since the bunker's construction. The narrow rectangles of the five camera slits, their shapes and positions determined by the instruments, studded the west wall like runic ideograms. Variations on these ciphers decorated the walls of the other bunkers, the unique signature of the island. In the mornings, if Traven was awake, he would always find the sun divided into its five emblematic beacons.

Most of the time the chamber was filled only by a damp gloomy light. In the control tower at the landing field Traven found a collection of discarded magazines, and used these to make a bed. One day, lying in the bunker shortly after the first attack of beri-beri, he pulled out a magazine pressing into his back and found inside it a full-page photograph of a six-year-old girl. This blonde-haired child, with her composed expression and self-immersed eyes, filled him with a thousand painful memories of his son. He pinned the page to the wall and for days gazed at it through his reveries.

For the first few weeks Traven made little attempt to leave the bunker, and postponed any further exploration of the island. The symbolic journey through its inner circles set its own times of arrival and departure. He evolved no routine for himself. All sense of time soon vanished, and his life became completely existential, an absolute break separating one moment from the next like two quantal events. Too weak to forage for food, he lived on the old ration packs he found in the wrecked Superfortresses. Without any implement, it took him all day to open the cans. His physical decline continued, but he watched his spindling legs and arms with indifference.

By now he had forgotten the existence of the sea and vaguely assumed the atoll to be part of some continuous continental table. A hundred yards to the north and south of the bunker a line of dunes, topped by the palisade of enigmatic palms, screened the lagoon and sea, and the faint muffled drumming of the waves at night had fused with his memories of war and childhood. To the east was the emergency landing strip and the abandoned aircraft. In the afternoon light their shifting rectilinear shadows made them appear to writhe and pivot. In front of the bunker, where he would sit, was the system of target lakes, the shallow basins extending across the atoll.

Above him, the five apertures looked out upon this scene like the tutelary symbols of a futuristic myth.

The Lakes and the Spectres

The lakes had been designed to reveal any radiobiological changes in a selected range of fauna, but the specimens had long since bloomed into grotesque parodies of themselves and been destroyed.

Sometimes in the evenings, when a sepulchral light lay over the concrete bunkers and causeways, and the basins seemed like ornamental lakes in a city of deserted mausoleums, abandoned even by the dead, he would see the spectres of his wife and son standing on the opposite bank. Their solitary figures appeared to have been watching him for hours. Although they never moved, Traven was sure they were beckoning to him. Roused from his reverie, he would stumble forward across the dark sand to the edge of the lake and wade through the water, shouting soundlessly at the two figures as they moved away hand in hand among the lakes and disappeared across the distant causeways.

Shivering with cold, Traven would return to the bunker and lie on the bed of old magazines, waiting for their return. The image of their faces, the pale lantern of his wife's cheeks, floated on the river of his memory.

The Blocks (II)

It was not until he discovered the blocks that Traven realized he would never leave the island.

At this stage, some two months after his arrival, Traven had exhausted his small cache of food, and the symptoms of beri-beri had become more acute. The numbness in his hands and feet, and the gradual loss of strength, continued. Only by an immense effort, and the knowledge that the inner sanctum of the island still lay unexplored, did he manage to leave the palliasse of magazines and make his way from the bunker.

As he sat in the drift of sand by the doorway that evening, he noticed a light shining through the palms far into the distance around the atoll. Confusing this with the image of his wife and son, and visualizing them waiting for him at some warm hearth among the dunes, Travern set off towards the light. Within a hundred yards he lost his sense of direction. He blundered about for several hours on the edges of the landing strip, and succeeded only in cutting his foot on a broken coca-cola bottle in the sand.

After postponing his search for the night, he set out again in earnest the next morning. As he moved past the towers and blockhouses the heat lay over the island in an unbroken mantle. He had entered a zone devoid of time. Only the narrowing perimeters warned him that he was crossing the inner field of the fire-table.

He climbed the ridge which marked the furthest point in his previous exploration of the island. From the plain below it the recording towers rose into the air like obelisks. Traven walked down towards them. On their grey walls were the faint outlines of human forms in stylized poses, the flash-shadows of the target community burnt into the cement. Here and there, where the concrete apron had cracked, a line of palms hung in the motion-

less air. The target lakes were smaller, filled with the broken
bodies of plastic models. Most of them lay in the inoffensive
domestic postures into which they had been placed before the
tests.

Beyond the furthest line of dunes, where the camera towers
began to turn and face him, were the tops of what seemed to be a
herd of square-backed elephants. They were drawn up in precise
ranks in a hollow that formed a shallow corral, the sunlight reflected off their backs.

Traven advanced towards them, limping on his cut foot. On
either side of him the loosening sand had excavated the dunes,
and several of the blockhouses tilted on their sides. This plain of
bunkers stretched for some quarter of a mile, the half-submerged
hulks, bombed out onto the surface in some earlier test, like
the abandoned wombs that had given birth to this herd of
megaliths.

The Blocks (III)

To grasp something of the vast number and oppressive size of
the blocks, and their impact upon Traven, one must try to visualize sitting in the shade of one of these concrete monsters, or walking about in the centre of this enormous labyrinth that extended
across the central table of the island. There were two thousand of
them, each a perfect cube 15 feet in height, regularly spaced at
ten-yard intervals. There were arranged in a series of tracts, each
composed of two hundred blocks, inclined to one another and to
the direction of the blast. They had weathered only slightly in the
years since they were first built, and their gaunt profiles were like
the cutting faces of a gigantic die-plate, devised to stamp out rectilinear volumes of air the size of a house. Three of the sides were
smooth and unbroken, but the fourth, facing away from the blast,
contained a narrow inspection door.

It was this feature of the blocks that Traven found particularly
disturbing. Despite the considerable number of doors, by some
freak of perspective only those in a single aisle were visible at any
point within the maze. As he walked from the perimeter line into
the centre of the massif, line upon line of the small metal doors
appeared and receded.

Approximately twenty of the blocks, those immediately below ground zero, were solid: the walls of the remainder were of varying thicknesses. From the outside they appeared to be of uniform solidity.

As he entered the first of the long aisles, Traven felt the sense of fatigue that had dogged him for so many months begin to lift. With their geometric regularity and finish, the blocks seemed to occupy more than their own volumes of space, imposing on him a mood of absolute calm and order. He walked on into the centre of the maze, eager to shut out the rest of the island. After a few random turns to left and right, he found himself alone, the vistas to the sea, lagoon and island closed.

Here he sat down with his back to one of the blocks, the quest for his wife and son forgotten. For the first time since his arrival at the island the sense of dissociation set off by its derelict landscape began to recede.

One development he did not expect. With dusk, and the need to leave the blocks and find food, he realized that he had lost himself. However he retraced his steps, struck out left or right at an oblique course, oriented himself around the sun and pressed on resolutely north or south, he found himself back again at his starting point. Only when darkness came did he manage to make his escape.

Abandoning his former home near the aircraft dump, Traven collected together what canned food he could find in the waist turret and cockpit lockers of the Superfortresses. He pulled them across the atoll on a crude sledge. Fifty yards from the perimeter of the blocks he took over a tilting bunker, and pinned the fading photograph of the blonde-haired child to the wall beside the door. The page was falling to pieces, like a fragmenting mirror of himself. Since the discovery of the blocks he had become a creature of reflexes, kindled from levels above those of his existing nervous system (if the autonomic system was dominated by the past, Traven sensed, the cerebro-spinal reached towards the future). Each evening when he woke he would eat without appetite and then wander among the blocks. Sometimes he took a canteen of water with him and remained there for two or three days on end.

The Submarine Pens

This precarious existence continued for the following weeks. As he walked out to the blocks one evening, he again saw his wife and son, standing among the dunes below a solitary camera tower, their faces watching him expressionlessly. He realized that they had followed him across the island from their former haunt among the dried-up lakes. At about this time he once again saw the distant light beckoning, and decided to continue his exploration of the island.

Half a mile further along the atoll he found a group of four submarine pens, built over an inlet, now drained, which wound through the dunes from the sea. The pens still contained several feet of water, filled with strange luminescent fish and plants. The warning light winked at intervals from the apex of a metal scaffold. The remains of a substantial camp, only recently vacated, stood on the pier outside. Greedily, Traven heaped his sledge with the provisions stored inside one of the metal shacks.

With this change of diet, the beri-beri receded, and during the next days he returned often to the camp. It appeared to be the site of a biological expedition. In the field office he came across a series of large charts of mutated chromosomes. He rolled them up and took them back to his bunker. The abstract patterns were meaningless, but during his recovery he amused himself by devising suitable titles for them. (Later, passing the aircraft dump on one of his forays, he found the half-buried juke-box, and tore the list of records from the selection panel, realizing that these were the most appropriate captions. Thus embroidered, the charts took on many layers of associations).

Traven: In Parenthesis

Elements in a quantal world:
    The terminal beach.
    The terminal bunker.
    The blocks.

The landscape is coded.

Entry points into the future=Levels in a spinal landscape= zones of significant time.

*August 5. Found the man Traven. A strange derelict figure,
hiding in a bunker in the deserted interior of the island. He is
suffering from severe exposure and malnutrition, but is unaware of this or, for that matter, of any other events in the
world around him. . . .*

*He maintains that he came to the island to carry out some
scientific project—unstated—but I suspect that he understands
his real motives and the unique role of the island. . . . In some
way its landscape seems to be involved with certain unconscious
notions of time, and in particular with those that may be a
repressed premonition of our own deaths. The attractions and
dangers of such an architecture, as the past has shown, need no
stressing. . . .*

*August 6. He has the eyes of the possessed. I would guess that
he is neither the first, nor the last, to visit the island.*

—from Dr. C. Osborne, ' Eniwetok Diary.'

Traven lost within the Blocks

With the exhaustion of his supplies, Traven remained within
the perimeter of the blocks almost continuously, conserving what
strength remained to him to walk slowly down their empty corridors. The infection in his right foot made it difficult for him to
replenish his supplies from the stores left by the biologists, and as
his strength ebbed he found progressively less incentive to make
his way out of the blocks. The system of megaliths now provided
a complete substitute for those functions of his mind which gave
to it its sense of the sustained rational order of time and space.
Without them, his awareness of reality shrank to little more than
the few square inches of sand beneath his feet.

On one of his last ventures into the maze, he spent all night and
much of the following morning in a futile attempt to escape.
Dragging himself from one rectangle of shadow to another, his
leg as heavy as a club and apparently inflamed to the knee, he
realized that he must soon find an equivalent for the blocks or he
would end his life within them, trapped inside this self-con-
structed mausoleum as surely as the retinue of Pharaoh.

He was sitting helplessly somewhere in the centre of the system,
the faceless lines of tomb-booths receding from him, when the

sky was slowly divided by the drone of a light aircraft. This passed overhead, and then returned five minutes later. Seizing his opportunity, Traven struggled to his feet and made his exit from the blocks, his head raised to follow the faintly glistening beacon of the exhaust trail.

As he lay in the bunker he dimly heard the aircraft return and carry out an inspection of the site.

A Belated Rescue

"Who are you? Do you realize you're on your last legs?"

"Traven.... I've had some sort of accident. I'm glad you flew over."

"I'm sure you are. But why didn't you use our radio-telephone? Anyway, we'll call the Navy and have you picked up."

"No...." Traven sat up on one elbow and felt weakly in his hip pocket. "I have a pass somewhere. I'm carrying out research."

"Into what?" The question assumed a complete understanding of Traven's motives. He lay in the shade under the lee of the bunker, and drank weakly from a canteen as Dr. Osborne dressed his foot. "You've also been stealing our stores."

Traven shook his head. Fifty yards away the striped blue Cessna stood on the concrete apron like a brilliant dragonfly. "I didn't realize you were coming back."

"You must be in a trance."

The young woman sitting at the controls of the aircraft climbed out and walked over to them. She glanced at the grey bunkers and towers, and seemed uninterested in the decrepit figure of Traven. Osborne spoke to her and after a downward glance at Traven she went back to the aircraft. As she turned Traven rose involuntarily, recognizing the child in the photograph he had pinned to the wall of the bunker. Then he remembered that the magazine could not have been more than four or five years old.

The engine of the aircraft started. As Traven watched, it turned on to one of the roadways and took off into the wind.

Later that afternoon the young woman drove over to the blocks by jeep and unloaded a small camp-bed and a canvas awning. During the intervening hours Traven had slept. He woke re-

freshed when Osborne returned from his scrutiny of the surrounding dunes.

"What are you doing here?" the young woman asked as she
secured the guy-ropes to the roof of the bunker.

Traven watched her move about. "I'm . . . searching for my
wife and son."

"They're on this island?" Surprised, but taking the reply at
face value, she looked around her. "Here?"

"In a manner of speaking."

After inspecting the bunker, Osborne joined them. "The child
in the photograph—is she your daughter?"

Traven hesitated. "No. She's adopted *me*."

Unable to make any sense of his replies, but accepting his
assurances that he would leave the island, Osborne and the young
woman drove back to their camp. Each day Osborne returned to
change the dressing, driven by the young woman, who seemed
now to grasp the role cast for her by Traven. Osborne, when he
learned of Traven's previous career as a military pilot, appeared
to suspect that he might be a latter-day martyr left high and dry
by the moratorium on thermonuclear tests.

"A guilt complex isn't an indiscriminate supply of moral sanc-
tions. I think you may be over-stretching your's." When he mentioned the name Eatherly, Traven shook his head.

Undeterred, Osborne pressed: "Are you sure you're not making similar use of the image of Eniwetok—waiting for your
Pentecostal wind?"

"Believe me, Doctor, no," Travel replied firmly. "For me the
hydrogen bomb was a symbol of absolute *freedom*. I feel it's
given me the right—the obligation, even—to do anything I want."

"That seems strange logic," Osborne commented. "Aren't we
at least responsible for our physical selves, if for nothing else?"

"Not now, I think," Traven replied. "After all, in effect we
are men raised from the dead."

Often, however, he thought of Eatherly: the prototypal Pre-
Third Man—dating the Pre-Third from August 6, 1945—carrying
a full load of cosmic guilt.

Shortly after Traven was strong enough to walk, he had to be rescued from the blocks for a second time. Osborne became less conciliatory.

"Our work is almost complete," he said warningly. "You'll die here, Traven. What *are* you looking for among those blocks?"

To himself, Traven murmured: the tomb of the unknown civilian, *Homo hydrogenensis*, Eniwetok Man. "Doctor," he said, "your laboratory is at the wrong end of this island."

Tartly, Osborne replied: "I'm aware of that, Traven. There are rarer fish swimming in your head than in any submarine pen."

On the day before they left, the young woman drove Traven over to the lakes where he had first arrived. As a final present, an ironic gesture unexpected from the elderly biologist, she had brought from Osborne the correct list of legends for the chromosome charts. They stopped by the derelict juke-box and she pasted them on to the selection panel.

They wandered among the supine wrecks of the Superfortresses. Traven lost sight of her, and for the next ten minutes searched in and out of the dunes. He found her standing in a small amphitheatre formed by the sloping mirrors of a solar energy device built by one of the visiting expeditions. She smiled to Traven as he stepped through the scaffolding. A dozen fragmented images of herself were reflected in the broken panes—in some she was sans head, in others multiples of her arms circled about her like the serpent limbs of a Hindu goddess. Confused, Traven turned and walked back to the jeep.

As they drove away he recovered himself. He described his glimpses of his wife and son. "Their faces are always calm," he said. "My son's particularly, though really he was always laughing. The only time his face was grave was when he was being born—then he seemed millions of years old."

The young woman nodded. "I hope you find them." As an afterthought she added: "Dr. Osborne is going to tell the Navy that you're here. Hide somewhere."

Traven thanked her.

From the centre of the blocks he waved to her the following day when she flew away for the last time.

The Naval Party

When the search party came for him Traven hid in the only logical place. Fortunately the search was perfunctory, and was called off after a few hours. The sailors had brought a supply of beer with them and the search soon turned into a drunken ramble.

On the walls of the recording towers Traven later found balloons of obscene dialogue chalked into the mouths of the shadowy figures, giving their postures the priapic gaiety of the dancers in cave drawings.

The climax of the party was the ignition of a store of gasoline in an underground tank near the air-strip. As he listened, first to the megaphones shouting his name, the echoes receding among the dunes like the forlorn calls of dying birds, then to the boom of the explosion and the laughter as the landing craft left, Traven felt a premonition that these were the last sounds he would hear.

He had hidden in one of the target basins, lying among the broken bodies of the plastic models. In the hot sunlight their deformed faces gaped at him sightlessly from the tangle of limbs, their blurred smiles like those of the soundlessly laughing dead.

Their faces filled his mind as he climbed over the bodies and returned to his bunker. As he walked towards the blocks he saw the figures of his wife and son standing in his path. They were less than ten yards from him, their white faces watching him with a look of almost overwhelming expectancy. Never had Traven seen them so close to the blocks. His wife's pale features seemed illuminated from within, her lips parted as if in greeting, one hand raised to take his own. His son's face, with its curiously fixed expression, regarded him with the same enigmatic smile of the child in the photograph.

"Judith! David!" Startled, Traven ran forwards to them. Then, in a sudden movement of light, their clothes turned into shrouds, and he saw the wounds that disfigured their necks and chests. Appalled, he cried out. As they vanished, he ran off into the safety of the blocks.

The Catechism of Good-bye

This time he found himself, as Osborne had predicted, unable to leave the blocks.

Somewhere in the centre of the maze, he sat with his back against one of the concrete flanks, his eyes raised to the sun. Around him the lines of cubes formed the horizon of his world. At times they would appear to advance towards him, looming over him like cliffs, the intervals between them narrowing so that they were little more than an arm's length apart, a labyrinth of corridors running between them. They then would recede from him, separating from each other like points in an expanding universe, until the nearest line formed an intermittent palisade along the horizon.

Time had become quantal. For hours it would be noon, the shadows contained within the blocks, the heat reflected off the concrete floor. Abruptly, he would find that it was early afternoon or evening, the shadows everywhere like pointing fingers.

" *Good-bye, Eniwetok,*" he murmured.

Somewhere there was a flicker of light, as if one of the blocks, like a counter on an abacus, had been plucked away.

Good-bye, Los Alamos. Again, a block seemed to vanish. The corridors around him remained intact, but somewhere in his mind had appeared a small interval of neutral space.

Good-bye, Hiroshima.

Good-bye, Alamagordo.

" *Good-bye, Moscow, London, Paris, New York....*

Shuttles flickered, a ripple of lost integers. He stopped, realizing the futility of this megathlon farewell. Such a leave-taking required him to fix his signature upon every one of the particles in the universe.

Total Noon: Eniwetok

The blocks now occupied positions on an endlessly revolving circus wheel. They carried him upwards into the sky, from where he could see the whole island and the sea, and then down again through the opaque disc of the concrete floor. From here he looked up at the under-surface of the concrete cap, an inverted landscape of rectilinear hollows, the dome-shaped mounds of the lake-system, the thousands of empty cubic pits of the blocks.

"Good-bye, Traven."

Near the end, he found to his disappointment that this ultimate rejection gained him nothing.

In the interval of lucidity, he looked down at his emaciated arms and legs, decorated with a lace-work of ulcers. To his right was a trail of disturbed dust, the wavering marks of slack heels.

To his left lay a long corridor between the blocks, joining an oblique series a hundred yards away. Among these, where a narrow interval revealed the open space beyond, was a crescent-shaped shadow, poised in the air above the ground.

During the next half an hour it moved slowly, turning as the sun swung, the profile of a dune.

The Crevice

Seizing on this cipher, which hung before him like a symbol on a shield, Traven pushed himself through the dust. He climbed precariously to his feet, and shielded his eyes from the blocks. He moved forward a few paces at a time.

Ten minutes later he emerged from the western perimeter of the blocks, like a tottering mendicant leaving behind a silent desert city. The dune lay fifty yards in front of him. Beyond it, bearing the shadow like a screen, was a ridge of limestone that ran away among the hillocks of the wasteland beyond this point of the atoll. The remains of an old bulldozer, bales of barbed wire and fifty-gallon drums lay half-buried in the sand. Traven approached the dune, reluctant to leave this anonymous swell of sand. He shuffled around its edges, and sat down in the mouth of a shallow crevice below the brow of the ridge.

After dusting his clothes, he gazed out patiently at the great circle of blocks.

Ten minutes later he noticed that someone was watching him.

The Marooned Japanese

This corpse, whose eyes stared up at Traven, lay to his left at the bottom of the crevice. That of a man of middle age and strong build, it rested on its back with its head on a pillow of stone, hands outstretched at its sides, as if surveying the window of the sky. The fabric of the clothes had rotted to a bleached grey vestment, but in the absence of any small animal predators on the island the skin and musculature of the corpse had been preserved. Here and there, at the angle of knee or wrist, a bony point glinted through the leathery integument of the skin, but the facial mask was still intact, and revealed a male Japanese of the professional classes. Looking down at the strong nose, high forehead and broad mouth, Traven guessed that the Japanese had been a doctor or lawyer.

Puzzled as to how the corpse had found itself here, Traven slid a few feet down the slope. There were no radiation burns on the skin, which indicated that the Japanese had been there for five years or less. Nor did he appear to be wearing a uniform, so had not been some unfortunate member of a military or scientific party.

To the left of the corpse, within reach of his left hand, was a frayed leather case, the remains of a map wallet. To the right was the husk of a haversack, open to reveal a canteen of water and a small mess-tin.

Traven slid down the slope until his feet touched the splitting soles of the corpse's shoes, the reflex of starvation making him for the moment ignore that the Japanese had deliberately chosen to die in the crevice. He reached out and seized the canteen. A cupful of flat water swilled around the rusting bottom. Traven gulped down the water, the dissolved metal salts cloaking his lips and tongue with a bitter film. The mess-tin was empty except for a tacky coating of condensed syrup. Traven prised at this with the lid, and chewed at the tarry flakes, letting them dissolve in his mouth with an almost intoxicating sweetness. After a few moments he felt light-headed and sat back beside the corpse. Its sightless eyes regarded him with unmoving compassion.

The Fly
(*A small fly, which Traven presumes has followed him into the fissure, now buzzes about the corpse's face. Guiltily, Traven leans forward to kill it, then reflects that perhaps this miniscule sentry has been the corpse's faithful companion, in return fed*

on the rich liqueurs and distillations of its pores. Carefully, to avoid injuring the fly, he encourages it to alight on his wrist.)

DR. YASUDA: Thank you, Traven. In my position, you understand ...

TRAVEN: Of course, Doctor. I'm sorry I tried to kill it—these ingrained habits, you know, they're not easy to shrug off. Your sister's children in Osaka in '44, the exigencies of war, I hate to plead them. Most known motives are so despicable, one searches the unknown in the hope that ...

YASUDA: Please, Traven, do not be embarrassed. The fly is lucky to retain its identity for so long. That son you mourn, not to mention my own two nieces and nephew, did they not die each day? Every parent in the world grieves for the lost sons and daughters of their earlier childhoods.

TRAVEN: You're very tolerant, Doctor. I wouldn't dare——

YASUDA: Not at all, Traven. I make no apologies for you. Each of us is little more than the meagre residue of the infinite unrealized possibilities of our lives. But your son, and my nephew, are fixed in our minds forever, their identities as certain as the stars.

TRAVEN: (*not entirely convinced*) That may be so, Doctor, but it leads to a dangerous conclusion in the case of this island. For instance, the blocks——

YASUDA: They are precisely what I refer to, Traven. Here among the blocks you at last find an image of yourself free of the hazards of time and space. This island is an ontological Garden of Eden, why seek to expel yourself into a world of quantal flux?

TRAVEN: Excuse me (*The fly has flown back to the corpse's face and sits in one of the dried-up orbits, giving the good doctor an expression of quizzical beadiness. Reaching forward, Traven entices it on to his palm. He examines it carefully*) Well, yes, these bunkers may be ontological objects, but whether this is the ontological fly is doubtful. It's true that on this island it's the *only* fly, which is the next best thing. ...

YASADA: You can't accept the plurality of the universe—ask yourself why, Traven. Why should this obsess you? It seems to me that you are hunting for the white leviathan, zero. The beach is a dangerous zone. Avoid it. Have a proper humility, pursue a philosophy of acceptance.

TRAVEN: Then may I ask why you came here, Doctor?

YASUDA: To feed this fly. ' What greater love——? '

TRAVEN: (*Still puzzling*) It doesn't really solve my problem. The blocks, you see . . .

YASUDA: Very well, if you must have it that way. . . .

TRAVEN: But, Doctor——

YASUDA: (*Peremptorily*) Kill that fly!

TRAVEN: That's not an end, or a beginning.

(*Hopelessly, he kills the fly. Exhausted, he falls asleep beside the corpse.*)

The Terminal Beach

Searching for a piece of rope in the refuse dump behind the dunes, Traven found a bale of rusty wire. After unwinding it, he secured a harness around the corpse's chest and dragged it from the crevice. The lid of a wooden crate made a crude sledge. Traven fastened the corpse to it in a sitting position, and set off along the perimeter of the blocks. Around him the island remained silent. The lines of palms hung in the sunlight, only his own motion varying the shifting ciphers of their criss-crossing trunks. The square turrets of the camera towers jutted from the dunes like forgotten obelisks.

An hour later, when Traven reached the awning by his bunker, he untied the wire cord he had fastened around his waist. He took the chair left for him by Dr. Osborne and carried it to a point midway between the bunker and the blocks. Then he tied the body of the Japanese to the chair, arranging the hands so that they rested on the wooden arms giving the moribund figure a posture of calm repose.

This done to his satisfaction, Traven returned to the bunker and squatted under the awning.

As the next days passed into weeks, the dignified figure of the Japanese sat in his chair fifty yards from him, guarding Traven from the blocks. He now had sufficient strength to rouse himself at intervals and forage for food. In the hot sunlight the skin of the Japanese became more and more bleached, and Traven would wake at night and find the sepulchral figure sitting there, arms resting at its sides, in the shadows that crossed the concrete floor. At these moments he would often see his wife and son watching him from the dunes. As time passed they came closer, and he would sometimes find them only a few yards behind him.

Patiently Traven waited for them to speak to him, thinking of the great blocks whose entrance was guarded by the seated figure of the dead archangel, as the waves broke on the distant shore and the burning bombers fell through his dreams.

DEEP END

THEY always slept during the day. By dawn the last of the townsfolk had gone indoors and the houses would be silent, heat curtains locked across the windows, as the sun rose over the deliquescing salt banks. Most of them were elderly and fell asleep
quickly in their darkened chalets, but Granger, with his restless
mind and his one lung, often lay awake through the afternoons,
while the metal outer walls of the cabin creaked and hummed,
trying pointlessly to read through the old log books Holliday had
salvaged for him from the crashed space platforms.

By six o'clock the thermal fronts would begin to recede south-
wards across the kelp flats, and one by one the air-conditioners in
the bedrooms switched themselves off. While the town slowly came
to life, its windows opening to the cool dusk air, Granger strode
down to breakfast at the Neptune Bar, gallantly doffing his sunglasses to left and right at the old couples settling themselves out
on their porches, staring at each other across the shadow-filled
streets.

Five miles to the north, in the empty hotel at Idle End, Holliday usually rested quietly for another hour, and listened to the
coral towers, gleaming in the distance like white pagodas, sing
and whistle as the temperature gradients cut through them.
Twenty miles away he could see the symmetrical peak of Hamil-
ton, nearest of the Bermuda Islands, rising off the dry ocean floor
like a flat-topped mountain, the narrow ring of white beach
still visible in the sunset, a scum-line left by the sinking
ocean.

That evening he felt even more reluctant than usual to drive

156

down into the town. Not only would Granger be in his private booth at the Neptune, dispensing the same mixture of humour and homily—he was virtually the only person Holliday could talk to, and inevitably he had come to resent his dependence on the older man—but Holliday would have his final interview with the migration officer and make the decision which would determine his entire future.

In a sense the decision had already been made, as Bullen, the migration officer, realized on his trip a month earlier. He did not bother to press Holliday, who had no special skills to offer, no qualities of character or leadership which would be of use on the new worlds. However, Bullen pointed out one small but relevant fact, which Holliday duly noted and thought over in the intervening month.

"Remember, Holliday," he warned him at the end of the interview in the requisitioned office at the rear of the sheriff's cabin, "the average age of the settlement is over sixty. In ten years' time you and Granger may well be the only two left here, and if that lung of his goes you'll be on your own."

He paused to let this prospect sink in, then added quietly: "All the kids are leaving on the next trip—the Merryweathers' two boys, Tom Juranda (*that lout, good riddance*, Holliday thought to himself, *look out Mars*)—do you realize you'll literally be the only one here under the age of fifty?"

"Katy Summers is staying," Holliday pointed out quickly, the sudden vision of a white organdy dress and long straw hair giving him courage.

The migration officer had glanced at his application list and nodded grudgingly. "Yes, but she's just looking after her grandmother. As soon as the old girl dies Katy will be off like a flash. After all, there's nothing to keep her here, is there?"

"No," Holliday had agreed automatically.

There wasn't now. For a long while he mistakenly believed there was. Katy was his own age, twenty-two, the only person, apart from Granger, who seemed to understand his determination to stay behind and keep watch over a forgotten Earth. But the grandmother died three days after the migration officer left, and the next day Katy had begun to pack. In some insane way Holli-

day had assumed that she would stay behind, and what worried
him was that all his assumptions about himself might be based on
equally false premises.

Climbing off the hammock, he went on to the terrace and
looked out at the phosphorescent glitter of the trace minerals in
the salt banks stretching away from the hotel. His quarters were
in the pent-house suite on the tenth floor, the only heat-sealed
unit in the building, but its steady settlement into the ocean bed
had opened wide cracks in the load walls which would soon reach
up to the roof. The ground floor had already disappeared. By the
time the next floor went—six months at the outside—he would
have been forced to leave the old pleasure resort and return to the
town. Inevitably, that would mean sharing a chalet with Granger.

A mile away, an engine droned. Through the dusk Holliday
saw the migration officer's helicopter whirling along towards the
hotel, the only local landmark, then veer off once Bullen identified
the town and circle slowly towards the landing strip.

Eight o'clock, Holliday noted. His interview was at 8.30 the next
morning. Bullen would rest the night with the Sheriff, carry out
his other duties as graves commissioner and justice of the peace,
and then set off after seeing Holliday on the next leg of his
journey. For twelve hours Holliday was free, still able to make
absolute decisions (or, more accurately, not to make them) but
after that he would have committed himself. This was the migration officer's last trip, his final circuit from the deserted cities near
St. Helena up through the Azores and Bermudas and on to the
main Atlantic ferry site at the Canaries. Only two of the big
launching platforms were still in navigable orbit—hundreds of
others were continuously falling out of the sky—and once they
came down Earth was, to all intents, abandoned. From then on
the only people likely to be picked up would be a few military
communications personnel.

Twice on his way into the town Holliday had to lower the salt-
plough fastened to the front bumper of the jeep and ram back the
drifts which had melted across the wire roadway during the afternoon. Mutating kelp, their genetic shifts accelerated by the radio-
phosphors, reared up into the air on either side of the road like

enormous cacti, turning the dark salt-banks into a white lunar garden. But this evidence of the encroaching wilderness only served to strengthen Holliday's need to stay behind on Earth. Most of the nights, when he wasn't arguing with Granger at the Neptune, he would drive around the ocean floor, climbing over the crashed launching platforms, or wander with Katy Summers through the kelp forests. Sometimes he would persuade Granger to come with them, hoping that the older man's expertise—he had originally been a marine biologist—would help to sharpen his own awareness of the bathypelagic flora, but the original sea bed was buried under the endless salt hills and they might as well have been driving about the Sahara.

As he entered the Neptune—a low cream and chromium saloon which abutted the landing strip and had formerly served as a passenger lounge when thousands of migrants from the Southern Hemisphere were being shipped up to the Canaries—Granger called to him and rattled his cane against the window, pointing to the dark outline of the migration officer's helicopter parked on the apron fifty yards away.

"I know," Holliday said in a bored voice as he went over with his drink. "Relax, I saw him coming."

Granger grinned at him. Holliday, with his intent serious face under an unruly thatch of blond hair, and his absolute sense of personal responsibility, always amused him.

"*You* relax," Granger said, adjusting the shoulder pad under his Hawaiian shirt which disguised his sunken lung. (He had lost it skin-diving thirty years earlier.) "*I'm* not going to fly to Mars next week."

Holliday stared sombrely into his glass. "I'm not either." He looked up at Granger's wry saturnine face, then added sardonically. "Or didn't you know?"

Granger roared, tapping the window with his cane as if to dismiss the helicopter. "Seriously, you're not going? You've made up your mind?"

"Wrong. And right. I haven't made up my mind yet—but at the same time I'm not going. You appreciate the distinction?"

"Perfectly, Dr. Schopenhauer." Granger began to grin again. He pushed away his glass. "You know, Holliday, your trouble is that you take yourself too seriously. You don't realize how ludicrous you are."

"Ludicrous? Why?" Holliday asked guardedly.

"What does it matter whether you've made up your mind or not? The only thing that counts now is to get together enough courage to head straight for the Canaries and take off into the wide blue yonder. For heaven's sake, what are you staying for? Earth is dead and buried. Past, present and future no longer exist here. Don't you feel any responsibility to your own biological destiny?"

"Spare me that." Holliday pulled a ration card from his shirt pocket, passed it across to Granger, who was responsible for the stores allocations. "I need a new pump on the lounge refrigerator. 30-watt Frigidaire. Any left?"

Granger groaned, took the card with a snort of exasperation. "Good God, man, you're just a Robinson Crusoe in reverse, tinkering about with all these bits of old junk, trying to fit them together. You're the last man on the beach who decides to stay behind after everyone else has left. Maybe you are a poet and dreamer, but don't you realize that those two species are extinct now?"

Holliday stared out at the helicopter on the apron, at the lights of the settlement reflected against the salt hills that encircled the town. Each day they moved a little nearer, already it was difficult to get together a weekly squad to push them back. In ten years' time his position might well be that of a Crusoe. Luckily the big water and kerosene tanks—giant cylinders, the size of gasometers —held enough for fifty years. Without them, of course, he would have had no choice.

"Let's give me a rest," he said to Granger. "You're merely trying to find in me a justification for your own enforced stay. Perhaps I am extinct, but I'd rather cling to life here than vanish completely. Anyway, I have a hunch that one day they'll be coming back. Someone's got to stay behind and keep alive a sense of what life here has meant. This isn't an old husk we can throw away when we've finished with it. We were born here. It's the only place we really remember."

Granger nodded slowly. He was about to speak when a brilliant white arc crossed the darkened window, then soared out of sight, its point of impact with the ground lost behind one of the storage tanks.

Holliday stood up and craned out of the window.

"Must be a launching platform. Looked like a big one, probably one of the Russians'." A long rolling crump reverberated through the night air, echoing away among the coral towers. Flashes of light flared up briefly. There was a series of smaller explosions, and then a wide diffuse pall of steam fanned out across the north-west.

"Lake Atlantic," Granger commented. "Let's drive out there and have a look. It may have uncovered something interesting."

Half an hour later, a set of Granger's old sample beakers, slides and mounting equipment in the back seat, they set off in the jeep towards the southern tip of Lake Atlantic ten miles away.

It was here that Holliday discovered the fish.

Lake Atlantic, a narrow ribbon of stagnant brine ten miles in length by a mile wide, to the north of the Bermuda Islands, was all that remained of the former Atlantic Ocean, and was, in fact, the sole remnant of the oceans which had once covered two-thirds of the Earth's surface. The frantic mining of the oceans in the previous century to provide oxygen for the atmospheres of the new planets had made their decline swift and irreversible, and with their death had come climatic and other geophysical changes which ensured the extinction of Earth itself. As the oxygen extracted electrolytically from sea-water was compressed and shipped away, the hydrogen released was discharged into the atmosphere. Eventually only a narrow layer of denser, oxygen-containing air was left, little more than a mile in depth, and those people remaining on Earth were forced to retreat into the ocean beds, abandoning the poisoned continental tables.

At the hotel at Idle End, Holliday spent uncounted hours going through the library he had accumulated of magazines and books about the cities of the old Earth, and Granger often described to him his own youth when the seas had been half-full and he had worked as a marine biologist at the University of

Miami, a fabulous laboratory unfolding itself for him on the lengthening beaches.

"The seas are our corporate memory," he often said to Holliday. "In draining them we deliberately obliterated out own pasts, to a large extent our own self-identities. That's another reason why you should leave. Without the sea, life is insupportable. We become nothing more than the ghosts of memories, blind and homeless, flitting through the dry chambers of a gutted skull."

They reached the lake within half an hour, worked their way through the swamps which formed its banks. In the dim light the grey salt dunes ran on for miles, their hollows cracked into hexagonal plates, a dense cloud of vapour obscuring the surface of the water. They parked on a low promontory by the edge of the lake and looked up at the great circular shell of the launching platform. This was one of the larger vehicles, almost three hundred yards in diameter, lying upside down in the shallow water, its hull dented and burnt, riven by huge punctures where the power plants had torn themselves loose on impact and exploded off across the lake. A quarter of a mile away, hidden by the blur, they could just see a cluster of rotors pointing up into the sky.

Walking along the bank, the main body of the lake on their right, they moved nearer the platform, tracing out its rivetted CCCP markings along the rim. The giant vehicle had cut enormous grooves through the nexus of pools just beyond the tip of the lake, and Granger waded through the warm water, searching for specimens. Here and there were small anemones and starfish, stunted bodies twisted by cancers. Web-like algae draped themselves over his rubber boots, their nuclei beading like jewels in the phosphorescent light. They paused by one of the largest pools, a circular basin 300 feet across, draining slowly as the water poured out through a breach in its side. Granger moved carefully down the deepening bank, forking specimens into the rack of beakers, while Holliday stood on the narrow causeway between the pool and the lake, looking up at the dark overhang of the space platform as it loomed into the darkness above him like the stern of a ship.

Deep End

He was examining the shattered air-lock of one of the crew domes when he suddenly saw something move across the surface of the deck. For a moment he imagined that he had seen a passenger who had somehow survived the vehicle's crash, then realized that it was merely the reflection in the aluminized skin of a ripple in the pool behind him.

He turned around to see Granger, ten feet below him, up to his knees in the water, staring out carefully across the pool.

"Did you throw something?" Granger asked.

Holliday shook his head. "No." Without thinking, he added: "It must have been a fish jumping."

"Fish? There isn't a single fish alive on the entire planet. The whole zoological class died out ten years ago. Strange, though."

Just then the fish jumped again.

For a few moments, standing motionless in the half-light, they watched it together, as its slim silver body leapt frantically out of the tepid shallow water, its short glistening arcs carrying it to and fro across the pool.

"Dog-fish," Granger muttered. "Shark family. Highly adaptable—need to be, to have survived here. Damn it, it may well be the only fish still living."

Holliday moved down the bank, his feet sinking in the oozing mud. "Isn't the water too salty?"

Granger bent down and scooped up some of the water, sipped it tentatively. "Saline, but comparatively dilute." He glanced over his shoulder at the lake. "Perhaps there's continuous evaporation off the lake surface and local condensation here. A freak distillation couple." He slapped Holliday on the shoulder. "Holliday, this should be interesting."

The dog-fish was leaping frantically towards them, its two-foot body twisting and flicking. Low mud banks were emerging all over the surface of the pool; in only a few places towards the centre was the water more than a foot deep.

Holliday pointed to the breach in the bank fifty yards away, gestured Granger after him and began to run towards it.

Five minutes later they had effectively dammed up the breach. Holliday returned for the jeep and drove it carefully through the winding saddles between the pools. He lowered the ramp and

163

began to force the sides of the fish-pool in towards each other. After two or three hours he had narrowed the diameter from a hundred yards to under sixty, and the depth of the water had increased to over two feet. The dog-fish had ceased to jump and swam smoothly just below the surface, snapping at the countless small plants which had been tumbled into the water by the jeep's ramp. Its slim white body seemed white and unmarked, the small fins trim and powerful.

Granger sat on the bonnet of the jeep, his back against the windshield, watching Holliday with admiration.

"You obviously have hidden reserves," he said ungrudgingly. "I didn't think you had it in you."

Holliday washed his hands in the water, then stepped over the churned mud which formed the boundary of the pool. A few feet behind him the dog-fish veered and lunged.

"I want to keep it alive," Holliday said matter-of-factly. "Don't you see, Granger, the fishes stayed behind when the first amphibians emerged from the seas two hundred million years ago, just as you and I, in turn, are staying behind now. In a sense all fish are images of ourselves seen in the sea's mirror."

He slumped down on the running board. His clothes were soaked and streaked with salt, and he gasped at the damp air. To the west, just above the long bulk of the Florida coastline, rising from the ocean floor like an enormous aircraft carrier, were the first dawn thermal fronts. "Will it be all right to leave it until this evening?"

Granger climbed into the driving seat. "Don't worry. Come on, you need a rest." He pointed up at the overhanging rim of the launching platform. "That should shade it for a few hours, help to keep the temperature down."

As they neared the town Granger slowed to wave to the old people retreating from their porches, fixing the shutters on the steel cabins.

"What about your interview with Bullen?" he asked Holliday soberly. "He'll be waiting for you."

"Leave here? After last night? It's out of the question."

Granger shook his head as he parked the car outside the

Neptune. "Aren't you rather over-estimating the importance of one dog-fish? There were millions of them once, the vermin of the sea."

"You're missing the point," Holliday said, sinking back into the seat, trying to wipe the salt out of his eyes. "That fish means that there's still something to be done here. Earth isn't dead and exhausted after all. We can breed new forms of life, a completely new biological kingdom."

Eyes fixed on this private vision, Holliday sat holding the steering wheel while Granger went into the bar to collect a crate of beer. On his return the migration officer was with him.

Bullen put a foot on the running board, looked into the car. "Well, how about it, Holliday? I'd like to make an early start. If you're not interested I'll be off. There's a rich new life out there, first step to the stars. Tom Juranda and the Merryweather boys are leaving next week. Do you want to be with them?'

"Sorry," Holliday said curtly. He pulled the crate of beer into the car and let out the clutch, gunned the jeep away down the empty street in a roar of dust.

Half an hour later, as he stepped out on to the terrace at Idle End, cool and refreshed after his shower, he watched the helicopter roar overhead, its black propeller scudding, then disappear over the kelp flats towards the hull of the wrecked space platform.

"Come on, let's go! What's the matter?"

"Hold it," Granger said. "You're getting over-eager. Don't interfere too much, you'll kill the damn thing with kindness. What have you got there?" He pointed to the can Holliday had placed in the dashboard compartment.

"Breadcrumbs."

Granger sighed, then gently closed the door. "I'm impressed. I really am. I wish you'd look after me this way. I'm gasping for air too."

They were five miles from the lake when Holliday leaned forward over the wheel and pointed to the crisp tyre-prints in the soft salt flowing over the road ahead.

"Someone's there already."

Granger shrugged. "What of it? They've probably gone to look at the platform." He chuckled quietly. "Don't you want to share the New Eden with anyone else? Or just you alone, and a consultant biologist?"

Holliday peered through the windshield. "Those platforms annoy me, the way they're hurled down as if Earth were a garbage dump. Still, if it wasn't for this one I wouldn't have found the fish."

They reached the lake and made their way towards the pool, the erratic track of the car ahead winding in and out of the pools. Two hundred yards from the platform it had been parked, blocking the route for Holliday and Granger.

"That's the Merryweathers' car," Holliday said as they walked around the big stripped-down Buick, slashed with yellow paint and fitted with sirens and pennants. "The two boys must have come out here."

Granger pointed. "One of them's up on the platform."

The younger brother had climbed on to the rim, was shouting down like an umpire at the antics of two other boys, one his brother, the other Tom Juranda, a tall broad-shouldered youth in a space cadet's jerkin. They were standing at the edge of the fish-pool, stones and salt blocks in their hands, hurling them into the pool.

Leaving Granger, Holliday sprinted on ahead, shouting at the top of his voice. Too preoccupied to hear him, the boys continued to throw their missiles into the pool, while the younger Merryweather egged them on from the platform above. Just before Holliday reached them Tom Juranda ran a few yards along the bank and began to kick the mud-wall into the air, then resumed his target throwing.

"Juranda! Get away from there!" Holliday bellowed. "Put those stones down!"

He reached Juranda as the youth was about to hurl a brick-sized lump of salt into the pool, seized him by the shoulder and flung him round, knocking the salt out of his hand into a shower of damp crystals, then lunged at the elder Merryweather boy, kicking him away.

The pool had been drained. A deep breach had been cut

through the bank and the water had poured out into the surrounding gulleys and pools. Down in the centre of the basin, in a
litter of stones and spattered salt, was the crushed but still wrig-
gling body of the dog-fish, twisting itself helplessly in the bare
inch of water that remained. Dark red blood poured from wounds
in its body, staining the salt.

Holliday hurled himself at Juranda, shook the youth savagely
by the shoulders.

"Juranda! Do you realize what you've done, you——" Exhausted, Holliday released him and staggered down into the
centre of the pool, kicked away the stones and stood looking at the
fish twitching at his feet.

"Sorry, Holliday," the older Merryweather boy said tentatively
behind him. "We didn't know it was your fish."

Holliday waved him away, then let his arms fall limply to his
sides. He felt numbed and baffled, unable to resolve his anger and
frustration.

Tom Juranda began to laugh, and shouted something derisively. Their tension broken, the boys turned and ran off together
across the dunes towards their car, yelling and playing catch with
each other, mimicing Holliday's outrage.

Granger let them go by, then walked across to the pool, wincing
when he saw the empty basin.

"Holliday," he called. "Come on."

Holliday shook his head, staring at the beaten body of the
fish.

Granger stepped down the bank to him. Sirens hooted in the
distance as the Buick roared off. "Those damn children." He took
Holliday gently by the arm. "I'm sorry," he said quietly. "But it's
not the end of the world."

Bending down, Holliday reached towards the fish, lying still
now, the mud around it slick with blood. His hands hesitated,
then retreated.

"Nothing we can do, is there?" he said impersonally.

Granger examined the fish. Apart from the large wound in its
side and the flattened skull the skin was intact. "Why not have it
stuffed?" he suggested seriously.

Holliday stared at him incredulously, his face contorting. For a moment he said nothing. Then, almost berserk, he shouted: "Have it stuffed? Are you crazy? Do you think I want to make a dummy of myself, fill my own head with straw?"

Turning on his heel, he shouldered past Granger and swung himself roughly out of the pool.

THE VOLCANO DANCES

THEY lived in a house on the mountain Tlaxihuatl half a mile below the summit. The house was built on a lava flow like the hide of an elephant. In the afternoon and evening the man, Charles Vandervell, sat by the window in the lounge, watching the fire displays that came from the crater. The noise rolled down the mountain side like a series of avalanches. At intervals a falling cinder hissed as it extinguished itself in the water tank on the roof. The woman slept most of the time in the bedroom overlooking the valley or, when she wished to be close to Vandervell, on the settee in the lounge.

In the afternoon she woke briefly when the 'devil-sticks' man performed his dance by the road a quarter of a mile from the house. This mendicant had come to the mountain for the benefit of the people in the village below the summit, but his dance had failed to subdue the volcano and prevent the villagers from leaving. As they passed him pushing their carts he would rattle his spears and dance, but they walked on without looking up. When he became discouraged and seemed likely to leave Vandervell sent the house-boy out to him with an American dollar. From then on the stick-dancer came every day.

"Is he still here?" the woman asked. She walked into the lounge, folding her robe around her waist. "What's he supposed to be doing?"

"He's fighting a duel with the spirit of the volcano," Vandervell said. "He's putting a lot of thought and energy into it, but he hasn't a chance."

"I thought you were on his side," the woman said. "Aren't you paying him a retainer?"

"That's only to formalize the relationship. To show him that I understand what's going on. Strictly speaking, I'm on the volcano's side."

A shower of cinders rose a hundred feet above the crater, illuminating the jumping stick-man.

"Are you sure it's safe here?"

Vandervell waved her away. "Of course. Go back to bed and rest. This thin air is bad for the complexion."

"I feel all right. I heard the ground move."

"It's been moving for weeks." He watched the stick-man conclude his performance with a series of hops, as if leap-frogging over a partner. "On his diet that's not bad."

"You should take him back to Mexico City and put him in one of the cabarets. He'd make more than a dollar."

"He wouldn't be interested. He's a serious artist, this Nijinsky of the mountain side. Can't you see that?"

The woman half-filled a tumbler from the decanter on the table. "How long are you going to keep him out there?"

"As long as he'll stay." He turned to face the woman. "Remember that. When he leaves it will be time to go."

The stick-man, a collection of tatters when not in motion, disappeared into his lair, one of the holes in the lava beside the road.

"I wonder if he met Springman?" Vandervell said. "On balance it's possible. Springman would have come up the south face. This is the only road to the village."

"Ask him. Offer him another dollar."

"Pointless—he'd say he had seen him just to keep me happy."

"What makes you so sure Springman is here?"

"He *was* here," Vandervell corrected. "He won't be here any longer. I was with Springman in Acapulco when he looked at the map. He came here."

The woman carried her tumbler into the bedroom.

"We'll have dinner at nine," Vandervell called to her. "I'll let you know if he dances again."

Left alone, Vandervell watched the fire displays. The glow shone through the windows of the houses in the village so that they seemed to glow like charcoal. At night the collection of hovels was deserted, but a few of the men returned during the day.

In the morning two men came from the garage in Ecuatan to reclaim the car which Vandervell had hired. He offered to pay a month's rent in advance, but they rejected this and pointed at the clinkers that had fallen on to the car from the sky. None of them was hot enough to burn the paint-work. Vandervell gave them each fifty dollars and promised to cover the car with a tarpaulin. Satisfied, the men drove away.

After breakfast Vandervell walked out across the lava seams to the road. The stick-dancer stood by his hole above the bank, resting his hands on the two spears. The cone of the volcano, partly hidden by the dust, trembled behind his back. He watched Vandervell when he shouted across the road. Vandervell took a dollar bill from his wallet and placed it under a stone. The stick-man began to hum and rock on the balls of his feet.

As Vandervell walked back along the road two of the villagers approached.

"Guide," he said to them. "Ten dollars. One hour." He pointed to the lip of the crater but the men ignored him and continued along the road.

The surface of the house had once been white, but was now covered with grey dust. Two hours later, when the manager of the estate below the house rode up on a grey horse Vandervell asked: "Is your horse white or black?"

"That's a good question, señor."

"I want to hire a guide," Vandervell said. "To take me into the volcano."

"There's nothing there, señor."

"I want to look around the crater. I need someone who knows the pathways."

"It's full of smoke, Señor Vandervell. Hot sulphur. Burns the eyes. You wouldn't like it.'

"Do you remember seeing someone called Springman?" Vandervell said. "About three months ago."

"You asked me that before. I remember two Americans with a scientific truck. Then a Dutchman with white hair."

"That could be him."

"Or maybe black, eh? As you say."

A rattle of sticks sounded from the road. After warming up, the stick-dancer had begun his performance in earnest.

"You'd better get out of here, Señor Vandervell," the manager said. "The mountain could split one day."

Vandervell pointed to the stick-dancer. "He'll hold it off for a while."

The manager rode away. "My respects to Mrs. Vandervell."

"*Miss* Winston."

Vandervell went into the lounge and stood by the window. During the day the activity of the volcano increased. The column of smoke rose half a mile into the sky, threaded by gleams of flame.

The rumbling woke the woman. In the kitchen she spoke to the houseboy.

"He wants to leave," she said to Vandervell afterwards.

"Offer him more money," he said without turning.

"He says everyone has left now. It's too dangerous to stay. The men in the village are leaving for good this afternoon."

Vandervell watched the stick-dancer twirling his devil-sticks like a drum-major. "Let him go if he wants to. I think the estate manager saw Springman."

"That's good. Then he was here."

"The manager sent his respects to you."

"I'm charmed."

Five minutes later, when the house-boy had gone, she returned to her bedroom. During the afternoon she came out to collect the film magazines in the bookcase.

Vandervell watched the smoke being pumped from the volcano. Now and then the devil-sticks man climbed out of his hole and danced on a mound of lava by the road. The men came down from the village for the last time. They looked at the stick-dancer as they walked on down the road.

At eight o'clock in the morning a police truck drove up to the village, reversed and came down again. Its roof and driving cabin were covered with ash. The policemen did not see the stick-dancer, but they saw Vandervell in the window of the house and stopped outside.

"Get out!" one of the policemen shouted. "You must go now! Take your car! What's the matter?"

Vandervell opened the window. "The car is all right. We're staying for a few days. Gracias, Sergeant."

"No! Get out!" The policeman climbed down from the cabin. "The mountain—pfft! Dust, burning!" He took off his cap and waved it. "You go now."

As he remonstrated Vandervell closed the window and took his jacket off the chair. Inside he felt for his wallet.

After he had paid the policemen they saluted and drove away. The woman came out of the bedroom.

"You're lucky your father is rich," she said. "What would you do if he was poor?"

"Springman was poor," Vandervell said. He took his hand-kerchief from his jacket. The dust was starting to seep into the house. "Money only postpones one's problems."

"How long are you going to stay? Your father told me to keep an eye on you."

"Relax. I won't come to any mischief here."

"Is that a joke? With this volcano over our heads?"

Vandervell pointed to the stick-dancer. "It doesn't worry him. This mountain has been active for fifty years."

"Then why do we have to come here now?"

"I'm looking for Springman. I think he came here three months ago."

"Where is he? Up in the village?"

"I doubt it. He's probably five thousand miles under our feet, sucked down by the back-pressure. A century from now he'll come up through Vesuvius."

"I hope not."

"Have you thought of that, though? It's a wonderful idea."

"No. Is that what you're planning for me?"

Cinders hissed in the roof tank, spitting faintly like boiling rain.

"Think of them, Gloria—Pompeiian matrons, Aztec virgins, bits of old Prometheus himself, they're raining down on the just and the unjust."

"What about your friend Springman?"

"Now that you remind me...." Vandervell raised a finger to the ceiling. "Let's listen. What's the matter?"

"Is that why you came here? To think of Springman being burnt to ashes?"

"Don't be a fool." Vandervell turned to the window.

"What are you worrying about, anyway?"

"Nothing," Vandervell said. "For once in a long time I'm not worrying about anything at all." He rubbed the pane with his sleeve. "Where's the old devil-boy? Don't tell me he's gone." He peered through the falling dust. "There he is."

The figure stood on the ridge above the road, illuminated by the flares from the crater. A pall of ash hung in the air around him.

"What's he waiting for?" the woman asked. "Another dollar?"

"A lot more than a dollar," Vandervell said. "He's waiting for me."

"Don't burn your fingers," she said, closing the door.

That afternoon, when she came into the lounge after waking up, she found that Vandervell had left. She went to the window and looked up towards the crater. The falls of ash and cinders obscured the village, and hundreds of embers glowed on the lava flows. Through the dust she could see the explosions inside the crater lighting up the rim.

Vandervell's jacket lay over a chair. She waited for three hours for him to return. By this time the noise from the crater was continuous. The lava flows dragged and heaved like chains, shaking the walls of the house.

At five o'clock Vandervell had not come back. A second crater had opened in the summit of the volcano, into which part of the village had fallen. When she was sure that the devil-sticks man had gone, the woman took the money from Vandervell's jacket and drove down the mountain.

BILLENNIUM

ALL day long, and often into the early hours of the morning, the tramp of feet sounded up and down the stairs outside Ward's cubicle. Built into a narrow alcove in a bend of the staircase between the fourth and fifth floors, its plywood walls flexed and creaked with every footstep like the timbers of a rotting windmill. Over a hundred people lived in the top three floors of the old rooming house, and sometimes Ward would lie awake on his narrow bunk until 2 or 3 a.m., mechanically counting the last residents returning from the all-night movies in the stadium half a mile away. Through the window he could hear giant fragments of the amplified dialogue booming among the rooftops. The stadium was never empty. During the day the huge four-sided screen was raised on its davit and athletics meetings or football matches ran continuously. For the people in the houses abutting the stadium the noise must have been unbearable.

Ward, at least, had a certain degree of privacy. Two months earlier, before he came to live on the staircase, he had shared a room with seven others on the ground floor of a house in 755th Street, and the ceaseless press of people jostling past the window had reduced him to a state of exhaustion. The street was always full, an endless clamour of voices and shuffling feet. By 6.30, when he woke, hurrying to take his place in the bathroom queue, the crowds already jammed it from sidewalk to sidewalk, the din punctuated every half minute by the roar of the elevated trains running over the shops on the opposite side of the road. As soon as he saw the advertisement describing the staircase cubicle he had left (like everyone else, he spent most of his spare time scanning the classifieds in the newspapers, moving his lodgings an average of once every two months) despite the higher rental. A cubicle on a staircase would almost certainly be on its own.

However, this had its drawbacks. Most evenings his friends from the library would call in, eager to rest their elbows after the bruising crush of the public reading room. The cubicle was slightly more than four and a half square metres in floor area, half a square metre over the statutory maximum for a single person, the carpenters having taken advantage, illegally, of a recess beside a nearby chimney breast. Consequently Ward had been able to fit a small straight-backed chair into the interval between the bed and the door, so that only one person at a time needed to sit on the bed—in most single cubicles host and guest had to sit side by side on the bed, conversing over their shoulders and changing places periodically to avoid neck-strain.

"You were lucky to find this place," Rossiter, the most regular visitor, never tired of telling him. He reclined back on the bed, gesturing at the cubicle. "It's enormous, the perspectives really zoom. I'd be surprised if you havn't got at least five metres here, perhaps six."

Ward shook his head categorically. Rossiter was his closest friend, but the quest for living space had forged powerful reflexes. "Just over four and a half, I've measured it carefully. There's no doubt about it."

Rossiter lifted one eyebrow. "I'm amazed. It must be the ceiling then."

Manipulating the ceiling was a favourite trick of unscrupulous landlords—most assessments of area were made upon the ceiling, out of convenience, and by tilting back the plywood partitions the rated area of a cubicle could be either increased, for the benefit of a prospective tenant (many married couples were thus bamboozled into taking a single cubicle), or decreased temporarily on the visits of the housing inspectors. Ceilings were criss-crossed with pencil marks staking out the rival claims of tenants on opposite sides of a party wall. Someone timid of his rights could be literally squeezed out of existence—in fact, the advertisement 'quiet clientele' was usually a tacit invitation to this sort of piracy.

"The wall does tilt a little," Ward admitted. "Actually, it's about four degrees out—I used a plumb-line. But there's still plenty of room on the stairs for people to get by."

Rossiter grinned. "Of course, John. I'm just envious, that's all. My room is driving me crazy." Like everyone, he used the term ' room ' to describe his tiny cubicle, a hangover from the days fifty years earlier when people had indeed lived one to a room, sometimes, unbelievably, one to an apartment or house. The microfilms in the architecture catalogues at the library showed scenes of museums, concert halls and other public buildings in what appeared to be everyday settings, often virtually empty, two or three people wandering down an enormous gallery or staircase. Traffic moved freely along the centre of streets, and in the quieter districts sections of sidewalk would be deserted for fifty yards or more.

Now, of course, the older buildings had been torn down and replaced by housing batteries, or converted into apartment blocks. The great banqueting room in the former City Hall had been split horizontally into four decks, each of these cut up into hundreds of cubicles.

As for the streets, traffic had long since ceased to move about them. Apart from a few hours before dawn when only the sidewalks were crowded, every thoroughfare was always packed with a shuffling mob of pedestrians, perforce ignoring the countless ' Keep Left ' signs suspended over their heads, wrestling past each other on their way to home and office, their clothes dusty and shapeless. Often ' locks ' would occur when a huge crowd at a street junction became immovably jammed. Sometimes these locks would last for days. Two years earlier Ward had been caught in one outside the stadium, for over forty-eight hours was trapped in a gigantic pedestrian jam containing over 20,000 people, fed by the crowds leaving the stadium on one side and those approaching it on the other. An entire square mile of the local neighbourhood had been paralysed, and he vividly remembered the mightmare of swaying helplessly on his feet as the jam shifted and heaved, terrified of losing his balance and being trampled underfoot. When the police had finally sealed off the stadium and dispersed the jam he had gone back to his cubicle and slept for a week, his body blue with bruises.

"I hear they may reduce the allocation to three and a half metres," Rossiter remarked.

Ward paused to allow a party of tenants from the sixth floor to pass down the staircase, holding the door to prevent it jumping off its latch. "So they're always saying," he commented. "I can remember that rumour ten years ago."

"It's no rumour," Rossiter warned him. "It may well be necessary soon. Thirty million people are packed into this city now, a million increase in just one year. There's been some pretty serious talk at the Housing Department."

Ward shook his head. "A drastic revaluation like that is almost impossible to carry out. Every single partition would have to be dismantled and nailed up again, the administrative job alone is so vast it's difficult to visualize. Millions of cubicles to be redesigned and certified, licences to be issued, plus the complete resettlement of every tenant. Most of the buildings put up since the last revaluation are designed around a four-metre modulus—you can't simply take half a metre off the end of each cubicle and then say that makes so many new cubicles. They may be only six inches wide." He laughed. "Besides, how can you live in just three and a half metres?"

Rossiter smiled. "That's the ultimate argument, isn't it? They used it twenty-five years ago at the last revaluation, when the minimum was cut from five to four. It couldn't be done they all said, no one could stand living in only four square metres, it was enough room for a bed and suitcase, but you couldn't open the door to get in." Rossiter chuckled softly. "They were all wrong. It was merely decided that from then on all doors would open outwards. Four square metres was here to stay."

Ward looked at his watch. It was 7.30. "Time to eat. Let's see if we can get into the food-bar across the road."

Grumbling at the prospect, Rossiter pulled himself off the bed. They left the cubicle and made their way down the staircase. This was crammed with luggage and packing cases so that only a narrow interval remained around the banister. On the floors below the congestion was worse. Corridors were wide enough to be chopped up into single cubicles, and the air was stale and dead, cardboard walls hung with damp laundry and makeshift larders.

Each of the five rooms on the floors contained a dozen tenants, their voices reverberating through the partitions.

People were sitting on the steps above the second floor, using the staircase as an informal lounge, although this was against the fire regulations, women talking to the men queueing in their shirtsleeves outside the washroom, children diving around them. By the time they reached the entrance Ward and Rossiter were having to force their way through the tenants packed together on every landing, loitering around the notice boards or pushing in from the street below.

Taking a breath at the top of the steps, Ward pointed to the food-bar on the other side of the road. It was only thirty yards away, but the throng moving down the street swept past like a river at full tide, crossing them from right to left. The first picture show at the stadium started at 9 o'clock, and people were setting off already to make sure of getting in.

"Can't we go somewhere else?" Rossiter asked, screwing his face up at the prospect of the food-bar. Not only was it packed and take them half an hour to be served, but the food was flat and unappetizing. The journey from the library four blocks away had given him an appetite.

Ward shrugged. "There's a place on the corner, but I doubt if we can make it." This was two hundred yards upstream; they would be fighting the crowd all the way.

"Maybe you're right." Rossiter put his hand on Ward's shoulder. "You know, John, your trouble is that you never go anywhere, you're too disengaged, you just don't realize how bad everything is getting."

Ward nodded. Rossiter was right. In the morning, when he set off for the library, the pedestrian traffic was moving with him towards the down-town offices; in the evening, when he came back, it was flowing in the opposite direction. By and large he never altered his routine. Brought up from the age of ten in a municipal hostel, he had gradually lost touch with his father and mother, who lived on the east side of the city and had been unable, or unwilling, to make the journey to see him. Having surrendered his initiative to the dynamics of the city he was reluctant to try to win it back merely for a better cup of coffee. Fortunately his job at the library brought him into contact with a wide range of young people of similar interests. Sooner or later he would marry, find a double cubicle near the library and settle down. If they had enough children (three was the required minimum) they might even one day own a small room of their own.

They stepped out into the pedestrian stream, carried along by it for ten or twenty yards, then quickened their pace and side-stepped through the crowd, slowly tacking across to the other side of the road. There they found the shelter of the shop-fronts, slowly worked their way back to the food-bar, shoulders braced against the countless minor collisions.

"What are the latest population estimates?" Ward asked as they circled a cigarette kiosk, stepping forward whenever a gap presented itself.

Rossiter smiled. "Sorry, John, I'd like to tell you but you might start a stampede. Besides, you wouldn't believe me."

Rossiter worked in the Insurance Department at the City Hall, had informal access to the census statistics. For the last ten years these had been classified information, partly because they were felt to be inaccurate, but chiefly because it was feared they might set off a mass attack of claustrophobia. Minor outbreaks had taken place already, and the official line was that world population had reached a plateau, levelling off at 20,000 million. No one believed this for a moment, and Ward assumed that the 3 per cent annual increase maintained since the 1960's was continuing.

How long it could continue was impossible to estimate. Despite the gloomiest prophecies of the Neo-Malthusians, world agriculture had managed to keep pace with the population growth, although intensive cultivation meant that 95 per cent of the population was permanently trapped in vast urban conurbations. The outward growth of cities had at last been checked; in fact, all over the world former suburban areas were being reclaimed for agriculture and population additions were confined within the existing urban ghettos. The countryside, as such, no longer existed. Every single square foot of ground sprouted a crop of one type or other. The one-time fields and meadows of the world were now, in effect, factory floors, as highly mechanized and closed to the public as any industrial area. Economic and ideological rivalries had long since faded before one over-riding quest—the internal colonization of the city.

Reaching the food-bar, they pushed themselves into the entrance and joined the scrum of customers pressing six deep against the counter.

"What is really wrong with the population problem," Ward confided to Rossiter, "is that no one has ever tried to tackle it. Fifty years ago short-sighted nationalism and industrial expansion put a premium on a rising population curve, and even now the hidden incentive is to have a large family so that you can gain a little privacy. Single people are penalized simply because there are more of them and they don't fit neatly into double or triple cubicles. But it's the large family with its compact, space-saving logistic that is the real villain."

Rossiter nodded, edging nearer the counter, ready to shout his order. "Too true. We all look forward to getting married just so that we can have our six square metres."

Directly in front of them, two girls turned around and smiled. "Six square metres," one of them, a dark-haired girl with a pretty oval face, repeated. "You sound like the sort of young man I ought to get to know. Going into the real estate business, Peter?"

Rossiter grinned and squeezed her arm. "Hello, Judith. I'm thinking about it actively. Like to join me in a private venture?"

The girl leaned against him as they reached the counter. "Well, I might. It would have to be legal, though."

The other girl, Helen Waring, an assistant at the library, pulled Ward's sleeve. "Have you heard the latest, John? Judith and I have been kicked out of our room. We're on the street right at this minute."

"What?" Rossiter cried. They collected their soups and coffee and edged back to the rear of the bar. "What on earth happened?"

Helen explained: "You know that little broom cupboard outside our cubicle? Judith and I have been using it as a sort of study hole, going in there to read. It's quiet and restful, if you can get used to not breathing. Well, the old girl found out and kicked up a big fuss, said we were breaking the law and so on. In short, out." Helen paused. " Now we've heard she's going to let it as a single."

Rossiter pounded the counter ledge. " A broom cupboard? Someone's going to live there? But she'll never get a licence."

Judith shook her head. " She's got it already. Her brother works in the Housing Department."

Ward laughed into his soup. " But how can she let it? No one will live in a broom cupboard."

Judith stared at him sombrely. " You really believe that, John? "

Ward dropped his spoon. " No, I suppose you're right. People will live anywhere. God, I don't know who I feel more sorry for— you two, or the poor devil who'll be living in that cupboard. What are you going to do? "

" A couple in a place two blocks west are sub-letting half their cubicle to us. They've hung a sheet down the middle and Helen and I'll take turns sleeping on a camp bed. I'm not joking, our room's about two feet wide. I said to Helen that we ought to split up again and sublet one half at twice our rent."

They had a good laugh over all this. Then Ward said good night to the others and went back to his rooming house.

There he found himself with similar problems.

The manager leaned against the flimsy door, a damp cigar butt revolving around his mouth, an expression of morose boredom on his unshaven face.

" You got four point seven two metres," he told Ward, who was standing out on the staircase, unable to get into his room. Other tenants pressed by on to the landing, where two women in curlers and dressing gowns were arguing with each other, tugging angrily at the wall of trunks and cases. Occasionally the manager glanced at them irritably. " Four seven two. I worked it out twice." He said this as if it ended all possibility of argument.

" Ceiling or floor? " Ward asked.

" Ceiling, whaddya think? How can I measure the floor with all this junk? " He kicked at a crate of books protruding from under the bed.

Ward let this pass. " There's quite a tilt on the wall," he pointed out. " As much as three or four degrees."

The manager nodded vaguely. " You're definitely over the four. Way over." He turned to Ward, who had moved down several steps to allow a man and woman to get past. " I can rent this as a double."

"What, only four and a half? " Ward said incredulously. " How? "

The man who had just passed him leaned over the manager's shoulder and sniffed at the room, taking in every detail in a one-second glance. " You renting a double here, Louie? "

The manager waved him away and then beckoned Ward into the room, closing the door after him.

" It's a nominal five," he told Ward. " New regulation, just came out. Anything over four five is a double now." He eyed Ward shrewdly. " Well, whaddya want? It's a good room, there's a lot of space here, feels more like a triple. You got access to the staircase, window slit——" He broke off as Ward slumped down on the bed and started to laugh. " Whatsa matter? Look, if you want a big room like this you gotta pay for it. I want an extra half rental or you get out."

Ward wiped his eyes, then stood up wearily and reached for the shelves. " Relax, I'm on my way. I'm going to live in a broom cupboard. ' Access to the staircase '—that's really rich. Tell me, Louie, is there life on Uranus? "

Temporarily, he and Rossiter teamed up to rent a double cubicle in a semi-derelict house a hundred yards from the library. The neighbourhood was seedy and faded, the rooming houses crammed with tenants. Most of them were owned by absentee landlords or by the city corporation, and the managers employed were of the lowest type, mere rent-collectors who cared nothing about the way their tenants divided up the living space, and never ventured beyond the first floors. Bottles and empty cans littered the corridors, and the washrooms looked like sumps. Many of the tenants were old and infirm, sitting about listlessly in their narrow cubicles, wheedling at each other back to back through the thin partitions.

Their double cubicle was on the third floor, at the end of a corridor that ringed the building. Its architecture was impossible to follow, rooms letting off at all angles, and luckily the corridor was a cul de sac. The mounds of cases ended four feet from the end wall and a partition divided off the cubicle, just wide enough for two beds. A high window overlooked the area ways of the buildings opposite.

Possessions loaded on to the shelf above his head, Ward lay back on his bed and moodily surveyed the roof of the library through the afternoon haze.

"It's not bad here," Rossiter told him, unpacking his case. "I know there's no real privacy and we'll drive each other insane within a week, but at least we haven't got six other people breathing into our ears two feet away."

The nearest cubicle, a single, was built into the banks of cases half a dozen steps along the corridor, but the occupant, a man of seventy, was deaf and bed-ridden.

"It's not bad," Ward echoed reluctantly. "Now tell me what the latest growth figures are. They might console me."

Rossiter paused, lowering his voice. "Four per cent. *Eight hundred million extra people in one year*—just less than half the earth's total population in 1950."

Ward whistled slowly. "So they will revalue. What to? Three and a half?"

"Three. From the first of next year."

"Three square metres!" Ward sat up and looked around him. "It's unbelievable! The world's going insane, Rossiter. For God's sake, when are they going to do something about it? Do you realize there soon won't be room enough to sit down, let alone lie down?"

Exasperated, he punched the wall beside him, on the second blow knocked in one of the small wooden panels that had been lightly papered over.

"Hey!" Rossiter yelled. "You're breaking the place down." He dived across the bed to retrieve the panel, which hung downwards supported by a strip of paper. Ward slipped his hand into the dark interval, carefully drew the panel back on to the bed.

"Who's on the other side?" Rossiter whispered. "Did they hear?"

Ward peered through the interval, eyes searching the dim light. Suddenly he dropped the panel and seized Rossiter's shoulder, pulled him down on to the bed.

" Henry! Look! "

Directly in front of them, faintly illuminated by a grimy sky-light, was a medium-sized room some fifteen feet square, empty except for the dust silted up against the skirting boards. The floor was bare, a few strips of frayed linoleum running across it, the walls covered with a drab floral design. Here and there patches of the paper peeled off and segments of the picture rail had rotted away, but otherwise the room was in habitable condition.

Breathing slowly, Ward closed the open door of the cubicle with his foot, then turned to Rossiter.

" Henry, do you realize what we've found? Do you realize it, man? "

" Shut up. For Pete's sake keep your voice down." Rossiter examined the room carefully. " It's fantastic. I'm trying to see whether anyone's used it recently."

" Of course they haven't," Ward pointed out. " It's obvious. There's no door into the room. We're looking through it now. They must have panelled over this door years ago and forgotten about it. Look at that filth everywhere."

Rossiter was staring into the room, his mind staggered by its vastness.

" You're right," he murmured. " Now, when do we move in? "

Panel, by panel, they pried away the lower half of the door and nailed it on to a wooden frame, so that the dummy section could be replaced instantly.

Then, picking an afternoon when the house was half empty and the manager asleep in his basement office, they made their first foray into the room, Ward going in alone while Rossiter kept guard in the cubicle.

For an hour they exchanged places, wandering silently around the dusty room, stretching their arms out to feel its unconfined emptiness, grasping at the sensation of absolute spatial freedom. Although smaller than many of the sub-divided rooms in which they had lived, this room seemed infinitely larger, its walls huge cliffs that soared upward to the skylight.

Finally, two or three days later, they moved in.

For the first week Rossiter slept alone in the room, Ward in the cubicle outside, both there together during the day. Gradually they smuggled in a few items of furniture: two armchairs, a table, a lamp fed from the socket in the cubicle. The furniture was heavy and victorian; the cheapest available, its size emphasized the emptiness of the room. Pride of place was taken by an enormous mahogany wardrobe, fitted with carved angels and castellated mirrors, which they were forced to dismantle and carry into the house in their suitcases. Towering over them, it reminded Ward of the micro-films of gothic cathedrals, with their massive organ lofts crossing vast naves.

After three weeks they both slept in the room, finding the cubicle unbearably cramped. An imitation japanese screen divided the room adequately and did nothing to diminish its size. Sitting there in the evenings, surrounded by his books and albums, Ward steadily forgot the city outside. Luckily he reached the library by a back alley and avoided the crowded streets. Rossiter and himself began to seem the only real inhabitants of the world, everyone else a meaningless by-product of their own existence, a random replication of identity which had run out of control.

It was Rossiter who suggested that they ask the two girls to share the room with them.

"They've been kicked out again and may have to split up," he told Ward, obviously worried that Judith might fall into bad company. "There's always a rent freeze after a revaluation but all the landlords know about it so they're not re-letting. It's damned difficult to find anywhere."

Ward nodded, relaxing back around the circular red-wood table. He played with the tassel of the arsenic-green lamp shade, for a moment felt like a victorian man of letters, leading a spacious, leisurely life among overstuffed furnishings.

"I'm all for it," he agreed, indicating the empty corners.

"There's plenty of room here. But we'll have to make sure they don't gossip about it."

After due precautions, they let the two girls into the secret, enjoying their astonishment at finding this private universe.

"We'll put a partition across the middle," Rossiter explained, "then take it down each morning. You'll be able to move in within a couple of days. How do you feel?"

"Wonderful!" They goggled at the wardrobe, squinting at the endless reflections in the mirrors.

There was no difficulty getting them in and out of the house. The turnover of tenants was continuous and bills were placed in the mail rack. No one cared who the girls were or noticed their regular calls at the cubicle.

However, half an hour after they arrived neither of them had unpacked her suitcase.

"What's up, Judith?" Ward asked, edging past the girls' beds into the narrow interval between the table and wardrobe.

Judith hesitated, looking from Ward to Rossiter, who sat on the bed, finishing off the plywood partition. "John, it's just that..."

Helen Waring, more matter-of-fact, took over, her fingers straightening the bed-spread. "What Judith's trying to say is that our position here is a little embarrassing. The partition is——"

Rossiter stood up. "For heaven's sake, don't worry, Helen," he assured her, speaking in the loud whisper they had all involuntarily cultivated. "No funny business, you can trust us. This partition is as solid as a rock."

The two girls nodded. "It's not that," Helen explained, "but it isn't up all the time. We thought that if an older person were here, say Judith's aunt—she wouldn't take up much room and be no trouble, she's really awfully sweet—we wouldn't need to bother about the partition—except at night," she added quickly.

Ward glanced at Rossiter, who shrugged and began to scan the floor.

"Well, it's an idea," Rossiter said. "John and I know how you feel. Why not?"

"Sure," Ward agreed. He pointed to the space between the girls' beds and the table. "One more won't make any difference."

The girls broke into whoops. Judith went over to Rossiter and kissed him on the cheek. "Sorry to be a nuisance, Henry." She smiled at him. "That's a wonderful partition you've made. You couldn't do another one for Auntie—just a little one? She's very sweet but she is getting on."

"Of course," Rossiter said. "I understand. I've got plenty of wood left over."

Ward looked at his watch. "It's seven-thirty, Judith. You'd better get in touch with your aunt. She may not be able to make it tonight."

Judith buttoned her coat. "Oh she will," she assured Ward. "I'll be back in a jiffy."

The aunt arrived within five minutes, three heavy suitcases soundly packed.

"It's amazing," Ward remarked to Rossiter three months later. "The size of this room still staggers me. It almost gets larger every day."

Rossiter agreed readily, averting his eyes from one of the girls changing behind the central partition. This they now left in place as dismantling it daily had become tiresome. Besides, the aunt's subsidiary partition was attached to it and she resented the continuous upsets. Ensuring she followed the entrance and exit drills through the camouflaged door and cubicle was difficult enough.

Despite this, detection seemed unlikely. The room had obviously been built as an afterthought into the central well of the house and any noise was masked by the luggage stacked in the surrounding corridor. Directly below was a small dormitory occupied by several elderly women, and Judith's aunt, who visited them socially, swore that no sounds came through the heavy ceiling. Above, the fanlight let out through a dormer window, its lights indistinguishable from the hundred other bulbs in the windows of the house.

Rossiter finished off the new partition he was building and held it upright, fitting it into the slots nailed to the wall between his bed and Ward's. They had agreed that this would provide a little extra privacy.

"No doubt I'll have to do one for Judith and Helen," he confided to Ward.

Ward adjusted his pillow. They had smuggled the two armchairs back to the furniture shop as they took up too much space. The bed, anyway, was more comfortable. He had never become completely used to the soft upholstery.

"Not a bad idea. What about some shelving around the wall? I've got nowhere to put anything."

The shelving tidied the room considerably, freeing large areas of the floor. Divided by their partitions, the five beds were in line along the rear wall, facing the mahogany wardrobe. In between was an open space of three or four feet, a further six feet on either side of the wardrobe.

The sight of so much spare space fascinated Ward. When Rossiter mentioned that Helen's mother was ill and badly needed personal care he immediately knew where her cubicle could be placed—at the foot of his bed, between the wardrobe and the side wall.

Helen was over-joyed. "It's awfully good of you, John," she told him, "but would you mind if Mother slept beside me? There's enough space to fit an extra bed in."

So Rossiter dismantled the partitions and moved them closer together, six beds now in line along the wall. This gave each of them an interval two and a half feet wide, just enough room to squeeze down the side of their beds. Lying back on the extreme right, the shelves two feet above his head, Ward could barely see the wardrobe, but the space in front of him, a clear six feet to the wall ahead, was uninterrupted.

Then Helen's father arrived.

Knocking on the door of the cubicle, Ward smiled at Judith's aunt as she let him in. He helped her swing out the made-up bed which guarded the entrance, then rapped on the wooden panel. A moment later Helen's father, a small, grey-haired man in an undershirt, braces tied to his trousers with string, pulled back the panel.

Ward nodded to him and stepped over the luggage piled

around the floor at the foot of the beds. Helen was in her mother's cubicle, helping the old woman to drink her evening broth. Rossiter, perspiring heavily, was on his knees by the mahogany wardrobe, wrenching apart the frame of the central mirror with a jemmy. Pieces of the wardrobe lay on his bed and across the floor.

"We'll have to start taking these out tomorrow," Rossiter told him. Ward waited for Helen's father to shuffle past and enter his cubicle. He had rigged up a small cardboard door, and locked it behind him with a crude hook of bent wire.

Rossiter watched him, frowning irritably. "Some people are happy. This wardrobe's a hell of a job. How did we ever decide to buy it?"

Ward sat down on his bed. The partition pressed against his knees and he could hardly move. He looked up when Rossiter was engaged and saw that the dividing line he had marked in pencil was hidden by the encroaching partition. Leaning against the wall, he tried to ease it back again, but Rossiter had apparently nailed the lower edge to the floor.

There was a sharp tap on the outside cubicle door—Judith returning from her office. Ward started to get up and then sat back. "Mr. Waring," he called softly. It was the old man's duty night.

Waring shuffled to the door of his cubicle and unlocked it fussily, clucking to himself.

"Up and down, up and down," he muttered. He stumbled over Rossiter's tool-bag and swore loudly, then added meaningly over his shoulder: "If you ask me there's too many people in here. Down below they've only got six to our seven, and it's the same size room."

Ward nodded vaguely and stretched back on his narrow bed, trying not to bang his head on the shelving. Waring was not the first to hint that he move out. Judith's aunt had made a similar suggestion two days earlier. Since he had left his job at the library (the small rental he charged the others paid for the little food he needed) he spent most of his time in the room, seeing rather more of the old man than he wanted to, but he had learned to tolerate him.

Settling himself, he noticed that the right-hand spire of the wardrobe, all he had been able to see of it for the past two months, was now dismantled.

It had been a beautiful piece of furniture, in a way symbolizing this whole private world, and the salesman at the store told him there were few like it left. For a moment Ward felt a sudden pang of regret, as he had done as a child when his father, in a moment of exasperation, had taken something away from him and he had known he would never see it again.

Then he pulled himself together. It was a beautiful wardrobe, without doubt, but when it was gone it would make the room seem even larger.

THE GIOCONDA OF THE TWILIGHT NOON

"THOSE confounded gulls!" Richard Maitland complained to his
wife. "Can't you drive them away?"

Judith hovered behind the wheelchair, her hands glancing
around his bandaged eyes like nervous doves. She peered across
the lawn to the river bank. "Try not to think about them, darling.
They're just sitting there."

"Just? That's the trouble!" Maitland raised his cane and
struck the air vigorously. "I can feel them all out there, watching
me!"

They had taken his mother's house for his convalescence, partly
on the assumption that the rich store of visual memories would in
some way compensate for Maitland's temporary blindness—a
trivial eye injury had become infected, eventually requiring surg-
ery and a month's bandaged darkness. However, they had failed
to reckon with the huge extension of his other senses. The house
was five miles from the coast, but at low tide a flock of the greedy
estuarine birds would fly up the river and alight on the exposed
mud fifty yards from where Maitland sat in his wheelchair in the
centre of the lawn. Judith could barely hear the gulls, but to
Maitland their ravenous pecking filled the warm air like the cries
of some savage Dionysian chorus. He had a vivid image of the
wet banks streaming with the blood of thousands of dismembered
fish.

Fretting impotently to himself, he listened as their voices suddenly fell away. Then, with a sharp sound like tearing cloth, the
entire flock rose into the air. Maitland sat up stiffly in the wheel
chair, the cane clasped like a cudgel in his right hand,
half-expecting the gulls to swerve down on to the placid

lawn, their fierce beaks tearing at the bandages over his eyes. As if to conjure them away, he chanted aloud:

> " *The nightingales are singing near*
> *The Convent of the Sacred Heart,*
> *And sang within the bloody wood*
> *When Agamemnon cried aloud ... ! "*

During the fortnight since his return from the hospital Judith had read most of the early Eliot aloud to him. The flock of unseen gulls seemed to come straight out of that grim archaic landscape.

The birds settled again, and Judith took a few hesitant steps across the lawn, her dim form interrupting the even circle of light within his eyes. "They sound like a shoal of piranha," he said with a forced laugh. "What are they doing—stripping a bull?"

"Nothing, dear, as far as I can see...." Judith's voice dipped on this last word. Even though Maitland's blindness was only temporary—in fact, by twisting the bandages he could see a blurred but coherent image of the garden with its willows screening the river—she still treated him to all the traditional circumlocutions, hedging him with the elaborate taboos erected by the seeing to hide them from the blind. The only real cripples, Maitland reflected, were the perfect in limb.

"Dick, I have to drive into town to collect the groceries. You'll be all right for half an hour?"

"Of course. Just sound the horn when you come back."

The task of looking after the rambling country house single-handed—Maitland's widowed mother was on a steamer cruise in the Mediterranean—limited the time Judith could spend with him. Fortunately his long familiarity with the house saved her from having to guide him around it. A few rope hand-rails and one or two buffers of cotton wool taped to dangerous table corners had been enough. Indeed, once upstairs Maitland moved about the winding corridors and dark back staircases with more ease than Judith, and certainly with far more willingness—often in the evening she would go in search of Maitland and be startled to see her blind husband step soundlessly from a doorway two or three feet from her as he wandered among the old attics and dusty lofts. His rapt expression, as he hunted some memory of childhood, reminded her in a curious way of his mother, a tall, handsome woman whose bland smile always seemed to conceal some potent private world.

To begin with, when Maitland had chafed under the bandages, Judith had spent all morning and afternoon reading the newspapers aloud to him, then a volume of poems and even, heroically, the start of a novel, *Moby Dick*. Within a few days, however, Maitland had come to terms with his blindness, and the constant need for some sort of external stimulation faded. He discovered what every blind person soon finds out—that its external optical input is only part of the mind's immense visual activity. He had expected to be plunged into a profound Stygian darkness, but instead his brain was filled with a ceaseless play of light and colour. At times, as he lay back in the morning sunlight, he would see exquisite revolving patterns of orange light, like huge solar discs. These would gradually recede to brilliant pinpoints, shining above a veiled landscape across which dim forms moved like animals over an African veldt at dusk.

At other times forgotten memories would impinge themselves on this screen, what he assumed to be visual relics of his childhood long buried in his mind.

It was these images, with all their tantalizing associations, that most intrigued Maitland. By letting his mind drift into reverie he could almost summon them at will, watching passively as these elusive landscapes materialized like visiting spectres before his inner eye. One in particular, composed of fleeting glimpses of steep cliffs, a dark corridor of mirrors and a tall, high-gabled house within a wall, recurred persistently, although its unrelated details owed nothing to his memory. Maitland tried to explore it, fixing the blue cliffs or the tall house in his mind and waiting for their associations to gather. But the noise of the gulls and Judith's to and fro movements across the garden distracted him.

"'Bye, darling! See you later!"

Maitland raised his cane in reply. He listened to the car move off down the drive, its departure subtly altering the auditory profile of the house. Wasps buzzed among the ivy below the kitchen windows, hovering over the oil stains in the gravel. A line of trees swayed in the warm air, muffling Judith's last surge of acceleration. For once the gulls were silent. Usually this would have roused Maitland's suspicions, but he lay back, turning the wheels of the chair so that he faced the sun.

Thinking of nothing, he watched the aureoles of light mushroom soundlessly within his mind. Occasionally the shifting of the willows or the sounds of a bee bumping around the glass water jug on the table beside him would end the sequence. This extreme sensitivity to the faintest noise or movement reminded him of the hypersensitivity of epileptics, or of rabies victims in their grim terminal convulsions. It was almost as if the barriers between the deepest levels of the nervous system and the external world had been removed, those muffling layers of blood and bone, reflex and convention. . . .

With a barely perceptible pause in his breathing, Maitland relaxed carefully in the chair. Projected on to the screen within his mind was the image he had glimpsed before, of a rocky coastline whose dark cliffs loomed through an off-shore mist. The whole scene was drab and colourless. Overhead low clouds reflected the pewter surface of the water. As the mist cleared he moved nearer the shore, and watched the waves breaking on the rocks. The plumes of foam searched like white serpents among the pools and crevices for the caves that ran deep into the base of the cliff.

Desolate and unfequented, the coast reminded Maitland only of the cold shores of Tierra del Fuego and the ships' graveyards of Cape Horn, rather than of any memories of his own. Yet the cliffs drew nearer, rising into the air above him, as if their identity reflected some image deep within Maitland's mind.

Still separated from them by the interval of grey water, Maitland followed the shoreline, until the cliffs divided at the mouth of a small estuary. Instantly the light cleared. The water within the estuary glowed with an almost spectral vibrancy. The blue rocks of the surrounding cliffs, penetrated by small grottoes and caverns, emitted a soft prismatic light, as if illuminated by some subterranean lantern.

Holding this scene before him, Maitland searched the shores of the estuary. The caverns were deserted, but as he neared them the luminous archways began to reflect the light like a hall of mirrors. At the same time he found himself entering the dark, high-gabled house he had seen previously, and which had now superimposed itself on his dream. Somewhere within it, masked by the mirrors, a tall, green-robed figure watched him, receding through the caves and groins....

A motor-car horn sounded, a gay succession of toots. The gravel grating beneath its tyres, a car swung into the drive.

"Judith here, darling," his wife called. "Everything all right?"

Cursing under his breath, Maitland fumbled for his cane. The image of the dark coast and the estuary with its spectral caves had gone. Like a blind worm, he turned his blunted head at the unfamiliar sounds and shapes in the garden.

"Are you all right?" Judith's footsteps crossed the lawn. "What's the matter, you're all hunched up—have those birds been annoying you?"

"No, leave them." Maitland lowered his cane, realizing that although not visibly present in his inward vision, the gulls had played an oblique role in its creation. The foam-white sea-birds, hunters of the albatross....

With an effort he said: "I was asleep."

Judith knelt down and took his hands. "I'm sorry. I'll ask one of the men to build a scare-crow. That should——"

"No!" Maitland pulled his hands away. "They're not worrying me at all." Levelling his voice, he said: "Did you see anyone in the town?"

"Dr. Phillips. He said you should be able to take off the bandages in about ten days."

"Good. There's no hurry, though. I want the job done properly."

After Judith had walked back to the house Maitland tried to return to his reverie, but the image remained sealed behind the screen of his consciousness.

At breakfast the next morning Judith read him the mail.

"There's a postcard from your mother. They're near Malta, somewhere called Gozo."

"Give it to me." Maitland felt the card in his hands. "Gozo—

that was Calypso's island. She kept Ulysses there for seven years, promised him eternal youth if he'd stay with her forever."

"I'm not surprised." Judith inclined the card towards her. "If we could spare the time you and I should go there for a holiday. Wine-dark seas, a sky like heaven, blue rocks. Bliss."

"Blue?"

"Yes. I suppose it's the bad printing. They can't really be like that."

"They are, actually." Still holding the card, Maitland went out into the garden, feeling his way along the string guide-rail. As he settled himself in the wheelchair he reflected that there were other correspondences in the graphic arts. The same blue rocks and spectral grottos could be seen in Leonardo's *Virgin of the Rocks*, one of the most forbidding and most enigmatic of his paintings. The madonna sitting on a bare ledge by the water beneath the dark overhang of the cavern's mouth was like the presiding spirit of some enchanted marine realm, waiting for those cast on to the rocky shores of this world's end. As in so many of Leonardo's paintings, all its unique longings and terrors were to be found in the landscape in the background. Here, through an archway among the rocks, could be seen the crystal blue cliffs that Mait-land had glimpsed in his reverie.

"Shall I read it out to you?" Judith had crossed the lawn.

"What?"

"Your mother's postcard. You're holding it in your hand."

"Sorry. Please do."

As he listened to the brief message, Maitland waited for Judith to return to the house. When she had gone he sat quietly for a few minutes. The distant sounds of the river came to him through the trees, and the faint cry of gulls swooping on to the banks further down the estuary.

This time, almost as if recognizing Maitland's need, the vision came to him quickly. He passed the dark cliffs, and the waves vaulting into the cave mouths, and then entered the twi-light world of the grottoes beside the river. Outside, through the stone galleries, he could see the surface of the water glittering like a sheet of prisms, the soft blue light reflected in the vitreous mirrors which formed the cavern walls. At the same time he sensed that he was entering the high-gabled house, whose surrounding wall was the cliff face he had seen from the sea. The rock-like vaults of the house glowed with the olive-black colours of the marine deeps, and curtains of old lace-work hung from the doors and windows like ancient nets.

A staircase ran through the grotto, its familiar turnings leading to the inner reaches of the cavern. Looking upwards, he saw the green-robed figure watching him from an archway. Her face was hidden from him, veiled by the light reflected off the damp mirrors on the walls. Impelled forward up the steps, Maitland reached towards her, and for an instant the face of the figure cleared....

"Judith!" Rocking forward in his chair, Maitland searched helplessly for the water jug on the table, his left hand drumming at his forehead in an attempt to drive away the vision and its terrifying lamia.

"Richard! What is it?"

He heard his wife's hurried footsteps across the lawn, and then felt her hands steadying his own.

"Darling, what on earth's going on? You're pouring with perspiration!"

That afternoon, when he was left alone again, Maitland approached the dark labyrinth more cautiously. At low tide the gulls returned to the mud flats below the garden, and their archaic cries carried his mind back into its deeps like mortuary birds bearing away the body of Tristan. Guarding himself and his own fears, he moved slowly through the luminous chambers of the subterranean house, averting his eyes from the green-robed enchantress who watched him from the staircase.

Later, when Judith brought his tea to him on a tray, he ate carefully, talking to her in measured tones.

"What did you see in your nightmare?" she asked.

"A house of mirrors under the sea, and a deep cavern," he told her. "I could see everything, but in a strange way, like the dreams of people who have been blind for a long time."

Throughout the afternoon and evening he returned to the grotto at intervals, moving circumspectly through the outer chambers, always aware of the robed figure waiting for him in the doorway to its innermost sanctum.

The next morning Dr. Phillips called to change his dressing.

"Excellent, excellent," he commented, holding his torch in one hand as he retaped Maitland's eyelids to his cheeks. "Another week and you'll be out of this for good. At least you know what it's like for the blind."

"One can envy them," Maitland said.

"Really?"

"They see with an inner eye, you know. In a sense everything there is more real."

"That's a point of view." Dr. Phillips replaced the bandages. He drew the curtains. "What have you seen with your's?"

Maitland made no reply. Dr. Phillips had examined him in the darkened study, but the thin torch beam and the few needles of light around the curtains had filled his brain like arc lights. He waited for the glare to subside, realizing that his inner world, the grotto, the house of mirrors and the enchantress, had been burned out of his mind by the sunlight.

"They're hypnagogic images," Dr. Phillips remarked, fastening his bag. "You've been living in an unusual zone, sitting around doing nothing but with your optic nerves alert, a no-man's land between sleep and consciousness. I'd expect all sorts of strange things."

After he had gone Maitland said to the unseen walls, his lips whispering below the bandages: "Doctor, give me back my eyes."

It took him two full days to recover from this brief interval of external sight. Laboriously, rock by rock, he re-explored the hidden coastline, willing himself through the enveloping sea-mists, searching for the lost estuary.

At last the luminous beaches appeared again.

"I think I'd better sleep alone tonight," he told Judith. "I'll use mother's room."

"Of course, Richard. What's the matter?"

"I suppose I'm restless. I'm not getting much exercise and there are only three days to go. I don't want to disturb you."

He found his own way into his mother's bedroom, glimpsed only occasionally during the years since his marriage. The high bed, the deep rustle of silks and the echoes of forgotten scents carried him back to his earliest childhood. He lay awake all night, listening to the sounds of the river reflected off the cut-glass ornaments over the fireplace.

At dawn, when the gulls flew up from the estuary, he visited the blue grottoes again, and the tall house in the cliff. Knowing its tenant now, the green-robed watcher on the staircase, he decided to wait for the morning light. Her beckoning eyes, the pale lantern of her smile, floated before him.

However, after breakfast Dr. Phillips returned.

"Right," he told Maitland briskly, leading him in from the lawn. "Let's have those bandages off."

"For the last time, Doctor?" Judith asked. "Are you sure?"

"Certainly. We don't want this to go on for ever, do we?" He steered Maitland into the study. "Sit down here, Richard. You draw the curtains, Judith."

Maitland stood up, feeling for the desk. "But you said it would take three more days, Doctor."

"I dare say. But I didn't want you to get over-excited. What's the matter? You're hovering about there like an old woman. Don't you want to see again?"

"*See?*" Maitland repeated numbly. "Of course." He subsided limply into a chair as Dr. Phillips' hands unfastened the bandages. A profound sense of loss had come over him. "Doctor, could I put it off for——"

"Nonsense. You can see perfectly. Don't worry, I'm not going to fling back the curtains. It'll be a full day before you can see freely. I'll give you a set of filters to wear. Anyway, these dressings let through more light then you imagine."

At eleven o'clock the next morning, his eyes shielded only by a pair of sunglasses, Maitland walked out on to the lawn. Judith stood on the terrace, and watched him make his way around the wheelchair. When he reached the willows she called: "All right, darling? Can you see me?"

The Gioconda of the Twilight Noon

Without replying, Maitland looked back at the house. He removed the sunglasses and threw them aside on to the grass. He
gazed through the trees at the estuary, at the blue surface of the
water stretching to the opposite bank. Hundreds of the gulls stood
by the water, their heads turned in profile to reveal the full curve
of their beaks. He looked over his shoulder at the high-gabled
house, recognizing the one he had seen in his dream. Everything
about it, like the bright river which slid past him, seemed dead.

Suddenly the gulls rose into the air, their cries drowning the
sounds of Judith's voice as she called again from the terrace. In a
dense spiral, gathering itself off the ground like an immense
scythe, the gulls wheeled into the air over his head and swirled
over the house.

Quickly Maitland pushed back the branches of the willows and
walked down on to the bank.

A moment later, Judith heard his shout above the cries of the
gulls. The sound came half in pain and half in triumph, and she
ran down to the trees uncertain whether he had injured himself
or discovered something pleasing.

Then she saw him standing on the bank, his head raised to the
sunlight, the bright carmine on his cheeks and hands, an eager,
unrepentant Oedipus.

THE LOST LEONARDO

The disappearance—or, to put it less euphemistically—the theft of the *Crucifixion* by Leonardo da Vinci from the Museum of the Louvre in Paris, discovered on the morning of April 19, 1965, caused a scandal of unprecedented proportions. A decade of major art thefts, such as those of Goya's *Duke of Wellington* from the National Gallery, London, and collections of impressionists from the homes of millionaires in the South of France and California, as well as the obviously inflated prices paid in the auction rooms of Bond Street and the Rue de Rivoli, might have been expected to accustom the general public to the loss of yet another over-publicized masterpiece, but in fact the news of its disappearance was received by the world with genuine consternation and outrage. From all over the globe thousands of telegrams poured in daily at the Quai d'Orsay and the Louvre, the French consulates at Bogota and Guatemala City were stoned, and the panache and finesse of press attaches at every embassy from Buenos Aires to Bangkok were strained to their not inconsiderable limits.

I myself reached Paris over twenty-four hours after what was being called 'the great Leonardo scandal' had taken place, and the atmosphere of bewilderment and indignation was palpable. All the way from Orly Airport the newspaper headlines on the kiosks blazoned the same story.

As the *Continental Daily Mail* put it succinctly:

LEONARDO'S CRUCIFIXION STOLEN
£5 Million Masterpiece Vanishes from Louvre

Official Paris, by all accounts, was in uproar. The hapless director of the Louvre had been recalled from a Unesco conference in Brasilia and was now on the carpet at the Elysée Palace, reporting personally to the President, the Deuxieme Bureau had been alerted, and at least three ministers without portfolio had been appointed, their political futures staked to the recovery of the painting. As the President himself had remarked at his press conference the previous afternoon, the theft of a Leonardo was an affair not only for France, but for the entire world, and in a passionate plea he enjoined everyone to help effect its speedy return (despite the emotionally charged atmosphere, cynical observers noticed that this was the first crisis of his career when the Great Man did not conclude his peroration with 'Vive La France').

My own feelings, despite my professional involvement with the fine arts—I was, and am, a director of Northeby's, the world-famous Bond Street auctioneers—by and large coincided with those of the general public. As the taxi passed the Tuileries Gardens I looked out at the crude half-tone illustrations of da Vinci's effulgent masterpiece reproduced in the newspapers, recalling the immense splendour of the painting, with its unparalleled composition and handling of chiaroscuro, its unsurpassed technique, which together had launched the High Renaissance and provided a beacon for the sculptors, painters and architects of the Baroque.

Despite the two million reproductions of the painting sold each year, not to mention the countless pastiches and inferior imitations, the subject matter of the painting still retained its majestic power. Completed two years after da Vinci's *Virgin and St. Anne*, also in the Louvre, it was not only one of the few Leonardos to have survived intact the thousand eager hands of the retouchers of four centuries, but was the only painting by the master, apart from the dissolving and barely visible *Last Supper*, in which he handled a composition with a large landscape and a huge gallery of supporting figures.

It was this latter factor, perhaps, which gave the painting its terrifying, hallucinatory power. The enigmatic, almost ambivalent expression on the face of the dying Christ, the hooded serpentine eyes of the Madonna and Magdalene, these characteristic signatures of Leonardo became more than mere mannerisms when set against the huge spiral concourse of attendant figures that seemed to swirl up into the distant sky across the Place of Bones, transforming the whole image of the crucifixion into an apocalyptic vision of the resurrection and judgment of mankind. From this single canvas had come the great frescoes of Michelangelo and Raphael in the Sistine Chapel, the entire schools of Tintoretto and Veronese. That someone should have the audacity to steal it was a tragic comment on mankind's respect for its greatest monuments.

And yet, I wondered as we arrived at the offices of Galleries Normande et Cie in the Madeleine, had the painting really been stolen at all? It's size, some 15 feet by 18 feet, and weight—it had been transferred from the original canvas to an oak panel—precluded a single fanatic or psychopath, and no gang of professional art thieves would waste their time stealing a painting for which there would be no market. Could it be, perhaps, that the French government was hoping to distract attention from some other impending event, though nothing less than the re-introduction of the monarchy and the coronation of the Bourbon Pretender in Notre Dame would have required such an elaborate smoke-screen.

At the first opportunity I raised my doubts with Georg de Stael, the director of Galleries Normande with whom I was staying during my visit. Ostensibly I had come to Paris to attend a conference that afternoon of art dealers and gallery directors who had also suffered from thefts of major works of art, but to any outsider our mood of elation and high spirits would have suggested some other motive. This, of course, would have been correct. Whenever a large stone is cast into the turbid waters of international art, people such as myself and Georg de Stael immediately take up our positions on the bank, watching for any unusual ripple or malodorous bubble. Without doubt the theft of the Leonardo would reveal a good deal more than the identity of some crack-pot cat burglar. All the darker fish would now be swimming frantically for cover, and a salutary blow had been struck at the official establishment of senior museum curators and directors.

Such feelings of revenge obviously animated Georg as he moved with dapper, light-footed ease around his desk to greet me. His blue silk summer suit, well in advance of the season, glittered like his smooth brilliantined hair, his svelte rapacious features breaking into a smile of roguish charm.

"My dear Charles, I assure you, categorically, the confounded picture has actually gone—" Georg shot out three inches of elegant chalk-blue cuff and snapped his hands together "—puff! For once everyone is speaking the truth. What is even more remarkable, the painting was genuine."

"I don't know whether I'm glad to hear that or not," I admitted. "But it's certainly more that you can say for most of the Louvre—and the National Gallery."

"Agreed." Georg straddled his desk, his patent leather shoes twinkling in the light. "I had hoped that this catastrophe might induce the authorities to make a clean breast of some of their so-called treasures, in an attempt, as it were to dispel some of the magic surrounding the Leonardo. But they are in a complete fuddle."

For a moment we both contemplated what such a sequence of admissions would do to the art markets of the world—the prices of anything even remotely genuine would soar—as well as to the popular image of Renaissance painting as something sacrosanct and unparalleled. However, this was not to gainsay the genius of the stolen Leonardo.

"Tell me, Georg," I asked. "Who stole it?" I assumed he knew.

For the first time in many years Georg seemed at a loss for an answer. He shrugged helplessly. "My dear Charles, I just do not know. It's a complete mystery. Everyone is as baffled as you are."

"In that case it must be an inside job."

"Definitely not. The present crowd at the Louvre are beyond reproach." He tapped the telephone. "This morning I was speaking to some of our more dubious contacts—Antweiler in Messina and Kolenskya in Beirut—and they are both mystified. In fact they're convinced that either the whole thing is a put-up affair by the present regime, or else the Kremlin itself is involved."

"The Kremlin?" I echoed incredulously. At the invocation of

this name the atmosphere heightened, and for the next half an hour we spoke in whispers.

The conference that afternoon, at the Palais de Chaillot, offered no further clues. Chief Detective-Inspector Carnot, a massive gloomy man in a faded blue suit, took the chair, flanked by other agents of the Deuxieme Bureau. All of them looked tired and dispirited; by now they were having to check up on some dozen false alarms each hour. Behind them, like a hostile jury, sat a sober-faced group of investigators from Lloyds of London and Morgan Guaranty Trust of New York. By contrast, the two hundred dealers and agents sitting on the gilt chairs below the platform presented an animated scene, chattering away in a dozen languages and flying a score of speculative kites.

After a brief resumé, delivered in a voice of sepulchral resignation, Inspector Carnot introduced a burly Dutchman next to him, Superintendent Jurgens of the Interpol bureau at The Hague, and then called on M. Auguste Pecard, assistant director of the Louvre, for a detailed description of the theft. This merely confirmed that the security arrangements at the Louvre were first-class and that it was absolutely impossible for the painting to have been stolen. I could see that Pecard was still not entirely convinced that it had gone.

"...the pressure panels in the floor surrounding the painting have not been disturbed, nor have the two infra-red beams across its face been broken. Gentlemen, I assure you it is impossible to remove the painting without first dismantling the bronze frame. This alone weighs eight hundred pounds and is bolted into the wall behind it. But the electric alarm circuit which flows through the bolts was not interrupted...."

I was looking up at the two life-size photographs of the front and reverse faces of the painting fastened to the screens behind the dais. The latter showed the back of the oak panel with its six aluminium ribs, contact points for the circuit and a mass of chalked graffiti enscribed over the years by the museum laboratories. The photographs had been taken the last time the picture was removed for cleaning, and after a brief bout of questioning it transpired that this had been completed only two days before the theft.

At this news the atmosphere of the conference changed. The hundred private conversations ceased, coloured silk handkerchiefs were returned to their breast pockets.

I nudged Georg de Stael. "So that explains it." Obviously the painting had disappeared during its period in the laboratory, where the security arrangements would be less than fool-proof. "It was not stolen from the *gallery* at all."

The hubbub around us had re-started. Two hundred noses once again were lifted to scent the trail. So the painting *had* been stolen, and was somewhere at large in the world. The rewards to the discoverer, if not the Legion of Honour or a Knighthood, then at least complete freedom from all income tax and foreign exchange investigations, hovered like a spectre before us.

On the way back, however, Georg stared sombrely through the window of the taxi.

"The painting *was* stolen from the gallery," he said to me pensively. "I saw it there myself just twelve hours before it vanished." He took my arm and held it tightly. "We'll find it, Charles, for the glory of Northeby's and the Galleries Normande. But, my God, the man who stole it was a thief out of this world!"

So began the quest for the missing Leonardo. I returned to London the next morning, but Georg and I were in regular contact by telephone. Initially, like all the others on its trail, we merely listened, ears to the ground for an unfamiliar foot-fall. In the crowded auction rooms and galleries we waited for the indiscreet word, for the give-away clue. Business, of course, was buoyant; every museum and private owner with a third-rate Rubens or Raphael had now moved up a rung. With luck the renewed market activity would uncover some distant accomplice of the thief, or a previous substitute for the Leonardo—perhaps a pastiche *Mona Lisa* by one of Verrocchio's pupils—would be jettisoned by the thief and appear on one of the shadier markets. If the hunt for the vanished painting was conducted as loudly as ever in the outside world, within the trade all was quiet and watchful.

In fact, too quiet. By rights something should have materialized, some faint clue should have appeared on the fine filters of
the galleries and auction rooms. But nothing was heard. As the
wave of activity launched by the displaced Leonardo rolled past
and business resumed its former tempo, inevitably the painting
become just another on the list of lost masterpieces.

Only Georg de Stael seemed able to maintain his interest in the
search. Now and then he would put through a call to London,
requesting some obscure piece of information about an anonymous buyer of a Titian or Rembrandt in the late 18th century, or
the history of some damaged copy by a pupil of Rubens or
Raphael. He seemed particularly interested in works known to
have been damaged and subsequently restored, information with
which many private owners are naturally jealous of parting.

Consequently, when he called to see me in London some four
months after the disappearance of the Leonardo, it was not in a
purely jocular sense that I asked: "Well, Georg, do you know
who stole it yet?"

Unclipping a large briefcase, Georg smiled at me darkly.
"Would it surprise you if I said 'yes'? As a matter of fact, I don't
know, but I have an idea, an hypothesis, shall we say. I thought
you might be interested to hear it."

"Of course, Georg," I said, adding reprovingly: "So this is
what you've been up to."

He raised a thin forefinger to silence me. Below the veneer of
easy charm I noticed a new mood of seriousness, a cutting of
conversational corners. "First, Charles, before you laugh me out
of your office, let's say that I consider my theory completely
fantastic and implausible, and yet—" he shrugged deprecatingly
" —it seems to be the only one possible. To prove it I need your
help."

"Given before asked. But what is this theory? I can't wait to
hear."

He hesitated, apparently uncertain whether to expose his idea,
and then began to empty the briefcase, taking out a series of
looseleaf files which he placed in a row facing him along the desk.
These contained what appeared to be photographic reproductions
of a number of paintings, areas within them marked with white

ink. Several of the photographs were enlargements of details, all of a high-faced, goatee-bearded man in mediaeval costume.

Georg inverted six of the larger plates so that I could see them. "You recognize these, of course?"

I nodded. With the exception of one, Rubens' *Pieta* in the Hermitage Museum at Leningrad, I had seen the originals of them all within the previous five years. The others were the missing Leonardo *Crucifixion,* the *Crucifixions* by Veronese, Goya and Holbein, and that by Poussin, entitled *The Place of Golgotha.* All were in public museums—the Louvre, San Stefano in Venice, the Prado and the Ryksmuseum, Amsterdam—and all were familiar, well-authenticated master-works, centre-pieces, apart from the Poussin, of major national collections. "It's reassuring to see them. I trust they're all in good hands. Or are they next on the mysterious thief's shopping list?"

Georg shook his head. "No, I don't think he's very interested in these. Though he keeps a watching brief over them." Again I noticed the marked change in Georg's manner, the reflective private humour. "Do you notice anything else?"

I compared the photographs again. "They're all crucifixions. Authentic, except perhaps in minor details. They were all easel paintings." I shrugged.

"They all, at some time, have been stolen." Georg moved quickly from right to left. "The Poussin from the Chateau Loire collection in 1822, the Goya in 1806 from the Monte Cassino monastery, by Napoleon, the Veronese from the Prado in 1891, the Leonardo four months ago as we know, and the Holbein in 1943, looted for the Herman Goering collection."

"Interesting," I commented. "But few master-works haven't been stolen at some time. I hope this isn't a key point in your theory."

"No, but in conjuction with another factor it gains in significance. Now." He handed the Leonardo reproduction to me. "Anything unusual there?" When I shook my head at the familiar image he picked up another photograph of the missing painting. "What about that one?"

The photographs had been taken from slight different perspectives, but otherwise seemed identical. "They are both of the original *Crucifixion*," Georg explained, "taken in the Louvre within a month of its disappearance."

"I give up," I admitted. "They seem the same. No—wait a minute!" I pulled the table light nearer and bent over the plates, as Georg nodded. "They're slightly different. What is going on?"

Quickly, figure by figure, I compared the photographs, within a few moments seized on the minute disparity. In almost every particular the pictures were identical, but one figure out of the score or more on the crowded field had been altered. On the left, where the procession wound its way up the hillside towards the three crosses, the face of one of the bystanders had been completely repainted. Although, in the centre of the painting, the Christ hung from the cross some hours after the crucifixion, by a sort of spatio-temporal perspective—a common device in all Renaissance painting for overcoming the static nature of the single canvas—the receding procession carried the action backwards through time, so that one followed the invisible presence of the Christ on his painful last ascent of Golgotha.

The figure whose face had been repainted formed part of the crowd on the lower slopes. A tall powerfully built man in a black robe, he had obviously been the subject of special care by Leonardo, who had invested him with the magnificent physique and serpentine grace usually reserved for his depiction of angels. Looking at the photograph in my left hand, the original unretouched version, I realized that Leonardo had indeed intended the figure to represent an angel of death, or rather, one of those agents of the unconscious, terrifying in their enigmatic calm, in their brooding ambivalence, who seem to preside in his paintings over all man's deepest fears and longings, like the grey-faced statues that stare down from the midnight cornices of the necropolis at Pompeii.

All this, so typical of Leonardo and his curious vision, seemed to be summed up by the face of this tall angelic figure. Turned almost in profile over the left shoulder, the face looked up towards the cross, a faint flicker of pity investing the grey saturnine features. A high forehead, slightly flared at the temples, rose above the handsome semitic nose and mouth. A trace of a smile, of compassionate resignation and understanding, hung about the lips, providing a solitary source of light which illuminated the remainder of the face partly obscured by the shadows of the thundering sky.

In the photograph on my right, however, all this had been altered completely. The whole character of this angelic figure had been replaced by a new conception. The superficial likeness remained, but the face had lost its expression of tragic compassion. The later artist had reversed its posture altogether, and the head was turned away from the cross and over the right shoulder towards the earthly city of Jerusalem whose spectral towers rose like a city of Miltonic hell in the blue dusk. While the other bystanders followed the ascending Christ as if helpless to assist him, the expression on the face of the black-robed figure was arrogant and critical, the tension of the averted neck muscles indicating that he had swung his head away almost in disgust from the spectacle before him.

"What is this?" I asked, pointing to the latter photograph. "Some lost pupil's copy? I can't see why——"

Georg leaned forward and tapped the print. "*That* is the original Leonardo. Don't you understand, Charles? The version on your left which you were admiring for so many minutes was superimposed by some unknown retoucher, only a few years after da Vinci's death." He smiled at my scepticism. "Believe me, it's true. The figure concerned is only a minor part of the composition, no one had seriously examined it before, as the rest of the painting is without doubt original. These additions were discovered five months ago shortly after the painting was removed for painting. The infra-red examination revealed the completely intact profile below."

He passed two more photographs to me, both large-scale details of the head, in which the contrasts of characterization were even more obvious. "As you can see from the brush-work in the shading, the retouching was done by a right-handed artist, whereas we know, of course, that da Vinci was left-handed."

"Well...." I shrugged. "It seems strange. But if what you say is correct, why on earth was such a small detail altered? The whole conception of the character is different."

"An interesting question," Georg said ambiguously. "Incidentally, the figure is that of Ahasuerus, the Wandering Jew." He pointed to the man's feet. "He's always conventionally represented by the crossed sandal-straps of the Essene Sect, to which Jesus himself may have belonged."

I picked up the photographs again. "The Wandering Jew," I repeated softly. "How curious. The man who taunted Christ to move faster and was condemned to rove the surface of the earth until the Second Coming. It's almost as if the retoucher were an apologist for him, superimposing this expression of tragic pity over Leonardo's representation. There's an idea for you, Georg. You know how courtiers and wealthy merchants who gathered at painters' studios were informally incorporated into their paintings —perhaps Ahasuerus would move around, posing as himself, driven by a sort of guilt compulsion, then later steal the paintings and revise them. Now there *is* a theory."

I looked across at Georg, waiting for him to reply. He was nodding slowly, eyes watching mine in unspoken agreement, all trace of humour absent. "Georg!" I exclaimed. "Are you serious? Do you mean——"

He interrupted me gently but forcefully. "Charles, just give me a few more minutes to explain. I warned you that my theory was fantastic." Before I could protest he passed me another photograph. "The Veronese *Crucifixion*. See anyone you recognize? On the bottom left."

I raised the photograph to the light. "You're right. The late Venetian treatment is different, far more pagan, but it's quite obvious. You know, Georg, it's a remarkable likeness."

"Agreed. But it's not only the likeness. Look at the pose and characterization."

Identified again by his black robes and crossed sandal straps, the figure of Ahasuerus stood among the throng on the crowded canvas. The unusual feature was not so much that the pose was again that of the retouched Leonardo, with Ahasuerus now looking with an expression of deep compassion at the dying Christ—an altogether meaningless interpretation—but the remarkable likeness between the two faces, almost as if they had been painted from the same model. The beard was perhaps a little fuller, in the

Venetian manner, but the planes of the face, the flaring of the temples, the handsome coarseness of the mouth and jaw, the wise resignation in the eyes, that of some well-travelled physician witnessing an act of barbaric beauty and power, all these were exactly echoed from the Leonardo.

I gestured helplessly. "It's an amazing coincidence."

Georg nodded. "Another is that this painting, like the Leonardo, was stolen shortly after being extensively cleaned. When it was recovered in Florence two years later it was slightly damaged, and no further attempts were made to restore the painting." Georg paused. "Do you see my point, Charles?"

"More or less. I take it you suspect that if the Veronese were now cleaned a rather different version of Ahasuerus would be found. Veronese's original depiction."

"Exactly. After all, the present treatment makes no sense. If you're still sceptical, look at these others."

Standing up, we began to go through the remainder of the photographs. In each of the others, the Poussin, Holbein, Goya and Rubens, the same figure was to be found, the same dark saturnine face regarding the cross with an expression of compassionate understanding. In view of the very different styles of the artists, the degree of similarity was remarkable. In each, as well, the pose was meaningless, the characterization completely at odds with the legendary role of Ahasuerus.

By now the intensity of Georg's conviction was communicating itself to me physically. He drummed the desk with the palm of one hand. "In each case, Charles, all six paintings were stolen shortly after they had been cleaned—even the Holbein was looted from the Herman Goering collection by some renegade S.S. after being repaired by concentration camp inmates. As you yourself said, it's almost as if the thief was unwilling for the world to see the true image of Ahasuerus's character exposed and deliberately painted in these apologies."

"But Georg, you're making a large assumption there. Can you prove that in each case, apart from the Leonardo, there is an original version below the present one?"

"Not yet. Naturally galleries are reluctant to give anyone the opportunity to show that their works are not entirely genuine. I know all this is still hypothesis, but what other explanation can you find? "

Shaking my head, I went over to the window, letting the noise and movement of Bond Street cut through Georg's heady speculations. "Are you seriously suggesting, Georg, that the black-robed figure of Ahasuerus is promenading somewhere on those pavements below us now, and that all through the centuries he's been stealing and retouching paintings that represent him spurning Jesus? The idea's ludicrous! "

"No more ludicrous than the theft of the painting. Everyone agrees it could not have been stolen by anyone bounded by the laws of the physical universe."

For a moment we stared at each other across the desk. "All right," I temporized, not wishing to offend him. The intensity of his idée fixe had alarmed me. "But isn't our best plan simply to sit back and wait for the Leonardo to turn up again? "

"Not necessarily. Most of the stolen paintings remained lost for ten or twenty years. Perhaps the effort of stepping outside the bounds of space and time exhausts him, or perhaps the sight of the original paintings terrifies him so——" He broke off as I began to come forwards towards him. "Look, Charles, it *is* fantastic, but there's a slim chance it may be true. This is where I need your help. It's obvious this man must be a great patron of the arts, drawn by an irresistible compulsion, by unassuageable feelings of guilt, towards those artists painting crucifixions. We must begin to watch the sale rooms and galleries. That face, those black eyes and that haunted profile—sooner or later we'll see him, searching for another *Crucifixion* or *Pieta*. Cast your mind back, do you recognize that face? "

I looked down at the carpet, the image of the dark-eyed wanderer before me. *Go quicker,* he had taunted Jesus as he passed bearing the cross towards Golgotha, and Jesus had replied: *I go, but thou shalt wait until I return.* I was about to say 'no', but something restrained me, some reflex pause of recognition stirred through my mind. That handsome Levantine profile, in a different costume, of course, a smart dark-striped lounge suit, gold-topped cane and spats, bidding through an agent....

"You *have* seen him?" Georg came over to me. "Charles, I think I have too."

I gestured him away. "I'm not sure, Georg, but ... I almost wonder." Curiously it was the retouched portrait of Ahasuerus, rather than Leonardo's original, which seemed more real, closer to the face I felt sure I had actually seen. Suddenly I pivoted on my heel. "Confound it, Georg, do you realize that if this incredible idea of your's is true this man must have spoken to Leonardo? To Michelangelo, and Titian and Rembrandt?"

Georg nodded. "And someone else too," he added pensively.

For the next month, after Georg's return to Paris, I spent less time in my office and more in the sale rooms, watching for that familiar profile which something convinced me I had seen before. But for this undeniable conviction I would have dismissed Georg's hypothesis as obsessive fantasy. I made a few tactful enquiries of my assistant, and to my annoyance two of them also vaguely remembered such a person. After this I found myself unable to drive Georg de Stael's fancies from my mind. No further news was heard of the missing Leonardo—the complete absence of any clues mystified the police and the art world alike.

Consequently, it was with an immense feeling of relief, as much as of excitement, that I received five weeks later the following telegram:

CHARLES. COME IMMEDIATELY. I HAVE SEEN HIM. GEORG DE STAEL.

This time, as my taxi carried me from Orly Airport to the Madeleine, it was no idle amusement that made me watch the Tuileries Gardens for any sight of a tall man in a black slouch hat sneaking through the trees with a rolled-up canvas under his arm. Was Georg de Stael finally and irretrievably out of his mind, or had he in fact seen the phantom Ahasuerus?

When he greeted me at the doorway of Normande et Cie his handshake was as firm as ever, his face composed and relaxed. In his office he sat back and regarded me quizzically over the tips of his fingers, evidently so sure of himself that he could let his news bide its time.

"He's here, Charles," he said at last. "In Paris, staying at the Ritz. He's been attending the sales here of 19th and 20th Century masters. With luck you'll see him this afternoon."

For once my incredulity returned, but before I could stutter my objections Georg silenced me.

"He's just as we expected, Charles. Tall and powerfully built, with a kind of statuesque grace, the sort of man who moves easily among the rich and nobility. Leonardo and Holbein caught him exactly, that strange haunted intensity about his eyes, the wind of deserts and great ravines."

"When did you first see him?"

"Yesterday afternoon. We had almost completed the 19th century sales when a small Van Gogh—an inferior copy by the painter of *The Good Samaritan*—came up. One of those painted during his last madness, full of turbulent spirals, the figures like tormented beasts. For some reason the Samaritan's face reminded me of Ahasuerus. Just then I looked up across the crowded auction room." Georg sat forward. "To my amazement there he was, sitting not three feet away in the front row of seats, staring me straight in the face. I could hardly take my eyes off him. As soon as the bidding started he came in hard, going up in two thousands of francs."

"He took the painting?"

"No. Luckily I still had my wits about me. Obviously I had to be sure he was the right man. Previously his appearances have been solely as Ahasuerus, but few painters today are doing crucifixions in the *bel canto* style, and he may have tried to redress the balance of guilt by appearing in other roles, the Samaritan for example. He was left alone at 15,000—actually the reserve was only ten—so I leaned over and had the painting withdrawn. I was sure he would come back today if he was Ahasuerus, and I needed twenty-four hours to get hold of you and the police. Two of Carnot's men will be here this afternoon. I told them some vague story and they'll be unobtrusive. Anyway, naturally there was the devil's own row when this little Van Gogh was withdrawn. Everyone here thought I'd gone mad. Our dark-faced friend leapt up and demanded the reason, so I had to say that I suspected the authenticity of the painting and was protecting the reputation of the gallery, but if satisfied would put it up the next day."

" Clever of you," I commented.

Georg inclined his head. "I thought so too. It was a neat trap. Immediately he launched into a passionate defence of the painting—normally a man with his obvious experience of sale rooms would have damned it out of hand—bringing up all sorts of details about Vincent's third-rate pigments, the back of the canvas and so on. The *back* of the canvas, note, what the sitter would most remember about a painting. I said I was more or less convinced, and he promised to be back today. He left his address in case any difficulty came up." Georg took a silver-embossed card from his pocket and read out: "'*Count Enrique Danilewicz, Villa d'Est, Cadaques, Costa Brava.*'" Across the card was enscribed: '*Ritz Hotel, Paris.*'

'Cadaques," I repeated. "Dali is nearby there, at Port Lligat. Another coincidence."

"Perhaps more than a coincidence. Guess what the Catalan master is at present executing for the new Cathedral of St. Joseph at San Diego? One of his greatest commissions to date. Exactly! A crucifixion. Our friend Ahasuerus is once more doing his rounds."

Georg pulled a leather-bound pad from his centre drawer. "Now listen to this. I've been doing some research on the identity of the models for Ahasuerus—usually some petty princeling or merchant-king. The Leonardo is untraceable. He kept open house, beggars and goats wandered through his studio at will, anyone could have got in and posed. But the others were more select. The Ahasuerus in the Holbein was posed by a Sir Henry Daniels, a leading banker and friend of Henry VIII. In the Veronese by a member of the Council of Ten, none other than the Doge-to-be, Enri Danieli—we've both stayed in the hotel of that name in Venice. In the Rubens by Baron Henrik Nielson, Danish Ambassador to Amsterdam, and in the Goya by a certain Enrico Da Nella, financier and great patron of the Prado. While in the Poussin by the famous dilettante, Henri, Duc de Nile."

Georg closed the note-book with a flourish. I said: "It's certainly remarkable."

"You don't exaggerate. Danilewicz, Daniels, Danieli, Da Nella, de Nile and Nielson. Alias Ahasuerus. You know Charles, I'm a little frightened, but I think we have the missing Leonardo within our grasp."

Nothing was more disappointing, therefore, than the failure of our quarry to appear that afternoon.

The transfer of the Van Gogh from the previous day's sales had fortunately given it a high lot number, after some three dozen 20th century paintings. As the bids for the Kandinsky's and Leger's came in, I sat on the podium behind Georg, surveying the elegant assembly below. In such an international gathering, of American connoisseurs, English press lords, French and Italian aristocracy, coloured by a generous sprinkling of ladies of the demi-monde, the presence of even the remarkable figure Georg had described would not have been over-conspicuous. However, as we moved steadily down the catalogue, and the flashing of the photographers' bulbs became more and more wearisome, I began to wonder whether he would appear at all. His seat in the front row remained reserved for him, and I waited impatiently for this fugitive through time and space to materialize and make his magnificent entry promptly as the Van Gogh was announced.

As it transpired, both the seat and the painting remained untaken. Put off by Georg's doubts as to its authenticity, the painting failed to reach its reserve, and as the last sales closed we were left alone on the podium, our bait untaken.

"He must have smelled a rat," Georg whispered, after the attendants had confirmed that Count Danilewicz was not present in any of the other sale-rooms. A moment later a telephone call to the Ritz established that he had vacated his suite and left Paris for the south.

"No doubt he's expert at sidestepping such traps. What now?" I asked.

"Cadaques."

"Georg! Are you insane?"

"Not at all. There's only a chance, but we must take it! Inspector Carnot will find a plane. I'll invent some fantasy to please him. Come on, Charles, I'm convinced we'll find the Leonardo in his villa."

We arrived at Barcelona, Carnot in tow, with Superintendent Jurgens of Interpol to smooth our way through customs, and three hours later set off in a posse of police cars for Cadaques. The fast ride along that fantastic coast line, with its monstrous rocks like giant sleeping reptiles and the glazed light over the embalmed sea, reminiscent of all Dali's timeless beaches, was a fitting prelude to the final chapter. The air bled diamonds around us, sparkling off the immense spires of rock, the huge lunar ramparts suddenly giving way to placid bays of luminous water.

The Villa d'Est stood on a promontory a thousand feet above the town, its high walls and shuttered moorish windows glistening in the sunlight like white quartz. The great black doors, like the vaults of a cathedral, were sealed, and a continuous ringing of the bell brought no reply. At this a prolonged wrangle ensued between Jurgens and the local police, who were torn between their reluctance to offend an important local dignitary—Count Danilewicz had evidently founded a dozen scholarships for promising local artists—and their eagerness to partake in the discovery of the missing Leonardo.

Impatient of all this, Georg and I borrowed a car and chauffeur and set off for Port Lligat, promising the Inspector that we would return in time for the commercial airliner which was due to land at Barcelona from Paris some two hours later, presumably carrying Count Danilewicz. "No doubt, however," Georg remarked softly as we moved off, "he travels by other transport."

What excuse we would make to penetrate the private menage of Spain's most distinguished painter I had not decided, though the possibility of simultaneous one-man shows at Northeby's and Galleries Normande might have appeased him. As we drove down the final approach to the familiar tiered white villa by the water's edge, a large limousine was coming towards us, bearing away a recent guest.

Our two cars passed at a point where the effective width of the road was narrowed by a nexus of pot-holes, and for a moment the heavy saloons wallowed side by side in the dust like two groaning mastodons.

Suddenly, Georg clenched my elbow and pointed through the window.

"Charles! There he is!"

Lowering my window as the drivers cursed each other, I looked out into the dim cabin of the adjacent car. Sitting in the back seat, his head raised to the noise, was a huge Rasputin-like figure in a black pin-stripe suit, his white cuffs and gold tie-pin glinting in the shadows, gloved hands crossed in front of him over an ivory-handled cane. As we edged past I caught a glimpse of his great saturnine head, whose living features matched and corroborated exactly those which I had seen reproduced by so many hands upon so many canvases. The dark eyes glowed with an intense lustre, the black eyebrows rearing from his high forehead like wings, the sharp curve of the beard carrying the sweep of his strong jaw forward into the air like a spear.

Elegantly suited though he was, his whole presence radiated a tremendous restless energy, a powerful charisma that seemed to extend beyond the confines of the car. For a moment we exchanged glances, separated from each other by only two or three feet. He was staring beyond me, however, at some distant landmark, some invisible hill-crest forever silhouetted against the horizon, and I saw in his eyes that expression of irredeemable remorse, of almost hallucinatory despair, untouched by self-pity or any conceivable extenuation, that one imagines on the faces of the damned.

"Stop him!" Georg shouted into the noise. "Charles, warn him!"

Our car edged upwards out of the final rut, and I shouted through the engine fumes:

"Ahasuerus! Ahasuerus!"

His wild eyes swung back, and he rose forward in his seat, a black arm on the window ledge, like some immense half-crippled angel about to take flight. Then the two cars surged apart, and we were separated from the limousine by a tornado of dust. Enchanted from the placid air, for ten minutes the squall seethed backwards and forwards across us.

By the time it subsided and we had managed to reverse, the great limousine had vanished.

They found the Leonardo in the Villa d'Est, propped against the wall in its great gilt frame in the dining-room. To everyone's surprise the house was found to be completely empty, though two manservants who had been given the day off testified that when they left it that morning it had been lavishly furnished as usual. However, as Georg de Stael remarked, no doubt the vanished tenant had his own means of transport.

The painting had suffered no damage, though the first cursory glance confirmed that a skilled hand had been at work on a small portion. The face of the black-robed figure once again looked upwards to the cross, a hint of hope, perhaps even of redemption, in its wistful gaze. The brush-work had dried, but Georg reported to me that the thin layer of varnish was still tacky.

On our feted and triumphant return to Paris, Georg and I recommended that in view of the hazards already suffered by the painting no further attempts should be made to clean or restore it, and with a grateful sigh the director and staff of the Louvre sealed it back into its wall. The painting may not be entirely by the hand of Leonardo da Vinci, but we feel that the few additions have earned their place.

No further news was heard of Count Danilewicz, but Georg recently told me that a Professor Henrico Daniella was reported to have been appointed director of the Museum of Pan-Christian Art at Santiago. His attempts to communicate with Professor Daniella had failed, but he gathered that the Museum was extremely anxious to build up a large collection of paintings of the Cross.